THE LAST LINE

A PHOEBE KORNEAL

MYSTERY TRILOGY

BOOK 3

The Last Line

A Phoebe Korneal Mystery

GaGa Gabardi and Judilee Butler

The Last Line

A PHOEBE KORNEAL MYSTERY TRILOGY

BOOK 3

FIRST EDITION

This story is dedicated to our kids
**Anne, Barbara, Constance, Dennis,
Jon, Randy, and Robert**
We so love your encouragement
and the occasional unsolicited critiques.

CONTENTS

YOU ARE HERE

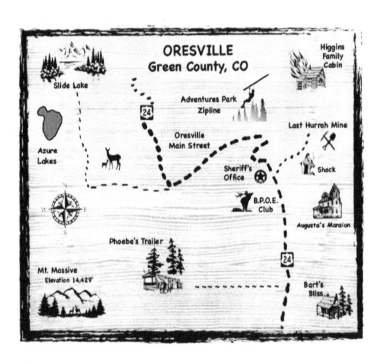

INTRODUCTION

Our fictional setting is the town of Oresville, Green County, Colorado, and a recent census puts the population near 2,000, including every known dog, cat, and various critters. The citizens of Oresville thrive in today's setting at over 10,000 feet in altitude with a foothold in the mining spirit of the mid-1800's. Although several of our characters have relocated to Oresville from other states, they feel the acceptance and camaraderie of those who were born and raised in this high mountain town.

Phoebe Korneal, Green County Deputy Sheriff and *detective as needed* is one of those transplants. She has enjoyed becoming part of this close knit community. Several months have passed since she solved the mystery of the truck off the road above the Azure Lakes. Another mystery has developed in Oresville. Phoebe has her work cut out for her and she is campaigning to become the first female Sheriff.

In a small town such as Oresville anything that happens to visitors or residents draws attention and concern, creating a headline. Phoebe's childhood friend, Carrie Jean, Ace Reporter for the High Mountain Gazette and the daily digital newsletter, the e-Blast!, stands ready to inform the public. CJ reports everything in the traditional role of newspapers in settling the western territories and bringing "community" to those roughshod settlements. Today newspapers remain integral players just as when the state was getting its footing settling the West in the 1800s.

Still today mining is part and parcel to the free-spirited, self-reliant people who seek their fortune in the high mountains of the Centennial State. The Rocky Mountains draw those who value the great out-of-doors and a culture of collective yet independent residents who appreciate and strive to preserve the environment. This is the perspective we bring to Oresville and our characters.

Join Phoebe and her crew of somewhat eccentric Green County citizens to unravel another mystery in Oresville. This cozy murder mystery will comfort you whether reading at the beach or relaxing at the end of a tough day. It will bring a smile as you escape to the high mountains of Colorado. Read on!

THE CRIME

R oz put down her nail file to pay attention to a call, "Good morning. Green County, Colorado, Sheriff's Office. Rosalind Marie Boudreaux-Diamond speakin'."

"Well, I just have a hard time getting used to your extended names, Roz. But, you know, when you see I'm callin' there's no need to blather on with all that introductory stuff." Augusta Higgins was out of her jeep and pacing at the base of a zipline ride, calling into the sheriff's official line.

Roz knew the early morning calls were never good—someone died in their sleep, a cat never came home, or "I can't find my car keys." She started work at six every weekday morning and relished the early morning calm, especially through the summer months when tourists doubled the population of Oresville and all of Colorado. Not to mention it gave her time to do nails, apply makeup, and try new hairstyles. Roz was no slouch when it came to how she wanted to look— *every day's a statement, y'all.*

"Don't y'all give me any grief, Augusta. I'm already miserable enough carryin' these twins. What's up, See-sta?"

"Sorry. What's the due date?"

"July 17th—seven in the morning as I see it. But I'm sure y'all didn't call to ask about the departure of these twins from this bod. Please, what's goin' on?"

"Yes. I called you. You're not gonna believe this one. I was headed out of town this morning. You know I spend weekends now ridin' motorcycles with Queennie, visiting other mountain towns. She heads back to Pikeview on Monday and then on Tuesday, butt-crack of dawn, I head up to the Last."

Tapping the nail file on a notepad, "Yeah, heard about the motorcycle. I can't see y'all on a Harley, right?"

"That makes two of us. Well, this morning I decided to swing by the new tourist park, High Mountain Adventures just to see how it's coming along. Did you know the Mickey kid from the county building has a fancy food truck in the parking lot? I was planning on getting some food to bring up to the Last, but he wasn't open. Usually he's open before sunup for breakfast and is busy, busy."

Roz halfway listened to Augusta ramble on and fell back to her to-do list. It got longer every day. At the top were possible names for the babies—still undecided and daylight's burnin' as the saying goes. To keep up with the subject at hand, she prompted Augusta, "Yup, it's Mickey Walker and he lasted barely three months with the county."

"Yeah, that's him, Mickey what's-his-name. I still have his dog. He neglected to pick him up, so possession is nine-tenths of the law, right?"

"So I've heard, but not from a lawyer."

Augusta let loose with her feelings at the mention of lawyers, "Hmph. Whatever. Back to the dog. I changed its name to Willie. It seemed to fit better than Fido. Who names a dog Fido? Mickey sure didn't last long at the county building job. But, oh well. The food truck business? It seems a tough row to hoe compared to 'retired in place' on the county payroll."

"Okay, so much for lawyers and dogs. Did you call to chat about breakfast? A dog? Or the Munchies' hours? This here's an emergency line and everythin' is recorded, ya know." Roz leaned back in her chair to give her back a rest. The twins showed no mercy if she sat in one position for even five minutes.

Augusta swapped subjects. Her voice dropped to a serious, strong level, "Roz, I can hardly believe my eyes. I'm parked at the food truck now. Hanging from the new zipline ride is a … a body." She hesitated and added, "Yup, a body. Nearly naked. Can't tell you who it is, but I do know we need the sheriff down here, like yesterday. And better call out the ladder truck from the fire department. You know, before the townsfolk arrive 'en masse'."

"No, no, no, hold on there. Are you sure it's a person? Maybe a manikin? Like some kids pullin' a prank? Or one of those kinky blow-up dolls? And y'all reportin' nearly naked? How's that?" Roz was talking fast and tapping her pen frantically trying to convince Augusta it was not a real body. Certainly not in the little old town of Oresville, population near two thousand if every pet or passerby were included.

Augusta's voice quivered as she took in the reality. What she was seeing was starting to soak in. The unmoving, hanging body now shocked her to the core of her fifty plus years on the planet. This was a real person high on the line. There was no mistaking it for otherwise.

"It's a human being all right, not looking too good either. When word gets out there's a nearly naked body hangin' high, the whole town'll be here. Maybe we should call it a naked body and then all the good Christians will behave themselves and stay away."

Roz was at full-attention now and trying to track Augusta's ramblings, "What did y'all mean by nearly naked?"

"There's some kind of hood over his head, but I can definitely see it's a guy. Just can't tell who it is. From what I know about men after several husbands and five marriages, I can say for sure he's young."

Roz straightened up, scooted forward to the edge of the chair, and started paging through her old Rolodex file of cards in search of the fire department number. Listening to the description, she was stuck on the vision, *Nearly naked on a zipline?*

Augusta continued, "I'm gonna stick with nearly naked on my report and you can play it from there. Sheriff'll have crowd control issues for sure. Who's the sheriff anyway since Joe abandoned the ship? Your new hubby, Bill Diamond?"

Roz's voice had hit a high note of impatience just below an over the top loud, excited yell, "Okay. Okay. Hang tight. Bill's only the actin' sheriff until the election for Joe's replacement. He won't be in for a couple more hours. Phoebe's at the office now and will be out there pronto. In the meantime, get in your Jeep and don't go anywhere. Ya hear me?" By the end of the directive, Roz was yelling into the headset as if volume could make a difference.

She was used to giving directions, "... stay out of harm's way until help arrives." In the past year, on two other occasions, Augusta had called in with a "dead body or worse" report.

The first time was last August. Augusta had found the dead body of Al Lewis up at the Sunshine Mine. He was nicknamed by the townsfolk Old Al because, well, he was old. Sheriff Joe Jackson wrote off the death to natural causes due to old age—sixty-nine at the time of his demise. The Deputy Sheriff and occasional Acting Detective, Phoebe Korneal, thought otherwise. She checked it out and determined death by arsenic poisoning was the culprit, not usually considered a natural cause.

The second occurrence was just before the end of last year. Augusta was out snowmobiling with the local club, Gettin' Higher, and came across a truck off the road, buried in snow, and a body she reported as "dead or worse." Again, Deputy Korneal did not go with the conventional wisdom from the good old boys—another example of female drivers' poor decision-making. This time Flight for Life saved the female at the wheel, Ellis Meredith Walker. Phoebe established the cause was intimate partner violence of the husband, Mickey Walker, coupled with Meredith's anger management issues. Very complicated.

With these two situations, Roz had started a pattern of telling Augusta what to do and the crux of it was to stay out of the way. Meanwhile, Augusta heard but did not listen and managed each event on her own terms. This morning would be no different. She swung back to a chatty level, "Roger that, Roz. If I find a donut around here, I'll have one sent over to you. Make that three, one for you and two for the twins, right?" and added a chuckle to this clever comment. She then blew off what Roz had advised and repositioned her ride nearer the body and stood at the base of the zipline to direct traffic should anyone happen to arrive.

The promise of a donut or three was ignored. Roz disconnected the line and let out with a Louisiana Cajun yell projected down the hallway. "Deputy Sheriff Korneal, front and center, now!" The office paging system worked on a limited basis and her voice projected—direct from the Atchafalaya Swamp, *Looseeann bayou country*.

Since the start of the year, Phoebe was on duty from six in the morning to four in the afternoon, Tuesday through Friday. The new four-tens schedule had landed her with the cherished three-day weekend. As Lead Patrol she had first choice for shift work and supported the other officers as needed to accommodate their family demands. Her life had taken on an expanded dimension with long weekends to enjoy "me time."

She had heard Roz's excited voice and was headed to the dispatch desk before Roz disconnected the line, half expecting an announcement, "I'm in labor."

"Everything good with you?" Phoebe was anxiously eyeing Roz's body for telltale signs of an impending birth, whatever that might involve. She was thinking, *Fingers crossed this morning's not gonna be the experience of hands-on Obstetrics 101.* Phoebe had no experience with labor and delivery but had read a booklet on emergency procedures and was ready for the event, should it occur during working hours. *How complicated can it be? Women have been birthin' babies forever.*

"That was Augusta callin' from the adventure park. There's a body, nearly naked, hangin' from the zipline ride. I told her you'd be right over." Roz took a deep breath and blew out through perfectly round lips. "Just practicin' my breathin' for the July excitement. It helps me calm down."

As she mentally leaped over the Roz breathing comments Phoebe launched into extreme professional modus operandi, "What? A body? Nearly naked? On a zipline? How does that happen? Is the person dead or alive?"

Roz was continuing the breathing practice and had freshened her lipstick at the same time, always multitasking, "Don't know."

Phoebe's brain went into high alert. In an excited, rising pitch, she yelled, "I'm on my way. Call search and rescue. Call the fire department. Call for an ambulance. Call for backup. I'll need some help out there and I'll be in touch when I know what's goin' on. Might need to call Bill to report in early and meet me." They were always slim on patrol officers covering all of Green County's three hundred plus square miles. Calling for officer assistance would bring Bill Diamond, Acting Green County Sheriff, into action. Not a good thing for Bill, as he liked to wander into the office at ten-ish after coffee at Becky's Buns Up.

Roz was listening, still breathing, now at a frantic level. Between hoots of breath, she gasped, "On it. Good luck."

Phoebe ran down the hallway into the patrol room, grabbed her duty belt from the desk and fastened it around her waist. *Check.* Then she shifted, bent, pushed, and wiggled the bulletproof vest into place above the thirty-pound belt. *Check.* Patted a pocket for the cell. *Check.* Tapped the holster for her trusty Glock 22. *Check.*

Rushing into the hallway at nearly six foot tall, her long legged stride carried her to the back door faster than most people of above average height. A heavy, chestnut brown head of hair pulled into a ponytail poked through the back opening of the Green County Sheriff's baseball cap. She carried a look of firm consternation on her face, lips pressed together, eyebrows pinched into a unibrow with alarm at this early morning call.

The Sheriff's patrol SUV was in the first parking slot with keys under the front seat. Making quick work of getting behind the wheel, she started the engine, slammed the shift arm down into Drive, and floored it. With lights on and no siren to break the serenity of this early morning, she raced to High Mountain Adventures.

ZIPPED TO DEATH

Two minutes later Phoebe roared into the parking lot and executed a drift power slide in front of the food truck, Mickey's Mountain Munchies. The sun was just short of clearing the mountains to the east of town at sixish in the morning. The day was beginning its wakeup stretch before offering sunlight for the vacationing tourists.

Temperatures hovered at a fresh, crisp thirty-five degrees. A bright sky held promise of a terrific summer day before the sun topped the mountain range. If the wind stayed behind Mt. Massive to the west, the day would warm nicely into the June average of mid-sixties. At nearly ten thousand five hundred feet above sea level, a sixty-degree temperature was a blessing.

As the SUV jerked to a stop, she was already surveying the scene, *The food truck's closed? That's odd. Mickey's is always open for those early risers who needed their coffee fix and more. He must have partied last night. What's with the two vehicles looking like they've been abandoned? Better check those out.*

The parking lot air felt heavy with apprehension. She moved through it leaving slow ripples in the atmosphere, quickly snapping pictures of the vehicles and adjacent areas. The context of the setting before the scene was filled with emergency workers mattered to her. Cell phone technology made work easier and now everyone was a pro at photography. In her early thirties, she had never known the days of waiting for film to be developed.

Augusta was standing next to her Rubicon near the base of the zipline. She was average in height, but her attitude made for added inches. After a lifetime in the mountains, equipped with the lineage of the Higgins Family women, she was a sharp, no-nonsense, tough-minded female. Five marriages later, she was still unsettled as her mother liked to remind her. She spent every summer in the mountains at her family's mining operations, The Last Hurrah.

The Higgins mine served as a teaching facility during the summer months and a production site otherwise. Engineering students applied from across the nation for the opportunity to learn the business, from the bottom up. They got paid for their work, including free board and lodging, and a scholarship awarded to the top achievers. She had a mine manager who coached, prodded, yelled, and in the end, released the students back to the universities better prepared to finish their education.

She watched Phoebe quickly closing the distance between them and pointed up to the body. It was several feet away from the launch platform, attached to a large carabiner on the zipline cable, rope wrapped around each wrist. The line's emergency brake device appeared to be holding the body in place.

Concerned for Augusta's well-being, Phoebe called out as

she approached, "Hey there, Augusta. You okay?" She placed a hand on Augusta's shoulder and searched her face.

Augusta appeared distraught with the seriousness of the scene. Shaking her head in disbelief, eyes round with excitement, "Oh yes. Since I've been here it's not moved. From ground level, I'd guess DOA without further measurements."

"Thanks for callin' it in. I might be able to gather evidence before the park opens or the entire Oresville population shows up." Phoebe made a quick assessment of the setting. Minus all clothing, the naked body confirmed it was a male. She could only guess that Augusta's description of nearly naked was an attempt to be politically correct as she practiced being a bit more "humanistic." Thus the influence of a close friend, Queennie Lewis, had brought a bit of humanism to the Augusta Higgins Attitude.

The male's head was covered with what appeared to be a hood. The entire body, torso, back, arms, and legs had been beaten. There was little blood to be seen, but some bruising and swelling looked raw, maybe fresh. He had not been there long. From Phoebe's perspective at ground zero, the body appeared lifeless but it was impossible to make the call—dead or alive. She grabbed her cell and rang dispatch.

Roz answered with her usual introduction, "Good morning. Green County, Colorado, Sheriff's Office. Rosalind Maric Boudreaux-Diamond speaking."

"Hey, Roz, when you see I'm calling there's no need to formally do your full-blown introduction."

Ignoring the intended training, Roz dropped into her early morning drawl, "Wadda Ya Want?"

Phoebe shot back, "What's the status of the emergency crew. We need all hands-on deck out here, ASAP."

"Already done and they should be a-pullin' up about now. I hear the sirens blaring from here. Lots of excitement for a Tuesday morning." Roz was sipping her Union brand of chicory coffee. She had been raised on Union coffee and in the digital age, it could be ordered online and delivered to her in Oresville. No need to stock up when she'd go to Louisiana for her yearly visit to Maw-maw, her Cajun grandma.

Rosalind Marie Boudreaux-Diamond AKA Roz was a newly married, first-time pregnant woman imported from the bayous of Louisiana. A Cajun beauty, she had thick, deep, shiny black slightly curly hair. She arrived in Colorado, complete with Maw-maw Anne's recipes, lots of Zydeco music, and a heavy swamp accent as needed. She'd left the bayou day two following high school graduation, headed north, and bounced off the town of Pikeview on the Front Range of Colorado. Ultimately, Roz landed in Oresville a few years back.

After a few cocktails at the Club, she liked to share her history. She was probably of Indigenous Peoples heritage. Many years ago, the family awoke from a weekend of reunion parties deep in the Atchafalaya Swamp. It was early morning. Her momma inquired of Maw-maw Choctaw, "What are we?" Their Maw-maw replied something that sounded akin to an expletive and the family members within hearing distance decided it was the ancient tribal family name. They claimed Fockarewe as the tribe, with no listed numbers on the government's tribal rolls.

As the call was disconnected, Phoebe cringed at the mention of sirens. Once they heard the emergency alarms, early risers would start rolling in to check the action. Before all the crews showed, she scurried up the steps to the zipline for a closer look. At the top step, she realized the platform could be the crime scene. There, strewn around was clothing, a baseball bat, and small vials of a white substance in glassine envelopes. She yelled at the body in case of a remote possibility of life. No answer. No movement. After taking several random photos of the platform and body, she climbed back to the ground knowing not to step into the mess on the platform.

The teams she needed were arriving. Cousin George rolled into the parking lot with the Moly Mine's bucket truck. Doc Watson, the county coroner, pulled up in his truck ready for transport should there be a need. They either had gotten a call from Roz or were monitoring the county's emergency dispatch channel. The parking lot was going to be crowded with all the emergency personnel.

"Morning, Cousin, Doc." Phoebe did a fist bump with Doc and a nod towards Cousin.

Cousin was looking around the parking lot and spoke first, "What'd we get this morning? Kind of early for a joyride on a zipline."

"For sure. Especially naked on a cool morning like this."

Just as she finished her sentence, the ambulance and fire truck rolled in with all the appropriate personnel.

At that moment Phoebe heard a noise above the commotion of the emergency teams. One of the vehicles that looked abandoned raced out of the parking area with a squeal of tires. She tried to get a glimpse of the driver and the license plate on the large SUV. *There's more than one person in that vehicle. The light's too weak to identify faces. Note to self, check the photos.*

Phoebe was looking around the parking lot at the other abandoned vehicle when Doc spoke up. "I heard the dispatch and came along to check out what *nearly nude* might entail." Both men looked at each other and popped a slight smile as they turned to where Augusta was standing. She gave them a nod and pointed up to where the body was hanging.

In unison they looked at the overhead zipline and the body. George released a slight whistle and got serious real fast. "Best get up there and check for signs of life before we jump

17

to conclusions." Thinking ahead, he added, "Doc, want a ride in an aerial bucket and we can save some time in the process?"

"Exactly. Let me get my coroner bag."

At nearly seven feet tall, Cousin George's usual stride was a running pace for others. He did a quick walk over to the staging area and the team of volunteers got the message without question or conversation. They went into action setting up the area for rescue, positioning the ambulance, moving the bucket truck into place, and adding equipment to the bucket in case resuscitation could save the life.

Cousin George was the head of safety at the nearby open pit molybdenum mine. It was nicknamed The Moly, short for the ore, molybdenum, atomic number 42 on the periodic table. He made sure the mine's machines and tools were readily available to Green County and the town of Oresville. The giant bucket truck brought from the mine would be perfect for this high line crime.

Cousin's nickname came from a complicated family history of marriage, divorces, stepchildren, and half-siblings that would send an ancestry expert into anaphylactic shock trying to diagram the extended relationships. Instead, he was known to everyone as Cousin George and no one bothered to clarify nor validate if he were, in fact, blood related.

Doc Watson had been the county's coroner for 30 years. He was also the only mortician in the area. At sixty years of age, he looked forty. A mountain bike was his primary vehicle, but he ran the trails around Oresville most days exercising his lifelong passion. He still participated in triathlons throughout Colorado but had dropped the Ironman competition.

Even though Doc resided in a small town with minimal crime, he was known at the state level for his knowledge and training as a coroner. Neighboring counties relied on his help when they had challenging cases. Over the years he had built a network of people associated with death, crime, and its analysis including members of the state forensics team. The coroner position did not require an MD license. The Doc title was a respectful courtesy given to the position.

There was a flurry of activity. Cousin George was guiding the setup for the rescue or recovery. Before going to his vehicle for the coroner gadgets, Doc hesitated and turned to Phoebe. "I think this is going to require some additional forensic expertise. What say we call the experts for help on this one?"

The forensic team was a division of the Colorado Bureau of Investigation (COBI). Calling them in would move the jurisdiction from local law enforcement to a broader scale and bring in high level forensic services. Green County had never needed this talent nor their expensive paraphernalia. Oresville historically had a low total crime rate of less than a quarter of one percent.

Phoebe slowly nodded, eyes fixed on the body, "It would certainly help. My experience and training with something like this is zilch. Thanks, Doc." She looked again in the direction of the departed SUV. *Where have I seen that supersized box of a vehicle?*

CAUGHT YA

As the ladder truck was lifting Doc and Cousin George to the suspended body, Oresville's newly installed constable, town cop Bartholomew Masterson—Bart pulled into the parking lot. Phoebe had labeled him Beautiful Man in her mind, Ponytail Guy to her friends, and Honeybun when they were alone.

A hundred miles or so east and slightly south of Green County, Bart had been a patrol officer in liberal-minded Greenstone. It was a small town adjacent to the larger conservative city of Pikeview on the Front Range of Colorado. When the *retired in place* constable-magistrate of Oresville officially retired on Valentine's Day, the position was opened and advertised. Bart was the best qualified applicant and was readily hired. The town had no police department per se and the one person "team" for law enforcement was mostly enough. Overflow demand and after-hours calls went to the Sheriff's office and budget.

At five feet eleven plus and built like a true athlete, he was the first choice in all team sports. Taking into account his black hair, blue eyes, and easy personality, he was the total package if ever there would be a centerfold opportunity. His personality was the binding agent for his attributes—humble enough to be enthralled with the pure athleticism of the pros, confident enough to go after what he wanted.

Bart and Phoebe's budding relationship prompted Bart's job change. Having moved at the end of March, the relocation interrupted his love for March Madness but brought him closer to her. He rationalized this as the complementary forces of yin and yang when faced with a choice—small sacrifice on his part considering how things were going.

They kept their relationship on the sideline during working hours. After hours, there was job overlap, as with every coincidental sharing. Their work-related conversations were limited like the crime level in Oresville. The base of their relationship was strengthening, feelings were deepening, and Oresville was the perfect scenario for next steps. Whatever that might bring, it worked for them.

On the heels of a relationship with a two timin' boyfriend in Salt Lake City, Phoebe had a motto, "One step at a time, Girly-girl". The coming special election for a sheriff could bring a change to the Bart and Phoebe Relationship. They chose to ignore whatever challenges winning the election might bring.

Acting Green County Sheriff, Bill Diamond, pulled into the parking lot following Constable Bart. Bill was on temporary status as Sheriff until the special election next week to replace the retired thirty-year veteran, Sheriff Joe Jackson. Joe was a local boy who had been the Sheriff of the county for thirty some years and no doubt was still running the show behind the scenes. Or trying to. There had never been a crime in Green

County Joe couldn't spin into "No Big Deal."

When an opening on the three-person Board of Commissioners (BOC) became available in April, he decided to go for the top of the political heap and quickly retired as Sheriff. Without any competition for the open seat, Joe moved easily into the position. Over his career he had gone from the basement as a janitor to the top floor office. No election had been needed, there being no other interest in the BOC opening. At least no candidates that anyone knew of.

The board then appointed Undersheriff Bill Diamond to the Sheriff's vacancy and business as usual was anticipated—a man in every top spot for the county.

Bill Diamond was a childhood friend to Phoebe and the stepbrother to reporter Carrie Jean, CJ. The three of them grew up together in Salt Lake City and now were enjoying life in the high mountains of Colorado. He had moved to Denver to attend college after graduating from high school in Salt Lake City. Good looking to a fault and knowing it, he dropped out of college without preamble and migrated to the Denver Police Department. He married the chief's daughter, and his law enforcement career path was launched. Two children later, his ten-year marriage was circling the drain and he was looking for a change.

Stepsister, CJ, called him from Oresville. The Sheriff was looking for help and Bill was the perfect fit. Seven years later, single and in line to be the next Green County Sheriff, he unexpectedly fell in love with Rosalind Marie Boudreaux. Life happens fast in the thin air of the Colorado mountains. Suddenly, he was married and the expectant father of twins. This new wife decided family was first, career was second. They were expecting twins in July and the timing was wrong for him to suddenly become Sheriff. It would be a distraction that Roz guaranteed would end their relationship and the family foursome before it was launched. She always won an argument.

CJ was the only reporter and therefore the ace reporter for Oresville's newspaper, the High Country Gazette and the e-Blast!, a digital newsletter. When Jesus Garcia married the third-generation owner of the Gazette, he became the editor-in-chief. As a newly married husband focused on his wife, he needed help in the reporting aspect of the business and CJ was the fix he needed. She was his willing-to-learn reporter and together they were the Green County news team.

Newspapers in the 1800s in Colorado were the major component of community growth and spirit. With this thought in mind, Garcia developed a daily twelve o'clock digital newsletter. The *e-Blast!* was born with CJ at the helm. She was a fast learner, and no news tidbit was ever too small for the weekday nooner—barometric pressure change coming, lost dog, so-and-so's birthday. All were likely prospects for a headline.

With a naturally buff physique, Garcia loved the great outdoors and worked out daily to preserve his image. His was the look of a hardened cowboy complete with hat, boots, and turquoise bolo tie. He radiated accountability for honest newspaper reporting.

Garcia was a born and raised citizen of Green County, a year younger than his high school friend, retired Sheriff, Joe Jackson. He was now a member of the Board of Commissioners and Garcia saw himself as Joe's conscience. The plan to appoint Bill as the new sheriff, without a call for candidates and election, put the friends at odds. Knowing the history and rules of the county, he recognized the lordly move on the part of the BOC and felt compromised in the lifelong friendship with Joe.

The law required a process enabling other candidates to

come forward. If there were none, then an appointment of a sheriff would be valid. However, in this case, no "Call for Candidates" had been put forth. Being honest to a fault, Garcia knew this was wrong.

Garcia was an avid history buff, especially of Green County. The county charter and statutes had developed out of necessity back in the 1860s when political corruption was rampant. The good old boys even back then locked in their closed ranks and silently agreed on the cost for any newcomer. The county rules outlined the first step for a job opening would be a call for candidates to come forward. If there were none, then an appointment could be made. *One and done* was the usual declaration.

Fast forward one hundred or so years. This time no opening had been advertised to test for any interest and the BOC went directly to a default of appointment. CJ jumped on this tidbit and the flagrant flouting of power like a rabid mouse on cheese and the brouhaha commenced. Her reporting was the wind fanning the fire of discontent directed at the political machine of Green County. Undersheriff Bill Diamond wanted nothing to do with scandal, infighting, or any kind of politically motivated antics. His lack of enthusiasm coupled with the newspaper articles criticizing the underhanded move by the good old boys of the three person BOC caused unheard embarrassment to the political machine. To save face, the machine backed off and a special election was announced for the first Tuesday in June.

The Green County Clerk ramped up the election process and hit the *action button*. She welcomed any and all candidates as long as they were of legal voting age, a Green County citizen, and had submitted the proper forms handwritten by the candidate. The last item was a county ordinance. The written form proved literacy.

When the town was formed in the mid-1800s many were not able to read or write. Building a schoolhouse was not on the horizon nor even the remotest possibility. Illiteracy was commonplace and therefore accepted. At least it had been accepted until the early pioneer women came to town, took one look, rode over to talk with Molly McDuff-Higgins, and plans were laid for a school and a church. They rammed the project through the white male political grinder.

Limited skills in reading and writing were the cause for improper recording of meetings, agreements, and title transfers. An X was the acceptable mark for a person's name. A gun fight could settle the differences, but the winner might be dead with the X still open to further interpretation. The occasional misspelled name on a death certificate would send future generations into a tailspin of embarrassment or pompous claims of heroism.

The current vacancy for Sheriff brought out many old white guys to file as candidates. The list was long at 12 names, and policing experience was thin such as a recently dismissed dog catcher, a grocery store clerk who knew everyone, and a lifetime member of the Optimist Club who was anything but. It was a list of candidates who were barely qualified, a few who were looking for employment, some who had read true crime books, and others who were in need of free transportation—a Sheriff's vehicle.

The public had been taking a collective yawn with each of the twelve candidates until the next to the last day to file. Thirty-one days prior to Special Election Tuesday, a group of women met at TuTu's Washateria and Deputy Phoebe Korneal had been convinced to file her papers for the opening. She would be the only candidate truly recognized as "qualified." Her experience would speak for itself with a little embellishment from the self-appointed Campaign Manager CJ, and community volunteer project manager, Roz.

CJ and Roz were eager to manage the thirty-day campaign for Phoebe. *We need a woman in a leadership role in this county.* With the two of them at the helm, they knew they could create a winning campaign for Phoebe. Now, rightfully, there was a woman on the all male slate. CJ could see a Pulitzer in her future for reporting on the shenanigans of the county leaders. *Vote for Phoebe* was the rallying cry with a sub note, "We're tired of voting for old white guys."

The immediate result of the newly initiated campaign was of high interest. Excitement was building for Phoebe to become the first female sheriff in Green County. Less than twelve percent of all law enforcement personnel in the United States were female. Every weekend for the last two weeks had been filled with door-to-door discussions, flier drops at screen doors, and general dialogue between Phoebe and the voting populace in the county. "Vote for Phoebe" rang out from one end of the county to the other. By Sunday afternoon, her feet hurt, a smile felt frozen in place, and doubt clouded the wisdom of the coerced decision to run.

COFFEE BLUES

The Acting Sheriff of Green County, Bill Diamond, was contemplating the scene standing with Phoebe, Bart, and Augusta. He wasn't the least bit interested in the title of Sheriff or this apparent crime. Standing near the food truck, Bill was in full whine mode, "I need a strong coffee with a 'donut back.' Wonder where Mickey is? He's usually open before dawn."

Phoebe looked at Bill and wondered if she would live long enough to see him actively engaged as an officer of the law. Friends since childhood, she loved and respected the friendship she shared with Bill and CJ. But Bill was way too preoccupied with his new life as a husband and upcoming father role.

Thinking today's crime scene would take a back seat in Bill's world, Phoebe looked at Bart. He ventured into the waters, "Tell you what, Bill, why don't you go to the office and take care of business for the county. Phoebe could take the lead on this and I'll be back up."

"Great idea, Bart." Bill exhaled a grateful look of thanks and jumped into his Sheriff's vehicle. He headed for Becky's Buns Up like a horse headed for the barn. Coffee and donuts were calling. It was across the street from the county office building. This would put Bill close enough to be considered *at work*. As Acting Sheriff, he had put in an appearance at the scene of the crime. Check that box.

The Buns, as the locals called it, was a bakery and cafe until two in the afternoon every day of the week. The owner, Becky Riney, had grown up in Oresville and stayed on for the joy of baking and running a business in her sleep at three in the morning everyday. She served the super early risers from the back door—take away donuts with a coffee back. Similar to ordering a shot of whiskey and water on the side.

With Bill out of the way, Phoebe and Bart went to work with crime scene tape cordoning off the entire area. Augusta tagged along and launched into a report on her weekend of motorcycle riding over Independence Pass to Aspen for a delightful lunch with a gang of newly minted friends. Listening to Augusta's observations, Phoebe kept one eye on what was going on overhead and the other eye on the whole area until the state help arrived. There were too many moving parts to focus on crime scene tape or motorcycle rides.

Cousin George and Doc were in the bucket truck by the body. Doc was checking vitals for a sign of life. He looked down to where Phoebe and Bart were standing and shook his head—no life. He called his state forensics contact person for "next step" advice. They were already responding to his earlier call and advising from afar to Doc's narrative. The decision was made not to bring the body to the ground until the forensic experts could analyze the scene or scenes or whatever this was. The state people were excited to get to Oresville as they had never cleared a zipline death before.

Doc called Phoebe on her cell to repeat the recommendation from the state forensic team. She had a short conversation with Bart and they concurred. They knew not to disturb a crime scene until a thorough analysis could be completed. All she could do now was to control the scene. *Hopefully the state team gets here soon.*

With tell-tale donut crumbs on their uniforms nearly a half hour after being called out, two deputies pulled into the parking lot. Observing the detritus, Phoebe was in no mood to make nice with them. She curtly directed them to stage a location near the east end of the lot where the curious townsfolk could gather, away from the zipline.

The entrance to the parking lot was cordoned off and large signs with arrows directed the looky-loos to the train depot at the east end of the parking lot. The locals of Oresville were starting to gather in hopes of adding details to the abbreviated remark of "nearly naked" over the police scanner airwaves. The deputies moved quickly to stage parking and keep nosy citizens at the depot—out of sight and out of mind.

Phoebe circled back to where Augusta was standing and called Bart over. "We need to take a statement from you. How did you find the body?"

Bart added. "Right. Even the smallest detail you can tell us might help."

Intently watching the action, "I can do this statement thing, but it'll have to be later this afternoon. Tuesday's a big day at the Last. I meet with my mine foreman, Thomas, and the students. We settle up for the coming week. I'm already late."

The Last Hurrah was Augusta's family mine. She owned it and lived nearby all summer, always saying, "...roughing it high in the Colorado Rockies." The truth of the living arrangement was a full sized, top of the line Airstream Classic 33FB model complete with electricity, cell tower, water, and food staples brought in every week with the full-time cook. This year was different in that she was off riding motorcycles every weekend with a new friend, Queennie Lewis. Tuesday was the start of the work week for her at the Last.

Every summer Augusta hired a crew of engineering students to learn mining with hands-on experience. This year she had added a young kid, Hank Williams Klingfus. Augusta had befriended Hank when he worked for gold prospector Al Lewis, who was called Old Al because he was, well, old.

After his junior year in high school, Hank dropped out of Greenstone High and declared an "early gap year" to get a head start on a career in gold prospecting. By the end of the summer with Old Al and his pet mule, Rose, he had gained little experience. Then Old Al unexpectedly died.

For thirty years Al and Rose had roamed the mountains around Oresville with some limited success in prospecting. At the ripe old age of 69, many believed the body just goes on to a brighter tomorrow or whatever. Phoebe did not subscribe to this theory and discovered he had died of poisoning. But that's a different story.

At Al's passing, Augusta stepped in and convinced Hank to return to his family and high school to get his diploma. If he graduated, he was guaranteed work at the Last Hurrah the following summer. They had agreed on a plan. Augusta would employ Hank every summer to teach him the mining trade since he was determined to be a gold prospector. Hank's side of the bargain was obtaining a high school diploma and admission into the Colorado School of Mines, her alma mater. She would provide tuition, books, room and board, and summer employment. Her personal influence at her alma mater helped him get accepted.

Additionally, the foreman at the Last, Thomas Walsh, was

getting up in age and Augusta needed to groom a replacement. The Walsh family men had been working at the Last through all three of the Higgins Family lady bosses—Connie, Anne Louise, and now Augusta. While Thomas had a natural instinct for mining ore, it was time to retire and move into the "follow the sun" years of life.

After a few cocktails at the Club, Thomas Walsh liked to brag to these engineering students, "The Walsh's of Oresville are *likely* related to the famous gold miner, Thomas Francis Walsh, out of Ireland."

Some listeners seriously considered what was being touted, "Lord knows the Oresville town cemetery is filled with Irish miners who lost life and limb to a career of mining. Their graves were unmarked other than being located in the Irish area of the cemetery. Therefore, these Walsh people are *likely* related. Yes."

As the engineering students moved on from the Last and graduated from college, they were convinced this Walsh guy had an instinct for the mining business and the *likely* could be correct. The well-known miner, Thomas Walsh, died in 1910 in Washington D.C. and the Oresville Walsh was a connection in name only. *Identity theft?* Thomas agreed to stay on until someone could take the reins.

Augusta was hoping that Hank could fill the shoes of the departing Walsh foreman down the line.

At the crime scene, Phoebe continued. "Okay Augusta. Bart and I'll be here until the state folks complete their work. When do you think you'll be done at the mine?"

"I can probably be back to town by three o'clock. Will that

work?"

"Depends. Give me a call when you leave the Last. We'll work something out."

"Got it. I'll make the meeting short. Thomas doesn't need any coaching, but we're tryin' to get Hank on board." She took one last look at the body on the zipline and shook her head. Her eyes conveyed sadness as they met Phoebe's. She headed to the Jeep.

PUNGENT PICS

As they sat in the SUV, Bart looked at the pictures Phoebe brought up on her phone. "I thought when I took the constable job in April it would be about barking dogs, cats in trees, and traffic tickets. What in the world happened here and why?"

"I have no idea why this man was beaten to death, but it's showing us the underbelly of Oresville. My bet is drugs are at the bottom of it. A whole new scenario. I think once we identify the victim, we can begin to understand what has happened and why. Don't ya think?"

Bart nodded, "When I look at these pictures, I'm shocked. This person was beaten with a vengeance. Those little envelopes scattered around the zipline platform are a tell— definitely drugs."

"Agreed. I'm thinking we're dealing with a level of crime

never seen in our small town before. Looks like it might be more than one constable can handle. Maybe it's time to form an Oresville PD."

Bart gave her a surprised look and silence overtook the SUV. Bart continued looking at the photos and stopped at the first picture of a vehicle. "Phoebe, I've seen this big box SUV, but I can't place it."

"I've seen it somewhere too. It flew out of here shortly after the search and rescue team arrived. I was so involved with them, the bucket truck, Doc, and Augusta I didn't see who was driving. I thought it looked like there was another person in it."

"Did you send the pictures to Roz?"

"No, I'll do it now and ask her to enhance the photos for a clearer shot of the license plates. We need to know who owns this vehicle and there's another one too. It's critical to know the owner of each."

The deputies had managed to get the crowd of citizens and otherwise moved back to the Short Line Train Depot and safely out of the way. The train depot, located at the east end of the lot, had not been used for years until an adventure park project came to town. The developer had fixed it up for offices and now it had some limited use. An enterprising soul had arrived at the depot with a side hustle of donuts and coffee from Becky's—five dollars for the bundle, no refills. People were using binoculars and sharing information as interpretation and speculation occurred, depending on the angle of the binoculars in use.

CJ had arrived and had been shuffled off to the depot. She badgered the deputies to "let the press in" and spouted first amendment rights—to no avail. As Augusta took off from the parking area, CJ flagged her down.

She swung the Jeep to the side of the road and CJ ran over, "Hey, good morning. What's happening over there, See-sta?"

Augusta and CJ had been friends for several years, despite the age difference of twenty-five years. Augusta had been married five times to three different men but had no children. She treated CJ like family and CJ enjoyed the camaraderie between the two of them. She loved to listen to Augusta's stories of her family over the generations here in Green County and Augusta loved an interested listener.

Augusta shook her head and shared what she had been through already and it was only seven something in the morning.

"What's this nearly naked talk?"

"Well, you did not hear this from me, not a headline, right?

"Right."

"There's a hood over the guy's head."

CJ stopped, "That's weird. A guy?"

Augusta lowered her voice, "Without a doubt, a guy."

"Who do ya think it is? Is Mickey open? I don't see his mountain bike." CJ was clearly excited and spewed the usual fountain of questions.

"I was here before seven and he wasn't anywhere in sight. No sign of his bicycle. He could be making a killing on breakfast with all these people arriving. I'll never understand this younger generation. Or is it two generations younger than me?"

CJ ignored the question and muttered agreement. She kept eyes on the bucket truck. Something was bothering her about Mickey's food truck. "Hey, have you ever heard anything about Mickey and the food truck?"

"I'm not around enough to keep track of much. I spent the winter down in Pikeview with Queennie and that took me out of the loop up here, ya know? I did help Hank get as far as graduation. Did you know he's working at the Last this summer?"

This is Augusta's usual talk and CJ let the question fade into thin air. She was hot on the trail of a headline for her nooner e-Blast!. "I'm headed to the Sheriff's Department to talk with Roz. That'll get me some answers. You take care and watch out for Big Foot." CJ tried to lighten the conversation, slapped the side of the jeep, and stepped back with a wave.

Augusta returned the wave and roared off, nearly hitting another vehicle vying for a parking space near the train depot. Horns honked, fingers flew, and she was off and running into the mountains.

PREGNANT PAUSE

Phoebe took advantage of a quiet moment to call back into the office. Blessedly, Roz answered without her usual litany. "Hey, Pheb'. How's it goin' out there?"

"As good as can be expected. Thanks for getting all the help called out. I'm here with Bart. We're waitin' for the state team of experts, making sure no one interferes with the parking lot, the zipline, the whatever scene. Looks like a murder, Roz. Pretty nasty stuff."

"Any idea who the Vic is?"

"Not yet, can't tell from here."

"No problemo. What about the *nearly naked* reported by Augusta? Inquiring minds want to know. Hint. Hint. Can you tell us what that's about?"

Phoebe was silent trying to figure out what Roz was talking about. Then it clicked. She lowered her voice, "Is our buddy, CJ, with you?"

Roz was trying to be as discreet as she could be and gave up. She was in no mood for guessing games. "That's a Roger. Ace Reporter CJ is here now. Yappin' about the Freedom of Information Act. I'm tellin' and tellin' her, we believe in free info alright, but seein' as how there is no information, there is no act, no First Amendment Rights or anything else. So, hold all horses."

"Humm, give her this. When you hear nearly naked what would a person be wearing?"

"That's likely the tightie-whities, right? I can see it now."

"That would be close, but only in horseshoes as we say in the crime business." Phoebe hesitated, thinking, *Should I release a tidbit of information here or not. Nope. Nothing public until the analysis is complete. The forensics team and Doc will disclose their findings via the Acting Sheriff, Bill. Follow the process, Girly-girl.*

"Gotta get back to business here. Until we have some results from our investigation, there will not be any announcements."

Roz announced in her broadcast voice, "Okay, Pheb', I'll handle it from here. Then she lowered her voice to a whisper, "What's the answer to the nearly naked?"

Phoebe matched her whisper, "Just between us girls, a hood over the victim's head qualifies as nearly naked."

CJ was acting nonchalant while listening closely to the Roz side of the conversation. She jumped in, "A hood! I got it from Augusta. Old news. I need something for my twelve noon headline. C'mon, Phoebe-girl."

Roz gave CJ *The Look* and reported back to Phoebe, "Uh-uh. Augusta already played that trump card."

CJ huffed and crossed her arms in frustration.

Phoebe jumped in. "Hey, that's not comin' from me, I've got work to do." She lowered her voice again to a whisper, "Roz, just listen so CJ can't guess what I need. The reason for this call. I took pictures of two cars in the parking lot this morning. I'll forward them to you. See if you can read the license plates and run a check. The one is a big box hearse looking thing. The other vehicle's still in the parking lot—a Ford Taurus. Let's see what you can dig up. Might as well start overthinking all possibilities. Sending pics now."

Roz was still in the stealth process, "You bet. I'm on it the minute the you-know-whats get here. It'll help take my mind off these twins beating me with their eight limbs from the inside out." She let out a yip, "Ouch, there goes a right hook to my bladder, Gotta goes. UGH."

CJ picked up the receiver as Roz hustled down the hallway to the lady's room. "Pheb', it's me. Just wanted to say you've got quite the mess on your hands and the timing couldn't be worse. Looks like you'll be busy with this and the rest of us will be doing the campaignin' for you. Count on us. 'Vote for Phoebe' will be loud and clear this week. Wrap up this deal and the election'll be yours." CJ was still hunting for a headline on her e-Blast! due at noon.

Phoebe had to chuckle over this election possibility. CJ made it sound so easy, "Thanks. Tell your stepbrother, Bill, nothing's going on here. We're waiting for the state people to roll in."

"He'll be happy to hear his help isn't needed. He's still at Becky's."

"Gotta go now. Later."

Roz returned to the desk just as CJ hung up. "Thanks for covering. I haven't seen much of you since our wedding. It was such a great day, wasn't it?"

CJ leaned against the desk, "You bet. I am glad we did the joint wedding for the four of us. I'm not good at taking center stage. Brian and I are still working on moving in together. Boxes all over the place. Not fun plus lots of distractions if you get my drift." With the last comment, CJ broke out a sexy, mischievous smile and wiggled her eyebrows.

Roz went into pregnant-woman-bitching sarcasm, "Not so much for us. Fun times ended with the twins getting stronger each day. Bill's move into my small house was easy for him. You know guys. The nursery is the 'long pole in the tent' hold-up. With a month to go, what's the hurry?"

"Roz, how about Brian and I come over, bring dinner this weekend, and we'll set up the nursery with you and you can check that box from your to-do list."

She dabbed her eyes and tried to stop the uncontrollable grateful tears. "You'd do that? Wonderful. See ya Saturday afternoon."

When Phoebe ended the call with CJ there was a tap at her window. One of the patrol deputies reported that the manager of the High Country Adventures, Oscar deHerrera, was anxious to open for the day. He was losing money while everything was locked down and was creating a scene at the depot holding area.

Bart did an eye roll and volunteered to talk with the guy. He took off with the deputy. No one would be doing any high flyin' until the crime scene was cleared for business—several hours from now. It could be days. Until then the area would be blocked off and the business closed. She knew this would be tough news for the owner, but Bart would be good at delivering it. Nothing could be done to undo this crime.

Cousin George and Doc finished what little they could with the body and joined her. The state people were firm in their instructions to not disturb the scene including the body.

She looked at Cousin George thinking out loud, "We need to keep track of everyone here in the parking lot. We're limited on staff with only two deputies busy managing the crowd. The depot helps to keep people from moving the line, but the deputies have their hands full. Is there anyone you trust who could start a clipboard of names, contact information, title or position, and purpose for being here?"

Phoebe spotted two of the three person Board of Commissioners pulling into the parking lot. Retired Sheriff Joe was driving. *There's already too many people here and we don't need the county commissioners to jump into the fray.*

She exited her vehicle and waved to Joe and his sidekick.

"Hey there. What brings you two here?"

"Just checking on this report over the air waves of a nearly naked body. Couldn't resist, ya know, Phoebe. What's happened here?"

"We're working on it, Joe. The Colorado Forensic Team is on its way. Can't say right now what happened. But what I can say is we have too many people here. And we don't need to add to the population. Would appreciate it if you could head back to your office. I'll keep you in the loop when we have some specific info."

Joe decided his help would not add value, "Call if you need an extra hand. After thirty years of being the Sheriff I still think like one. I might add, Phoebe, best play this out as a prank gone wrong. Let it ride the wave of public opinion and it will hit the sand and die—not a rip tide. There's always something that comes along to distract, right?"

Phoebe almost wrinkled her nose at Joe's image for this crime—a wave erasing everything? *Hum. I don't think so. I am not of the mind to make a crime go away.* "Thanks, Joe. I know I can count on you going forward." *Not.*

She was thinking more about the underhanded business

with the commissioners trying to lock in Bill as Sheriff instead of holding an election. *Yeah Joe. We'll see how willing you are to help.*

With a quick good-bye, they headed back to town. Phoebe turned to Cousin, "We can't stop everyone from being here who thinks they can help, but we certainly can log them if needed later. We can review it and set guidelines for who comes in and who does not if there is a next time."

"I've got a guy or two who could do it. I'll get that set up." He took off in the direction of the fire department's search and rescue team. Phoebe was relieved to know there were capable people who could get things moving without questioning the politically correct wisdom of doing so.

Doc reported, "The body's a real mess. Someone had a message for someone. From what I could see the zipline platform was involved, but there could be other areas of interest to the forensics people."

Phoebe was looking around, "If the parking lot's involved, all these people and emergency vehicles in here contaminate the evidence."

Bart came back and reported Oscar, the manager, understood, no opening today. He was not happy, but the message was clear. She was thinking, *Bart has a way of making people feel comfortable. They trust him.*

Bart looked at Doc, "The state people should be here soon and that'll move things along."

TIGER EYES

The state's three person forensics team rolled in. Phoebe, Doc, and Bart waved and walked over to them as they parked their van. After quick introductions and updates, the team lead, Kate, a forensic pathologist, added, "Has anybody been up to the platform? And has anyone touched the body?"

Phoebe raised her hand. "Yes, to both questions. I went up to the platform, but when I saw what was there, I did not step onto it. I just wrapped some crime scene tape around the supporting columns and the steps."

Doc stepped in, "Cousin George and I reached the body from a bucket truck to determine if the person was alive. That's when I called you for help. Phoebe and I were thinking this is too big for our limited resources."

"Great. Now who's in charge of this investigation here in Oresville?"

Bart piped up, "Phoebe's in charge. She's lead patrol and detective as needed for the Sheriff's department. We have one town constable to cover the city limits. That's me, but the sheriff's department covers any crime beyond the basics."

"The Acting Sheriff assigned this case to me and Bart is part of the team.

"Oh, you're Phoebe. We saw lots of signs as we came into town. "Vote For Phoebe" was everywhere."

"Sure is."

"I knew a woman was running for a sheriff spot in the state but didn't connect the dots. That's cool. Good luck with that."

"Thanks. But right now, it looks like we have bigger fish to fry than getting out the vote. Let's get to it."

Doc and Bart were listening to the election talk. Doc raised his eyebrows, smiled, and tilted his head to Bart, "We're looking forward to next Tuesday." Bart agreed.

Phoebe was eager to get the forensic team moving. She asked Kate how to help the process. Kate looked around and asked her to have the deputies keep the area clear of any additional contamination. No vehicles, no people in the parking area. Kate designated the entire parking lot as the crime scene. She would narrow the scope as they investigated.

Kate invited Phoebe to huddle with the team. It was decided that Kate would detail the body and the two men would search the platform and the ground under the body. They covered up with the standard level D hazmat suits and began the painstaking task of gathering forensic evidence. They searched in a grid beneath the body and detailed the crime scene with photos. The search included footprints, fingerprints, bodily fluids, hair—any trace evidence in the area and on the body. All was bagged and labeled, ready for the lab to analyze.

Phoebe was amazed at how this team of three worked together. There was little talking and they appeared to not need any discussion. An hour later they had completed the forensic scrub of the scene. Phoebe was told the complete area, including the zipline, must remain closed. The body could be removed and taken to the coroner's office. The team would follow to do more analysis of the body. They would work into the afternoon, write a preliminary report, spend the night, and give the Sheriff's office an update before they left town first thing in the morning.

Once the Denver forensics lab completed their analysis of the data, a written report would follow. The results would take a while as the lab was backed up with a recent spike in drug related crime along the Front Range. It was still less than other areas of the same size, but a recent spike perhaps brought on by competition.

Kate confirmed what Phoebe thought, the primary crime scene appeared to be the zipline platform. There was some blood, articles of clothing and a baseball bat in plain sight. In the pocket of a pair of discarded jeans, they had found a thick roll of small bills. The forensic team noted drugs were present—cocaine. Testing would lock down this fact.

The body was released to Doc, the county coroner. The fire department crew was standing by watching the state team do their work. Cousin George had already directed them to get suited up in hazmat gear, anticipating what would be needed. When drugs were present, the risk of contamination could not be overstated. This year, one volunteer had been taken to the hospital for treatment due to an oversight. It was hard enough to attract and keep volunteers without putting them in harm's way due to carelessness.

Cousin George fired up the bucket truck and two firemen were lifted to the zipline. The body was carefully bagged, zipped, and lowered to the ground where the ambulance crew was waiting.

Before the stretcher was loaded into the ambulance, Phoebe stepped over to it. She asked if they would unzip the bag far enough for her to check the identity of the victim in case it was someone she knew.

With a quick movement, George lifted the hood still covering the face. Her gasp could be heard throughout the county. "Doc, George, do you know who this is?" Phoebe's round, startled eyes were in full shock as she looked at the beaten and bruised head. Bart was standing next to her and felt the sag in her posture. He grabbed an arm to steady her.

In unison, "It's Mickey Walker."

She went on to explain, "The owner of the food wagon over there. Now we know why he didn't open this morning."

"Are you sure?" Doc asked.

"Absolutely."

Bart added, "He's the one who let his wife go up to Slide Lake last December, right?"

Directing the rest of her comments to Doc, she explained, "It was the end of last year, before Bart moved here from Greenstone. Mickey also came from Greenstone and Bart knew of him because of the abusive wife. He had a restraining order against her."

Phoebe looked at George, "You remember the Flight for Life out of Slide Lake last December, right?"

With her comment, his memory was significantly nudged and he spouted, "Of course. The red truck off the road below Slide Lake. Got it now. Thanks for the help."

There followed a brief reverent silence as each of them was trying to make sense of a domestic case in December and now a death in June. Then Bart spoke up, "Think the best thing I can do is go over to where he lived and see what's there."

"Good idea. See if you can locate his mountain bike. It's not parked at the food truck. I'll get a deputy to start interviewing the neighborhood around the Park."

George offered, "There might be some cameras nearby. Seems like everyone has cameras for safety after hours now."

Phoebe agreed. "Ah-ha, I'll add that to the interviews around the Park. There's one too many patrol deputies over at the train depot now. I'll pull one of them to start going door to door. Maybe someone heard something, saw something, photographed something. Catch up to you at the office when Augusta comes in for her statement?"

"You bet. I'll check with Roz for his address from the county records. He worked there when he first came to town." Bart gave a quick nod to the people standing around the body and left.

Phoebe leaned into the group, "Gentlemen, for now, let's keep this among us, okay? Besides, we need a formal ID through Doc's office." Other than correct procedure, she was not sure why she did not want the word to hit the street that the Vic was Mickey Walker. *My gut tells me there's something unique here—a delay in identification might help.*

ABSENT FOR CAUSE

P hoebe's cell rang, an incoming from Roz. "Well, while you were out there chattin' up the Denver guys, I was stuck back in the office working way too hard."

"I'm not sure that's the case. We've got a woman from Denver running the show here and two guys with her, lot's happening. But go ahead." She liked to keep pace with Roz. They were good friends, but more importantly, an ad hoc investigation team. They outguessed each other and dug into plain old detective work. Phoebe, in her spirit of over-thinking, solved the riddles of crime by interviewing, analyzing, and linking random pieces of information. Roz supported the process with her research talents.

"The black SUV is registered out of state. It's a rental from New Mexico. Picked up a week ago, with an open return date. Rented to a certain Alejandro Martinez of Albuquerque."

"That's the vehicle I saw leave the parking lot when I first got here. Couldn't tell who was driving, but I thought there was another person in it. What about the second vehicle?"

"The second one is registered to Suzanne Martinelli. You know the young woman who works the reception desk here in the county building? She was the chick with Mickey Walker at the Club for the New Year's Eve party. Remember? They were sitting at the bar, chattin' it up, havin' a gay old time."

"Oh yea, they were there and I overheard him talking, something about getting rid of his wife and starting over here in Oresville. I promised myself to check further and promptly forgot about it when Bart appeared at the front door."

"That was a great party and Bart's arrival was straight out of a movie scene. Not quite Hundred and One Dalmatians, closer to the drama of a *second coming* when he arrived." Roz laughed at the vision.

"Exactly. Quite the entrance. It feels like things have changed fast and for the better. Now he's working up here as the Oresville Constable, living in a tent while he restores the cabin he bought on a whim. We get to spend time together. Amazing how the planets align, if ya think about it."

"That's life, my Grandma used to say, 'Never bet on the Come Line'."

"What's that mean?"

"No idea, but it seems to fit what we're talkin' about here. Crap shoot."

"Hum, sure. Hey, back to business. See if Suzanne can tell us why her car is here in the parking lot. I'd guess it's been here overnight and no one seems interested in it. The fire department is cleaning up and I'm headed back to the office."

"Roger that," and Roz clicked off.

With a call over to the main entrance reception desk, Sparkle answered and Roz found out Suzanne had not shown up to work this morning.

They chatted at the gossip level. Sparkle loved to gather information on everyone in the county building and beyond for that matter, in what she called *background*. She was always willing to share with anyone and everyone. "Not only did Suzanne not show up this morning, she had skipped out yesterday also. No call or otherwise. Just no show. Of course, with her connections, she's not likely to be fired. She was hangin' with the building maintenance guy, Mickey something, and is majorly distracted. She moved here from Denver, so Oresville's beneath her."

"What connections does she have that'll save her job with a no show for two days?"

"Her family's out of the East Coast and somehow connected to mining in Colorado. Lots of Italian workers were here in the 1880s. Cheap labor, I guess. Not like Augusta's family money, but her family's connected, ya know. They've moved on into other business ventures. I hear it's not real legit, but ya didn't hear it from me."

"Does she call out sick a lot?"

"That's what's weird. She's never gone. People come to the information desk, talk with her, and leave. I guess I'll have to work this desk until she gets back, recovered or otherwise. People come in and are not pleased to see me. They ask about Suzanne and leave, not on a happy note. It's strange."

"That's different. Can you call me if you hear from her? It's nothing urgent, just a few questions about her latest squeeze, Mickey Walker."

"Well, he's a piece of work, right? Starts here and quits four months later. Then brings in a food truck and it's open all the time. I hear what he's servin' ain't just food, if ya get my drift."

"What else is he into?"

"No clue. Just *added sides* you could call it. Gotta go, citizens looking for help." Sparkle laughed as she disconnected the line and Roz heard a shiny, distant, "How can I help make your day?" Likely directed at the next Green County citizen looking for help or otherwise.

Back at the base of the zipline, the ambulance guys closed the body bag, loaded it, and headed to Doc's place. The forensics team packed their tools and followed the ambulance. Phoebe thanked Cousin George for all of his help and he headed the bucket truck back to the mine.

She went over to the train depot to check on the deputies. "Thanks for a great job, guys. Sure appreciate all you did this morning." Phoebe never missed an opportunity to praise other deputies. After all, they might all be working for her in just a few days.

There were few remaining citizens in the area. The coffee and donuts detritus was being picked up. The ride would not open today and would not be in action until the crime scene was released. With no more action, most of the citizens were already going about their daily business.

The park manager was nowhere to be seen. He was probably in his office upstairs at the depot trying to explain to the superiors what was going on.

Phoebe walked slowly back across the parking lot. It was hard to think about what had happened to Mickey. What he must have gone through sickened her. Over the years in law enforcement, she had seen most everything, but this level of inhumanity was unforgivable. She easily recognized her priorities, *There will be no politicking on my part until justice is served.*

With a survey of the area, Suzanne's car created an ominous presence.

MIA

Phoebe's cell rang. It was Roz again, "Well, what we have here is a no-show reception desk person, Suzanne. You know, the owner of the Taurus in the parking lot."

"What d'ya mean? No-show?"

"No-show as in missing. Somethin'. Spoke with Sparkle. Suzanne did not show up for work yesterday or today. No call, no nothin'. Just didn't make an appearance."

"Not good. Seems like I need to do a wellness check at her house."

"You're right on track and I'm one step ahead as per usual. Here's Suzanne's house address. I'm checking now to see if she owns it, rents, whatever. Let me know if you find her. In the meanwhile, I'll just stay here, watching the clock tick till these twins are born."

"Later, Roz."

Suzanne's was a five minute drive from the zipline.

Blinding sunshine showered energy to the solar panels throughout the neighborhood. Nothing in the driveway. The house emitted a quiet, empty aura. Phoebe rang the bell. No answer. She rang again and banged on the door with the palm of her hand. Still no response. Moving to the back door, she checked the side windows on the way. The blinds were lowered preventing visual access.

She used a utility flashlight to knock firmly on the back door—it opened. Phoebe knew if she went in and found anything remotely resembling a clue, it would be inadmissible in a court of law. On the other hand, this was a wellness check and it was important to be certain Suzanne was not in dire straits. It is a small community after all. *Only right to take the extra step to be certain citizens are safe. We're not ruled by laws like big cities.*

Decision made. "Deputy Korneal here. Anyone home?" No response and the air was fresh. Suzanne must have been here this morning, *Maybe.*

The door opened all the way and Phoebe nearly got run over by a large, gray, hissing, screeching cat. The green eyes flashed like an exploding camera bulb. Then it took flight from the countertop, ricocheted off her gun holster, shot off the back step, and flew across the weeds of the backyard in a matter of seconds.

Heart racing, she righted herself, pulled at her shirt, and wiggled to balance the bullet proof vest over her boobs. The design of the vest was clearly not built for females in law enforcement. The woman who would design such a vest would make a fortune.

Over the years, Phoebe had unconsciously developed a set of unique styles of shifting, pulling, and twisting to accommodate the vest. Entering and exiting vehicles was a class act of forceful shifting into a slight crawl with a headfirst motion, arms crossed over her stomach to land behind the steering wheel. From a chair to a standing position was a quick jerk—side to side. Sitting was a swift jab from the elbows to each side gracefully executed in sync with the motion landing her into the chair with an acceptable level of vest comfort. While making rounds on patrol, she used a careful, ballet-like gliding gait. This kept the vest secured to her chest.

These movements were automatic for her, but a source of snickers, eyebrow action, and tightlipped silent chuckles from newly hired fellow officers. The seasoned veterans were not entertained and occasionally speculated what a re-design of the vest would look like—accidental fortunes had been made by many garage inventors.

With the vest in place and heart rhythm slowing to normal, she took a deep, calming breath and gave out another yell to announce herself. She dabbed a sleeve at her forehead, reached to the ponytail and tightened the band with a hard pull, *Easy girl, the kitty is clearly an outdoor cat or from this point forward will be.*

The afternoon sun was hitting a kitchen skylight, reflecting off the bright, shiny yellow walls. Sunglasses would be needed in this room to avoid retina damage. The kitchen was spartan, just Phoebe's style. Her self-assessed slight register on an OCD scale approved of this kitchen. There was nothing on the countertops, no leftover dishware in the sink, but an undefined odor permeated the space. Her gut instinct jumped in. There was a note of tension in the air.

On the table was a wine bottle, two used juice glasses, crumpled napkins, and an empty bowl. With the neatness of the kitchen, the assortment on the table looked out of place. She pulled on a pair of rubber gloves from the duty belt pocket and smelled each glass. Clearly, there were two people drinking red wine here, not too long ago. The wine in the bottom of the glasses had not evaporated.

Phoebe announced again and moved into the other rooms. The house was small and a quick glance at each of the four rooms revealed nothing until the last room. This door was closed and she had to push to get it open. The room was a mess with papers piled on every flat surface, folders on the floor, and a chair pulled to a four drawer filing cabinet. On the desk next to the cabinet was a water glass. She leaned over to take a sniff. Someone had helped him or herself to the wine from the kitchen. The cabinet drawers were open and empty—contents tossed to the floor. Whoever it was, had taken their time.

Another more careful check of each room was in line. She went back through the house, room by room. The blinds in each room were closed. This time she turned on all the lights as she moved back through the house carefully, slowly noticing any little thing.

Only the living room appeared to have been used and not straightened. A rug had a corner flipped over, a pillow without a covering was on the floor, and there were scrape marks on the hardwood floor next to the rug. Phoebe got out her flashlight and got down on all fours to check under the furniture for anything left behind—no fuzz, no food, no funk.

Her phone rang. Startled, she flipped to a sitting position, simultaneously shifting, twisting, with upper arms trying to get the bulletproof vest into place. The whole thing had shifted upward and she could barely fumble the cell phone to her ear. She cleared her throat, "Korneal."

Bart came through loud and clear, "Hey, just checking in with you. I'm over at Doc's place and it'll be a while before they have anything. You sound out of breath or somethin.' Everything good with you?"

"Yeah, yeah. Roz told me about Mickey's close friend, Suzanne Martinelli, didn't show up for work now two days in a row. It's her car at the zipline parking lot. So, I'm checking here at the house. No sign of her. But it feels like someone was recently here, long gone now."

"It's been a long day. This morning I started a crock pot dinner. Do you want to come over to my lair? We'll have a glass of something. Eat. Relax. What d'ya say? Up for it?"

"Just what I need at this point. I'll go back to the office. Augusta might be there about now. Do you want to hang with the state team and Doc or meet at the office to talk with Augusta?"

"Hard pass on Augusta's statement. I'll stay here and get all I can from these state people."

"No worries. Alrighty then. See you around sixish. I'll bring the 'something'."

Since Bart had moved from Greenstone to the mountains outside of Oresville at the end of March, she had a better, healthier diet. He liked to cook, she liked to eat. Phoebe did not know how to cook, didn't like to cook, and had no desire to learn to cook. It was a match made in heaven. With Bart into healthy living and their attraction to one another, Phoebe embraced all the accoutrements of their time together after hours.

Before she resumed the search with a flashlight, she sat on the floor thinking about Bart. He was a kind, considerate guy. Life in Oresville had taken a monumental step forward. The thought of getting a dog for keeping her company was now in the rearview mirror, *Back to business, Girly-girl.*

She called into the office. Roz was already gone for the day. She worked a six a.m. shift and by three each afternoon was in a hurry to get home. The evening shift operator told Phoebe Augusta had not come in yet but had called to say she was on her way and would be in the Sheriff's office within an hour.

With little fact to go on, Phoebe's intuition told her something not so good had happened at Suzanne's place. Thinking she had some high level help in town, she called Doc's office. "Hi Doc. How're things goin'?"

"Going well. The team's almost finished with the body. Compiling their findings, they'll never get back to Denver by quittin' time, so I've arranged hotel rooms for tonight. Courtesy of the County, of course."

"Great. Is Kate available for a moment?"

"Let me check."

The next voice she heard was Kate's. "Hi, Phoebe. What's up?"

"I was doing a wellness check on Suzanne, the owner of a car at the zipline. My hunch is something is not kosher. I could use a second opinion. Just wondering if you or one of your team could come over."

"My guys have a few more things to do here. I'll come."

"Here's the address. It's just a few minutes from Doc's. I'll stand outside and watch for you."

Kate arrived and Phoebe greeted her, "That was quick. Thanks so much."

"No problem. What've we got here?"

They put on protective gloves, shoe covers, and entered the house through the backdoor. Phoebe took Kate through the rooms and shared her thoughts. Kate noted the rug and floor scuffs immediately in the living room.

After seeing the office, Kate agreed with Phoebe's suspicions, "Let's take this place on as well. After a call to the team, I'll get started." Kate took out evidence bags from her crime scene kit and began with collecting the glasses.

"If you don't need me here, I'll go to the office. Augusta Higgins discovered the body and she's coming in for an interview."

"That's fine. We can do this. You take off and we'll see you first thing in the morning? We'll have more information by then."

Earlier Phoebe had noticed a mountain bike leaning against the back side of the house. As she exited via the kitchen door for a closer look, she saw the lightweight carbon body equipped with adjustable air spring pressure. A top of the line all around traveling system—not just a bicycle at over ten thousand dollars. Not knowing what kind of bike Mickey used, an assumption of ownership was not made. This didn't look like a first choice for a smallish woman. She had to catch herself, *Mind your prejudices, Phoebe-girl.*

She stepped back into the house, "Hey Kate, please include the bike leaning against the back of the house. Fingerprints might settle the score on this one."

NOTHING NEW

I n the Sheriff's SUV Phoebe rounded the corner into the county's parking lot, just as Augusta was exiting the Rubicon. She had parked it next to the back door of the Green County Sheriff's Office. The door was quicker access and first choice for the few citizens who knew the entry code at the back of the building. Phoebe had a temporary thought, *I wonder when the code was last changed? Over the years how many people still have it? Oh well, that's a question for Roz.*

The fragile summer day was holding and the main streets of Oresville were crowded with tourists, citizens, and fresh air wannabes on skateboards, e-bikes, Segways, and rented jeeps. All were offered for the four wheeling mountain thrills at an altitude of almost ten thousand three hundred feet. The local Chamber of Commerce used the altitude to bill their motto, "Life's great at 10-5." A slight embellishment from the actual footage, but without question it captured the spirit. If the visitor was a pilot the altitude might be questioned.

The local emergency room was in constant motion from early June to mid-August with the onslaught of outdoor enthusiasts and their need for X-rays, stitches, and pain meds. The staff no longer tried to organize the closet of soft casts. Instead they were stacked in various corners for quick access along with crutches, Ace bandages and ice packs piled in portable freezers.

Frustrated locals were crowding the side streets for everyday routes, leaving Main Street and Highway 24 for the town constable. Bart's mission was to ensure balance and decorum from all. The town constable only worked Monday thru Friday and the weekends were a free-for-all. The Sheriff's people picked up the weekend action. Once again there was a discussion about the need for an Oresville Police Department. It would be nothing heavy, just daytime hours of nine to five but expanded to seven days a week. The sales tax collections were delightful as a steady 30 knot wind and promised another record-breaking year. With only the first official week of summer on the books, an Oresville PD looked like a distinct possibility.

Phoebe escorted Augusta through the door into the back hallway, and a quick left into the conference room. The recording app was started, "Alright Augusta, tell me the details from this morning."

She reiterated what had been reported to Roz, rushing over the details and providing little additional information. She thought there were two men getting into a large SUV but she didn't check it out. On second thought, she reported she was alone. The food truck was closed. The parking lot was empty. A body on the zipline wearing a hood, therefore nearly naked. Report completed.

"I gotta hunch there are drugs coming into town. It just

feels different. I talked with TuTu at the Washateria and she's run into some new people who give pause for caution. That Oscar deHerrera? He's the manager of the new park. TuTu knows the family from growing up and working in New Mexico. Maybe you should talk with her."

"I'll give it a try. She usually has an ear to the ground and picks up details before they become a CJ headline on the e-Blast!"

"Well, whatever. Gotta go. I'm headed to the county assessor's office. Looks like I've got some squatters in an old mining cabin on the edge of my property. Or maybe it's not my property. I want to be sure before I run them out. Or before the shack falls over, burns down, whatever. But you didn't hear it from me." She was exiting the room as she spoke over her shoulder in Phoebe's general direction.

In her recent past, Augusta had taken care of the Higgins homestead cabin by igniting it in an effort to improve the family business' bottom line. After the passing of her friend, partner, and cabin caretaker, Al Lewis, she decided the family cabin was no longer contributing to the business spreadsheets.

When it came to the Higgins Family enterprises—and most people—she liked to say, "You're either lift or drag." She was also not happy with her mother, Anne Louise. She was living *the life* in France with partner, Uncle Q. To lessen overhead, deliver revenge, and in general get even, she set fire to the cabin.

Ten months later, the chimney was still standing and great grandaddy's prize Elmira Wood cook stove, purchased in 1860 with matching nickel trivet, remained intact albeit heavily scorched. Augusta had located Old Al's stash of gold hidden under the floorboards of the kitchen. Now those pickle jars of gold coins, nuggets and flakes were safely stored in her safe deposit boxes at the bank. This was a constant source of struggle, *Only half of it's mine. Or is it?*

Phoebe could not resist a comment about the fire and yelled after her, "Just be careful no one gets hurt. Deep pockets are always liable. In this county that's you." She heard a chuckle as Augusta hustled down the hallway headed for the second floor assessor's office, *Did she flash a finger back at my comment?*

Augusta came from a long line of wealthy miners and businesswomen. When great grandaddy discovered gold in the 1860s the fever became part of the family DNA. To this day the Higgins women and money were known throughout the state for their built-in DNA of survivability.

Phoebe turned off the recording app. She would see TuTu tomorrow morning. The tight knit women of Oresville gathered at TuTu's Washateria every Wednesday morning. In the comfort of gentle machine noise, they could compare lives, share gossip, and now plot for Phoebe's victory in the election next week.

The Reverend Gabriella Trujillo-Tavarez, AKA TuTu, and the Retired Right Reverend Jorge Tavarez served a free breakfast six days a week for anyone in need. TuTu popped the quarters into machines for free laundry. Jorge proclaimed, "While I feed the soul, TuTu cleans it." Bloody Marys were also offered up if one knew to ask. As retired ministers of multiple faiths, both TuTu and Jorge practiced "Active Faith," not the study of faith. They applied what they had preached for so many years throughout New Mexico and parts of Colorado.

Together they knew what was going on or speculated on what was to come frequently before it occurred. Often by several months. Some said it was Divine Intervention. Nevertheless, TuTu sorted random bits of information into context before law enforcement was brought into play. With the events of today, whatever was going on was now at a criminal level. Too little too late for Mickey Walker.

Mind made up for tomorrow's plan, Phoebe pulled the Deputy Korneal timecard and punched out for the day. She headed home to the trailer on the south edge of town. The thought of going to Bart's little mountain cabin a bit further down the road brought a relaxed smile.

Mt. Massive was the boundary for the western edge of Green County. It was a solid mountain of granite, but its view varied with the ethereal drift of sun, moon, and stars. She looked forward to building up reserves from the unyielding mountain while sitting on the front porch of Bart's cabin.

She quickly changed her clothes, fixed her hair, and gave Bart a heads up call. "I'm five minutes out, Honeybun."

"Dinner and cocktails await your arrival, Sweet P. See you soon."

It had been nearly a year since Bart and Phoebe met, not under the most desirable circumstances. There was a spark between them from the first encounter. It was a chance meeting at the Greenstone Police Department. One look at who she later referred to as "Ponytail Man", Phoebe swooned. It proved to be the beginning of what would prompt his move to Oresville months later.

Both had experienced heartbreak following lengthy relationships and were wary of trusting anyone. Despite their pasts, things were working for them. At the end of March, Bart left his police position in Greenstone to take the constable's job in Oresville. The budding relationship took a sharp uptick with their shared interest in law enforcement and now they were co-located. As in Marketing 101—location, location, location. Their mutual interest moved from the entry level of *lust* to the second level of *attraction*, unspoken but recognized.

Phoebe thought Bart was fantastic and began to feel she could trust him. *Why would he move to Oresville and buy a cabin with land? A long term relationship for us?* Letting her guard down, Phoebe was beginning to open her heart to him. *Sometimes heartbreak is worth the risk.*

BART'S BLISS

As she headed south to Bart's cabin, Phoebe could feel her tension drain with the spectacular view of the mountain range. Her mind wandered, *Having Bart living here in Oresville has changed life. There was BB, before Bart and AB, after Bart. No doubt, AB is the winner. I had forgotten how awesome it is to have someone you can trust, company to enjoy, and he cooks, too—the trifecta.*

After the romantic disaster in Salt Lake City, the safest course of action for Phoebe was to leave that city and embrace a safe, single life in Colorado. Meeting Bart began a transformation of her life's perspective. Her perspective moved from job, friends, and more job. Now it could be called out as job, Bart, friends, and Phoebe's life. *Keep your head on straight and pay attention, Girlfriend. Meantime, enjoy.*

When Bart moved to Oresville, there was little planning, searching, or project management. He was offered the job as the constable, a somewhat misleading title, but no one cared to update the County Human Resource pamphlet. He gave notice at the Greenstone Police Department, listed his house for sale by owner, drove to Oresville, and followed the signs for a sale.

The garage sale was liquidating sixty years of minutia crammed into a vacant log building. He struck a chord with the owners and by the end of the weekend, he had bought the shack in the middle of twenty acres, a dream come true for him. The land was covered with quaking aspen, all from an original root. Aspen multiply by sending out their roots to start new trees, resulting in what is called a clone of aspen. Bart considered how a single Aspen created the beautiful grove surrounding his cabin. He wondered how this concept could apply to his new beginning in Oresville and his relationship with Phoebe.

The three room cabin was, mildly put, a fixer upper. When he called Phoebe to take a look, she came close to tears of disappointment at first sight. Bart explained he needed a weekend project and this would be the perfect fit. While working on his new home he would make do with a tent. Although a fast learner, this ability did not translate to construction skills.

Colorado gets more snow in April than any other month, so his temporary accommodations were tricky. The warm days between snow events melted most of the new accumulation, leaving a soggy mess under and around his tent. Of course, this was a great inspiration to get the cabin livable, sooner rather than later. It was slow going on the cabin repairs and multiple redo's of what he had accomplished. It was even slower going to hire the right talent to get it done.

Phoebe realized he would have no facilities for a while, so she offered him a key for needed showers, laundry, and electricity. Perhaps a warm overnight would be in order too.

Two months later, the cabin was at a level of comfort. The holes between most logs were chinked. The roof repair was done, albeit twice, first by Bart and followed by a redo of experienced roofers.

The resident Pack Rats had been "relocated" to their next life as part of Phoebe's contribution. Bart had designed a wood burning stove that provided a heating source through an infrastructure of water pipes. He took the time to start a small garden which was limping along with a small harvest of radishes early in the short mountain growing season.

At six in the afternoon on this beautiful June day, the sun was still bright in the western sky. Phoebe pulled the truck into his long, rutted, dirt driveway, and parked to the side, not blocking the view. Bart waited at the cabin's porch as she walked over. "Greetings, Sheriff Phoebe." Bart enjoyed teasing her about the upcoming election. He had confidence she'd win and felt compelled to get her used to the idea when they were alone. "So glad you're here." Bart wrapped her in a warm, loving embrace.

She relaxed into the comfortable, safe embrace and mumbled, "Me too, Honeybun. It's been one heck of a day."

"Well, c'mon in. Dinner's in the pot."

"Sounds perfect. My offering is a reasonable bottle of wine and I can manage the screw off top."

They were seated and lifted glasses in a toast, "Here's to us," and Bart leaned over with a kiss to her cheek. The wine tasted like heaven in the thin air at tree line. The quick kiss was the icing on the beginning of the evening.

Bart leaned back into the chair and prompted her, "So where are you with this murder?"

"It's gotten even more complicated, Bart. Let me put together what I know and see what you think."

"Just so you know, I did go over to his place and nothing looked out of sync."

"Was his mountain bike there?"

"Not that I could see. The bike rack was empty."

"Just so you know, Kate and her team did go over to Suzanne's house and did their CSI stuff. There's a bike there. I'd guess it's Mickey's."

"That'll help move this along. I'll report on the bike at the morning meeting."

"Great. Here's what we have so far." Phoebe took a deep breath, held up her right hand and started ticking off the events. "One, Augusta calls in a dead body on a zipline. Two, a pair of empty vehicles in the parking lot, one's a rental with New Mexico plates and the other belongs to Suzanne Martinelli. Three, drug paraphernalia, clothing, and a baseball bat on the zipline platform. Four, the hooded, naked body had been beaten and that connects it to the platform—a dangerous assumption here—it's probably the crime scene."

"Red alert, you know what assumptions do."

"Agreed, it's all about our experience and the gut instinct from it. So, it's okay to assume but we must validate. Once validated it moves us forward, maybe the right direction but we won't know until the case is solved. Hindsight, right?"

"Yes. And number five, Doc Watson, after reviewing the scene, suggested we call in the state forensics team on this one. I agreed."

"You're right, Pheb'. Hopefully the forensic report tomorrow will confirm this assumption on the crime scene location."

Bart reached over to her glass with the bottle of wine and added a splash, "The danger here is when we locals bring in the state's resources, they take over."

"That's a risk for sure, but we need their high dollar technology and experience for this situation."

He tipped his glass to emphasize, "Right. Just manage it— about all we can do. So here's another assumption. Is Suzanne somehow involved in this situation?"

"Yes. At her house today with Kate, we found some suspicious looking areas. Kate brought in her techs to do their magic at the house. I expect we'll hear those results in the morning."

Taking a sip, the two of them stared out the window for a mental break before continuing. Phoebe exhaled and reached for Bart's hand. "Suzanne's definitely involved—my guess, assumption, wild-goose chase, all of the above."

She turned back to Bart and leaned in for a kiss, followed with a delightful little "more-to-come" smile. *The man's incredible. In this mess, he can still deliver a killer kiss.*

He sat back with a serious smile, "Yup, I think your gut's right on with this Suzanne woman. Something's off with her, for sure. Remember, she hasn't shown up for work for two days."

"Right. And number seven, when the New Mexico vehicle took off like a bat out of hell, it appeared to have two people in it. It had tinted windows, giant off-road tires, the works, and it was hard to see inside. Couldn't make any ID, but sure looked like two heads to me. Wonder if Suzanne was in the vehicle?"

"If she's a small person it would be tough to even see her above the seats."

"You're right. You know, I've seen Suzanne and Mickey together and she was inches shorter than him. The first time I saw them was New Year's Eve at the Club, then once or twice around town. He looked to be about five foot nine or ten. She works the front desk at the county building—petite, friendly, frilly, and a giggle that's perky. I'm thinkin' there's something going on between the two of them, more than just kissy-kissy."

"Do you know where she comes from?"

"Not really. She started the county job about eight months ago, but never talked about where she moved from. Once

Mickey took the job as maintenance man for the county, they seemed to hit it off right away."

"Has anyone looked into her family? It might give up some clues as to what's going on. Maybe some insight into why he was killed and she's missing—if missing. She could have left her car at the park and someone else drove."

"At tomorrow morning's meeting, Doc, the state team, Bill, you, and I'll be there. We'll hear the readout from the state experts. Then I plan on going to Denver, find her family, meet the lead state investigator, and hopefully visit Ellis Meredith, Mickey's wife. She might be the ex-wife by now. So many questions, so few answers."

WISHY-WASHY

On Wednesday morning at six sharp, Phoebe was at her desk, lining up the schedule for the day. Looking at coverage for next week with the election on Tuesday. They never had enough deputies to cover twenty four by seven. For Tuesday, she planned to work all day, off at four and back to the Club at six for results at seven-ish. Show up in uniform or jeans and t-shirt? *Why does this not come naturally? If I'm the next Sheriff of Green County, maybe my uniform changes too? Hum, later for this one.*

There was a message from the state team, confirming they were ready with a preliminary report. The eight o'clock meeting was a go.

Phoebe updated Roz with what she saw at Suzanne's house. She dropped the nail file, picked up a pen, and tapped a notepad, "Y'all are gonna need her family details like names, relationships, addresses, any ex's lurking in Suzanne's history.

I will start a clean slate of information on her and the Martinelli Family."

"I'm headed to Denver and anything you can ferret out would help. Let's start with, does she show up for work today? Do ya think she could be on vacation somewhere and the boss forgot to make a note? It's happened before, not often mind you. It would explain why the backfill woman at the front desk says she's not going to be fired as a no-show."

Conversation over. Phoebe left and cruised over to TuTu's Washateria. At this early hour TuTu and Jorge were alone and into their morning rituals. As she entered, a bell jingled and they turned to see who was up this early.

"Wow, here comes the next Sheriff of Green County, Colorado! Morning," announced Jorge. TuTu was stacking coins in neat columns by denomination, the contributions from yesterday to their food and cleanliness faith-based mission, "Breakfast with a Spin." Jorge and TuTu never denied anyone food and clean clothes. The collection jug was always out. It was a repurposed laundry soap container and the take from the previous day usually covered the operating costs for the next day.

"Lots going on today. I wanted to get here first thing for your input about the excitement yesterday."

TuTu shifted to create space for Phoebe to help her count coins and Jorge offered her his seat, "We heard the abbreviated version of events from CJ, but no identification, no suspects, and no motive. I'll get you some breakfast. It's the midweek leftovers, a Jorge's 'Name That Food' scramble."

"Let's hope it's not recycled toast from last week," Phoebe was halfway kidding. Jorge and TuTu served breakfast all day, every day to fill the stomachs for those needing help over a hump in life's journey, not a long term handout solution.

These retired ministers practiced their faith in little ways making a 'hand up' kind of difference. The washateria provided a minimal living for them and offered an oasis for those who fought for survival each day. Phoebe had seen these two look at each other and recite with mutual smiles, "Cleanliness is next to Godliness." Phoebe loved this couple and their support to the community, their flock, without preaching, bible thumping, or qualification.

She stacked a short column of quarters, "Maybe identification today. But the next of kin notification takes precedence. You know how I am."

TuTu was recording the columns of coins and dipped her head to acknowledge the Phoebe protocol, "Next of kin first. Then we talk the details."

"TuTu, I wanted to talk with you about drugs in Oresville. What are you hearing?"

She let loose with a heavy sigh, put down the pen, and looked at Phoebe, "Just this year there's been an uptick in overdoses, young and old alike. You know this. By old we're thinkin' thirties and forties. By the time someone hits thirty five or so, maturity and common sense seem to come out of the mixmaster of growing up and the rates taper off. At least for Oresville. Lately this has not been the case. Some independent types can't afford surgery, dental fillings, physical therapy. Instead, painkillers are easier. Certainly cheaper. And they are still functional. When a bad shipment of drugs comes in, usually cocaine around here, their use cannot be managed."

"Any ideas on where it's coming from?"

"Oh yea, straight over the mountains from Denver. Strong Italian connections out of the East Coast. This isn't new, but what is new is there seems to be some competition to the Old Guard coming from our friendly Zia state to the south, New Mexico."

"Zia?"

"It's on their flag, license plates, tattoos, you name it. It's the four seasons and the cycle of life—a religious symbol for the Zia people. Most people moving to the state today have no idea of the religious significance."

"Okay, but what's with the competition? What have ya heard?"

"I know the deHerrera family. Jorge and I lived in New Mexico for many years and we are familiar with them, mostly by reputation. There was little doubt in our community they were into drug running. And surprise, surprise, a deHerrera is the manager of the new High Mountain Adventures Park. Coincidence? I don't think so."

"We've had two overdoses at the high school this year. Serious, but not fatal, thank the good Lord. Word on the street, its bad stuff comin' in. Cheap, plentiful, and laced with God knows what."

"Do you see a connection with this deHerrera or do you think it's coming from Denver?"

"If I was to follow my hunch on this, I'd definitely say deHerrera is playing a part in this increase. If we had a solid on this, we would have come to you. It's scuttlebutt from high schoolers. Jorge and I both agree the minister's zipped lips open if a crime or serious injury can be avoided."

"Please keep me posted. We've turned a blind eye to this threat for way too long. It's time we pony up and wade into the fray."

"We'd certainly appreciate support. The bad guys are few and far between, but they operate without filters. We're small enough to make an example out of them, if we can catch them at the point of sales or better yet stop the delivery."

Phoebe was listening intently, slowly nodding her head to understand the pieces. "It'll have to be more than responding to the situation. We need to get ahead of the distribution. Let's see how Tuesday comes out and see if we can build on what little we have."

"There are citizens who will come together to help if the need for support is recognized."

"I hope you're right. The Sheriff's Department is a drop of what is really needed. On another subject, remember Mickey Walker, Ellis Meredith's hubby? You're working with her."

"Oh yes, the case at Christmas when she hightailed it out of town and slid off the road below Slide Lake. I did work with her. She was in my anger management group, but she's moved on. I heard she moved to Denver, filed for divorce."

"I'm not surprised, but I thought he would seek a divorce. After all, she was the one abusing him."

"Humm. I shouldn't be telling you this, but it was not her. It was him. Hers was and probably still is the classic case of deny, deny, deny."

"What? All this time I had it wrong? You could have told me. Set me straight on my She thinking."

"Sorry, Pheb'. While counseling people, the rule I play by is *zipped lips.* People sharing the truth with others is healthier than me blabbing the truth."

"Whatever, but the way she acted, she seemed committed to controlling her temper, being nicer to him, making the marriage work."

"Classic."

"Man, oh man. Was I duped. Well, let's move on. Mickey quit the county job and opened a food truck at the new park."

"So I heard. That's suspect."

"How so?"

She slid a stack of quarters to the side and turned. "Think about it. Let's be skeptical. He's new to town. Quits a perfectly good job. Gets money from somewhere for that high dollar food truck. Those trucks are not cheap. And works day and night to make a go of it or somethin'."

"Hard worker, a real entrepreneur would explain it."

"It doesn't add up." TuTu went back to her record keeping and moved a column to the done side.

Phoebe sat in silence, thinking. "You're right. I'll check it out."

Fishing for information, only looking at coins, TuTu nonchalantly mentioned "What's with the *nearly* on the naked description?" She always watched for information to shelter their flock.

"Hood covering his head, beaten, hung out on the zipline. A clear message of some kind."

A sad innocent look at Phoebe with the real question in the room, "Who was strung up nearly naked?"

Phoebe did an air tap with a pointed finger, "I'll get back to you on that. Hint. Hint. I'm headed to Denver for the next of kin notification. Got an eight o'clock. See ya."

Jorge had listened from the kitchen. He converted Phoebe's breakfast to a carry-out and as he handed it to her smiled. "Here's a carry-out breakfast for Roz, too. She's eating for three this year."

With a thanks, she took the box, tossed a bill into the repurposed Tide laundry detergent collection jug, and headed back to the office, *Was Mickey Walker the Denver link? Maybe New Mexico? And where does Suzanne fit in this picture? Think, Girlfriend, think.*

CRIME SCENE REDUX

Entering the conference room, Phoebe noted the faces at the table. Bill Diamond, Doc Watson, Bart Masterson, and Kate plus her forensic team of two. From the talking around the table, introductions had been renewed. *Hmm, where's CJ?*

Once Phoebe was settled at the table she saluted, "Good morning. Looks like everyone has their coffee and is ready to go."

Acting Sheriff Bill Diamond welcomed everyone. He was not looking well. Usually his hair was carefully coiffed, his uniform flawless with knife sharp creases, and an eye shattering brilliant smile. This morning he looked wilted. Phoebe was thinking married life and the anticipation of being a new father of twins had taken away the glitz. He was a lifelong friend to Phoebe and she intended to give him a pep talk when the opportunity presented itself before the election next week.

Bill had plans for the morning. He announced that Phoebe, as lead detective, would head the discussion. He had to step out for some very important work. *Really? Where's he off to? What's more important than this? Did he take a management lesson from Sheriff Joe? Leave before you get roped into an assignment.*

Phoebe was shocked, shifted in the chair, repositioned her bulletproof vest, and started the recording app in an effort to buy time. "I guess we can get started," and looked at Kate. With this quick recovery she offered a confident facial expression, clenched her hands on the table, leaned forward, and assumed an "I'm ready to listen" countenance.

If Kate was irritated that Sheriff Bill had left the review it didn't show. She related the details from yesterday's investigation. They identified the body as Michael "Mickey" Walker using the fingerprints on file with the County. Doc could do the basics as coroner, but this case required more in-depth forensic investigation. He had brought in one of the local Medical Examiners.

The ME concluded the death was caused by blunt force trauma to the head. A vein was broken by a hit to head. The bleed created pressure inside the cavity and death was slow. The beating took place after death. There was bruising on the body and little blood was evident.

They sent out blood and tissue samples to the state lab for analysis. The packets found on the zipline landing were also sent. It could take several weeks for the final results. The field test showed positive for cocaine which was not a surprise. The ME noted there was damage to Mickey's septum typically attributed to long term use of the stuff.

Kate continued her report, segueing into her examination of Suzanne's house. Phoebe was most interested in what was found. "The fingerprints throughout the house matched

Suzanne's from the county files and Mickey's prints were also found. She is still missing, right?"

Phoebe interjected, "Yes, at least we're thinking that way. No one has been able to contact her so far. And it's rumored the two of them had some kind of a relationship. This explains his prints being at her house."

Bart chimed in, "And I went over to Mickey's house of record. There was nothing to indicate a break-in. Everything is locked up tight, blinds closed, doors locked. I couldn't check inside. No high end mountain bike. At least nothing parked outside in the rack."

Kate added, "I think the bike you're looking for might be the one at Suzanne's house. It's pretty sophisticated as they go. The prints on it belong to Mickey and there is a partial on the seat. It belongs to Suzanne. The prints on the wine glass in her home office did not match anything on file in the Integrated Automated Fingerprint Identification System, IAFIS. However, the same prints were found at the crime scene. Additionally, there is another set of prints also not in the system at both the crime scene and Suzanne's."

Phoebe raised her hand to interrupt, "So whomever was at her house was also at the zipline."

"Right."

"What about Suzanne's prints? Anything at the crime scene?"

"No, we did not find her prints there. Of course, there's plenty of latent prints from the use of the zipline ride and have all been submitted. It will take some effort to research these.

"What about the hood on the body?"

"It matches another pillowcase on the couch at her house. There is a matching pillow slip on a decorative cushion on her sofa and there is a pillow missing its cover. Both have been tagged, photographed, and sent in for analysis. The hood will be returned to you as evidence after the lab has analyzed it. We look for unique characteristics as to make and brand and where it might have been purchased. There's cat hair on the fabric, similar to what was found at Suzanne's house. There was not a cat in the house at the time we processed the location."

Phoebe held up a pointer finger, "I can solve that one. When I opened the back door into Suzanne's kitchen, a cat shot from the room and nearly knocked me over. It hit me, bounced off the back step, and high tailed it over a neighbor's fence."

"The glasses along with the other pieces of evidence found have been bagged, labeled, and sent off to the state. There was a small smear of blood at the bottom of the kitchen door frame. And another in the front room where we found scuff marks on the floor. The lab will look for a match. Phoebe, once we get the results, I'll call."

"Thanks, Kate. In the meanwhile, I'll be going over to Denver today. I need to find Ellis Meredith, Mickey's wife and inform her of his death. They may or may not be married. The trail is incomplete. I also plan to stop at State Police Headquarters to talk with the assigned detective you told me about."

"I can give you his name. The officer for this area is assigned automatically when our team is called in. Chief Detective Cliff Wingate makes the initial call on further state involvement. We are happy to help, but long term case management is his decision. He does all the tracking of the good, the bad, the ugly."

Doc agreed, "Oh, yea, I've talked with him. It was from the short file on what happened with Old Al last August. Death by arsenic poisoning caught a bit of attention at the state level."

"Old Al?" Kate asked.

"A local gold prospector who lived in the great out-of-doors, but in the end, it was not his sixty-nine years on the planet that did him in, it was the killer water in some home brew."

Phoebe clarified for Kate, "For years he was drinking Augusta Higgins's special tea, along with water from contaminated wells. It's all been fixed now with drilling a new well at the Last Hurrah and the other one, well, someone burned down the winter cabin he lived in early last fall. It was the Higgins homestead. Thanks for the memories, as is said."

With Phoebe's light explanation, Kate held back a laugh, "More than one way to negate the situation, I guess. I've heard of her or at least the family. The Higgins women settled this entire area—one way or another, legal or not. I heard they moved to France."

"Partially true. Just the Mom, Anne Louise, and her partner, but they're back as of the end of last year."

Doc added, "More like France kicked 'em out. Squatters without visas are not welcome."

Phoebe gave thought to what Doc was reporting and decided it wasn't worth adding details for this big city team's edification.

But he continued. "Augusta is the daughter and runs the family enterprises from the Last Hurrah in summertime and Oresville in winter. She decided to burn down the family cabin rather than drill a new well sans arsenic. I think there was a bit of angst on Augusta's part regarding her family."

Phoebe took issue with Doc's report and decided to add, "I like to think that she's a businesswoman and if the cabin did not contribute to the bottom line, it goes." She gave Doc *The Look* and he got the message, *Butt out*.

Katie sensed the opinions flavoring the air and moved the conversation back to topic, "I'll write up our findings and send it over to you and Detective Wingate. He's a good guy and will be easy to work with."

"Excuse my lack of understanding here, but we have so little crime I'm not clear how he will help."

"It's pretty straightforward. When we're called in, the state is funded to help in ways that the local rural areas could never afford. So, these expensive services are funded at the state level—the laboratories, computer programs, officers trained at FBI headquarters, and so forth.

"The state has dedicated people to develop understanding and expertise for specific areas around the state. Cliff Wingate is the head honcho for all of the areas. If never needed, you'd never meet an area detective specialist. There's enough work along the Front Range to keep us hoppin'."

"So, these services of yours will not cost Green County?"

"Nope, as I said, we are funded at the state level. You did the right thing by calling us in. What this crime could indicate is a new developing drug related enterprise. At the other end of the scale, a random killing. Who knows? I just do the crime scene investigations. Cliff'll work with you to figure it out."

Phoebe immediately felt cautious yet pleased to have the expertise to learn from. *Random? Like some passing tourist or an emerging psychopath in Oresville honing his or her skills? If this election works out, I'll at least have a contact and resources Green County could never afford ... Or need ... I hope.*

Kate was packing up her tablet while chatting with Doc. They were catching up on mutual acquaintances and some interesting work elsewhere in the state. Phoebe stopped the Record App.

CJ hustled into the conference room as everyone was clearing out, "Did I miss the memo on this meeting?"

Kate stepped over to CJ and reached out her hand, "Just visiting. I'm from State Forensics, CSI."

"Ah-ha. Do you have a statement for the citizens of

Oresville?"

She had to smile at CJ's request, "Nope, not in my job description. Detective Korneal will help you."

Phoebe stepped in and put her hand on CJ's shoulder, "Let's go to my desk and see what you can write for the citizens. It'll be short and sweet as I need to get moving' on over to Denver."

CJ planted a frown on her face and led the way into the hallway headed for the patrol bullpen. "How about I go with you and we can trade off driving? I can work on the way."

Bill Diamond was walking towards them, "I'm all caught up from the very important work. Did I miss anything?"

Phoebe avoided CJ's comment and herded them to Bill's office where she wanted to share the findings of the meeting they had both missed.

The crumbs on Bill's shirtfront told the tale of what 'caught up' included. Becky's Buns Up, the Oresville coffee shop and bakery, located across the street. The recently retired Sheriff of Green County, Joe Jackson, had never missed a morning of politicking at the Buns. Bill was following in his footsteps.

Even though Joe had retired as Sheriff he still went to Becky's. His new position as county commissioner required a fair amount of politicking and Becky's Buns was the place to be. Phoebe suspected he was still running the Sheriff's office by way of Bill.

Phoebe reacted to his comment, "Sheriff Joe's retired, Bill, and now you're the Sheriff around here. Acting for now. This is more than a prank gone sideways. Something bad has happened and we can't just blow it off. If we try to take the high road and spin this thing it will likely bite us in the you-know-what. Regardless of the Good Old Boy Network."

"Now. Phoebe. Joe's long-term experience with some practical advice can go a long way."

"Cool it, Bill. His approach is not going to work on this

one. The state's involved and will be taking over. Not our circus."

Bill knew better than to get into this discussion with Phoebe. He settled into his chair and tried to look interested in her readout of the CSI's early findings. Afterall, if the big time operators out of Denver were going to run the show, case closed on the local level, and the Sheriff's office could go back to the usual party line.

Phoebe recited the team's findings with practiced skill and added the Vic's name at the end.

"Mickey Walker? Wait till Sheriff Joe hears about this one." Bill was almost gleeful. "He thought the kid could be the next up and coming deputy around here."

CJ bounced over the comment from Bill, "So this is why the food truck's not open today. What happened? I can't believe, a murder? Our little burg of Oresville? Wait till this headline hits my e-Blast! nooner."

"CJ, we don't have any details to share. Not until the next of kin is notified. Remember? I'm heading out now to deliver the bad news to his wife, meet the state detective, and check in with Suzanne's family. No one here has seen her and I am hoping the parents might know her whereabouts. Roz is getting the contact information right now."

Bill was cautious, "Now let's not rush into anything here. First off, she's an adult and might be on a vacation or something. Shopping. Getting nails done. Meeting friends for lunch in Aspen. The stuff ladies like to do."

Phoebe leveled a look at Bill, *This guy has no clue.* "She didn't come to work on Monday or yesterday. Plus, her car is parked at the Mountain Adventures parking lot, apparently abandoned. That's enough for me to look for her."

He continued thinking out loud, "Has anyone reported her missing? She should be missing for a few days before we get all excited about some adult not reporting in for work. Ya know? Plus, we don't have the funds to let you go to Denver and spend a few days investigating when a phone call could do it."

"I'll be there and back today. I'll not spend any time having lunch, as you suggest ladies do."

Bill sat straighter in his chair and shifted his eyes in a practiced move to catch his reflection in the window behind where CJ and Phoebe were sitting. A hand went to the side of his head, he turned slightly for a profile, and the hand swept from front to back over his ear. Satisfied that all was right, he looked back at CJ and smiled.

Both CJ and Phoebe were trying to hold back a bark. The three of them had grown up together in Salt Lake City. Bill was CJ's stepbrother and Phoebe lived nearby. The ladies had gotten used to his conceited grooming. Every now and then they laid it on thick.

Each of them in turn looked at the window for a reflection and started a pattern of hair fussing. CJ had a head of wild, curly red hair that always appeared to lack control. Phoebe's hair was a dark chestnut color and the usual ponytail could always use a tightening yank. Together they could embarrass Bill and keep a straight face. With a deadpan, taunting look they turned back to him in unison.

Decision made, "I'm ready to go when you are, CJ."

Together they stood and walked to the door. Bill was overruled.

Bill's rebuttal, "By the way, we're short vehicles today. And there's a rule of no personal vehicle use on county business. Sorry, ladies."

From her desk outside of Bill's office, Roz overheard his comment and came to the rescue, "I knew this would be an issue. I was able to rent a vehicle for nothing. Expenses are paid if we can return a rental truck to Denver and bring one back here."

In her delicate state of pregnancy, Bill knew better than to take issue with his new wife and her plan. *I know when to fish or cut bait.* "That's my girl. Always one step ahead of the rest of us. Thank you, Sweetie." He gave her a winning smile, the ladies stood a little taller, and Roz related the rental details.

Game on.

ON THE ROAD AGAIN

White knuckled grip on the steering wheel while leaning to the windshield to induce speed, "Geez, CJ, this truck's a killer. I swear there's no shocks, the bench seat's a rock, and the steering needs work or fluid or I'm losin' strength in my arms. Don't these things come with power steering? And the windows are the old crank style, not even power. We look like a low rider with air shocks or a fancy hydraulics system bouncing down the highway."

"The wind's not helpin' us goin' over Fremont Pass. Just hang in there, Phoebe. The I-70 interstate's at the bottom of this twenty mile stretch, just beyond the Copper Mountain ski area."

"Well, I'm embarrassed, nonetheless. We're all juiced up in a U-Haul-Em panel truck. If you recognize someone, kindly duck down so we don't have to acknowledge. Okay?"

"Yes, Sheriff, but I don't think we have much to worry

about unless Roz blabs it around the Club before we get back."

"No chance. Roz is lucky to waddle home after her shift."

"Well, I could always offer it on the noon e-Blast! today. I can see the headline now, 'Who's the Funky Low Rider?' It could be something that gets you the votes of the younger crowd. What'd ya think?"

"I don't think. With this case going on, I have no time to remind people to vote for the first female sheriff of Green County, Colorado. It was a long shot from the get-go anyway. I'm just a patrol deputy who wants to be a detective when she grows up. Don't know why I let you talk me into this. What if I lose? Loser! Loser! I'll have to turn tail and run."

CJ rose to the occasion, "Don't go there. You're the right person for the job. The rest of the candidates are old white guys. No experience other than cheap talk and off the wall armchair quarterback strategy."

"But people don't trust young women. There are few female sheriffs in the country and fewer in Colorado. If I lose, I'll have to leave Oresville, probably the state and go where?"

"Look at it this way. If you don't win it creates a fork in the road for your life. You'll get to make a choice on what's next. Lots of people don't have the guts it takes to play a win or lose game. That's a life without risk and no fork in their road."

"Maybe I'm not cut out for a game of risk."

"So, what if you lose? Then what happens to you?"

She let out a laugh, "I'll figure it out when the fork appears."

"Besides, not to brag, but I'm running' the campaign and it looks promising. People are sick and tired of gray haired men, with their tired rhetoric and failure to take a stand unless it benefits them, or family members. And then there is the trite, old-hat party BS. This is your show. Now step up and run it. The rest of us will be out shaking' hands and talkin' you up all weekend."

Just then a gust of wind hit the truck. The bouncing, shifting, and fighting to stay in the right lane commenced. Phoebe held her breath as she struggled to right the ride.

There was a passing lane up ahead. A fully loaded semi-truck was bearing down on them from behind. The rental wheezed and gasped in a wasted effort to maintain speed on the uphill side of the mountain. The semi easily passed them and tooted the horn. Phoebe ignored the insult. CJ offered a hand gesture that did nothing to compensate for their waning speed.

"Hard Pass, please. And I'm not the Sheriff, just lead patrol and the occasional acting detective until next week. For now, let's pray this wreck gets us to Denver. I hope we get something with springs in the seat cushions for the trip back. A padded seat cushion would help."

"The U-Haul-Em folks told Roz the truck needed work so the trip down and back is free to the County. Hubby Brian reported the weather out of Denver predicted wind gusts on the high passes at fifty plus. Not good news if you're driving a cab-over truck. Keep it between the lines, See-sta. It's the mountains, remember?"

"He's exactly right, CJ. This wind's a challenge. Hey, you never said how married life's treating you."

"Brian's a great guy and it turns out he loves to cook, clean, and do laundry. I'm sayin' I married up."

"I have to laugh at that one. We've come a long way from Salt Lake City—dead end jobs and crappy relationships. Although there was a time when I never thought I'd be sayin' crappy relationship about my SL-Ick One True Love that turned out to be someone else's One True Love. Simultaneously."

CJ was partially reclined on the bench seat. Her feet were jammed on the dash in the hopes of trying to limit the bouncing in the cab. "I'm just glad I got you to Oresville with Bill and me. The old neighborhood back together in one town. Livin' large."

Another gust hit the truck and Phoebe sat forward righting the truck track. "Speaking of your brother, Bill. He seems about a half bubble off these days. What's up with that?"

"I think the circumstances are wearing on him. Married life is fine, but expecting twins is cause for angina for any sane person."

"He's sick?"

"No, no, no. He's just excited, worried, starting over. You know he's got the two teenagers in Denver, plus the ex. Then Roz wouldn't let him take the Sheriff's job. It's too much all at once."

"Hum. I get it. He probably assumed the next step for his career is Sheriff. Now these twins are the priority. Time to regroup."

"Sure, and kids born at this altitude are a handful. They'll be on oxygen for the first several weeks of their lives. Plus, they're a smaller weight at birth. Thin air equals less oxygen and this will affect their growth. Scary. But it's all set. They have an appointment in Denver for the birth at seven in the morning. Not seven thirty. Seven sharp. You know Roz, she's a control freak."

"If I win the election next week, I want him to stay on as Undersheriff. I should talk with him, but it feels too early for that subject. Mickey's murder is the priority. I'll worry about votes maybe never. First things first."

"You may not have much to say or do about the murder. Once the State Bureau of Investigation comes in, they pretty much run the show. They're good and it makes it easier for you."

"We'll see what they have for us today. First, a quick stop to see Mickey's wife, ex-wife, whatever she is and then,

Suzanne's family. Next stop, meet this Detective guy and then we'll exchange this POS for the return rental. Or call a tow truck for completing the ride, whatever comes first."

"No kidding. But for now, I'm just along for the ride, Phoebe."

"Ha, thank goodness. But, FYI, when we get to the SBI, let's cool it on the extended introductions. Let's let Mr. Hot Shot assume you're in law enforcement. And you know what "assume" makes of you and me, right?"

Another gust blasted down the mountainside, slammed the truck, and Phoebe yanked on the wheel to make the rig behave. She was now an old pro at the wheel but a newcomer to the world of big time SBI.

NO NEWS IS GOOD

C J was trying to calm down her Best Friend Forever, "Not to worry, BFF. We'll find a remote place to park and no one will see our wheels." *I hope.*

Phoebe was already nervous about meeting this state investigator and this bazaar fashion of transportation wasn't helping. "Well, we'll do our best to hide this monstrosity, but it does stick out like a sore thumb. Do we look legitimate in this ride? Ha. Not even!"

"Never mind, Phoebe. You find Ellis Meredith first and get the notification over with regarding Mickey's passing. Once that's completed, we'll find Suzanne's parents. Then we'll see about getting the return truck. Maybe it'll be smaller and in better shape. But you know, there is somethin' to be said about cruzin' in a low rider wannabe." CJ's laugh echoed in the cab of the wreck they were driving.

"That's the lack of functional shocks, not a high dollar

juicy ride. We're almost at Ellis' house. I guess she moved to Denver to be closer to her job. I hope she's working from home this morning."

They circled the block for a large enough parking spot to hide the ride, to no avail. Phoebe maneuvered the truck into a long space in front of the house. With the size of this moving van, her parking skills were maxed, "Good enough for government work."

Adjusting the bullet proof vest, she easily stepped her almost six foot frame down from the driver's seat to the street, She took in the neighborhood and adjusted the twenty-eight pound duty belt. The upscale quality of the street, the houses, the manicured lawns. Yup. *Definitely high dollar*.

CJ steadied her 'five foot nothin' on the floor of the truck cab, eyed the distance to the curb, shook her head with red curlettes bouncing, "No problem, I can jump to the curb from here." Phoebe gave her friend *The Look* and nothing more was needed regarding truck parking skills.

As they walked up the stone walkway toward the house, the front door opened with Ellis standing there. She was named after Ellis Meredith, a suffragette in the early 1900s, known as the Susan B. Anthony of Colorado. At birth, Mom hoped the name would channel strength to her daughter. The jury was still out on that.

"Hello. It's Deputy Kernal, right? I'm surprised to see you here. What brings you out of Oresville?" She was looking at Phoebe and then did a quick assessment of CJ who was dressed in her usual black ensemble—leggings, t-shirt, and canvas Tom's.

Phoebe offered her hand to Ellis, "It's Core-nell, but call me Phoebe. Sorry to drop in like this, unannounced." She tilted her head toward CJ, "This is Carrie Jean O'Brien-Friedrich." No further explanation was offered from Phoebe nor inquired from Ellis.

"What's with the U-Haul-Em ride? You're moving?"

Phoebe immediately went into her official business control technique. With a shrug of one shoulder and no smile, "We needed wheels and this was handy. Our Green County Coordinator orchestrated a creative acquisition. Very resourceful." She forged ahead, "Can we have a few minutes of your time? We'd like to talk with you about Mickey."

Ellis gave a small grunt of a chuckle, "Always ready to talk trash about the guy. How about a cup of coffee or stronger? It's always five o'clock somewhere."

"Coffee sounds about right. Can I help?" CJ offered as a diversion to the possible question of 'why's this civilian riding along with a deputy sheriff?' If the question came up, she was ready with a one word mumble, "Undercover." Followed with, "If I tell ya I'd have to kill ya."

"No help needed, I was just fixin' something for myself, so the water's hot."

Ellis led them into the house, gestured to a sofa in the small front room, "Have a seat. I'll be right back and then we can talk Mickey."

Phoebe and CJ made themselves comfortable on a flowered sofa next to an office desk. It looked as though Ellis worked from home. The desk was layered in photographs, newspapers, official looking grant requests, and a computer with two monitors.

CJ was leaning into the mess from the edge of the sofa. Phoebe suspected she might start peeping through the papers or worse yet take out her cell phone to snap photos. "Easy, CJ. We're not here to snoop on the Hysterical Fund."

Calling the State Historical Society 'Hysterical' was her way of bringing the bigtime organization to a working level. It was a well-funded group over the years from the money generated from the gambling approved in 1991. Three historical towns were blessed with the voter approval to offer casino gambling and at the same time build money for historical preservation throughout the state—riding on the backs of Cripple Creek, Black Hawk, and Central City. The state referendum for casino operations made gambling legal and removed some of the illegal activities going on after hours in the back rooms of various bars and restaurants.

In a conversation about how gambling was legalized in Colorado, Bart related the story of Mable Willie, the first female mayor of Greenstone. In the early 1950s, a corrupt police chief allowed gambling in bars after hours in exchange for a cut of the action. Mabel got wind of the talk and visited the late night action. She fired the Chief, shut down the bar, and declared her no nonsense position on gambling. Several elections later, thanks to the noble citizens of Greenstone, Mabel remained mayor. The message was clear to Phoebe. A strong woman as Sheriff (or Mayor as the case may be) can make a difference for the county and its residents.

CJ defended her nosey interest in the workspace with a whisper, "You know Oresville is after the Society's money for restoration of our downtown. I'm a supportive citizen trying to get a jump on the status, that's all."

Phoebe pressed her lips together and added a hard look at this lifelong friend sending a message of "Knock it off" just as Ellis came into the room, "Here ya go, Ladies, help yourselves—a midmorning snack." She set down a tray with cookies, almonds, dried fruit, drinks, and accouterments. A few minutes passed in silence as CJ dived into the food. She caught Phoebe's look and whined, "It was a long ride and I missed breakfast."

Ellis passed on the CJ action, looked at Phoebe, and prompted, "Now, what's the scuttlebutt on Mickey? I'm hoping he's in serious trouble or worse." With a mischievous grin she eagerly balanced on the edge of her desk chair.

Phoebe took out her cell phone and turned on the Recording App. "If you don't mind, I'll record our talk. My mind is still driving over Fremont Pass in the wind." She smiled at Ellis and without waiting for agreement went on, "Ellis Meredith, just to clarify for the record, Mickey Walker is still your legal husband?"

"Yes. The court has approved our divorce. In this mess on my desk are the papers waiting for my signature. I filed not long after he ran me off the road just before Christmas."

"What? He ran you off the road? In our interview after you got out of the hospital, you said he wasn't following you up the Wurtz Ditch side road."

"I was covering for him. I didn't want to get him in trouble."

"We had to call out Flight for Life to get you out of there. You could have died from the accident."

"Right. Classic case, I thought I could change him. Like other abused women, I had hopes he'd be a better man with a great woman like me—wrong! Luckily, I had TuTu Tavarez to help me think through the mess I was in. I still have my job at the Historical Society, my self-worth is coming back, and I'm back to Denver with my friends and family. Did you come here to talk about me?"

The silence fell heavy in the little room. Phoebe stared at Ellis, trying to understand this woman and mulling over what she heard. She had to remind herself, *Not my circus.* Then mentally moved forward and shifted her vest. CJ stopped the grazing, looked at Ellis trying to make sense out of this woman's disclosure. Ellis looked out the window to the street avoiding their stares. She was revisiting the incident of her truck off the road, the snowstorm, the rescue. It was the last slide into the reality of her situation, her marriage, the near miss on life.

"Well, Ellis. There's no easy way to say this, so I'll just get on with it. Mickey's body was found hanging from a zipline ride in Oresville yesterday. He died of a strike to the head. I'm sorry for your loss even though a divorce is pending."

Ellis quickly sat back and leaned over as if she had been gut punched. With a shocked look on her face and holding back tears, she took a deep breath. The silence was broken as she sighed, telling Phoebe she wasn't surprised. "I'm sorry too, Phoebe, but Mickey had gotten himself into a bad crowd. Who did this to him?"

"We're trying to figure it out. The state police are involved now and he has a friend who is missing. Or so we think she is missing."

Ellis appeared to listen to what Phoebe was saying. Staring at her coffee cup she took another deep breath and went on, "First he started selling drugs in Denver and then started sampling the product. We got in deep financial trouble. That's when I started putting my foot down, 'No more dealing. Stop it.' But he wouldn't listen, the money was great, but his spending was way beyond control. I think he got into gambling, but he'd never admit it.

"He got us in trouble with the drug dealers here in Denver and that's why we moved to Greenstone. When he got the Greenstone market going strong as a supplement to the legal pot shops there, the drug bosses sent him to Oresville to open that market. If he were successful, his debt would be forgiven. That's when I came to my senses and said I was done. TuTu's counseling helped me work through the anger, the hurt, and in the end, I think I was right to be ticked off with myself, done with married life, and him."

Phoebe steadied her look at Ellis, "Then he comes to Oresville. What happened up there?"

"I don't know. By then I was getting back on track with my life. He was a hundred miles away from where we were living in Greenstone—out of sight, out of mind."

Phoebe just shook her head in disbelief, "I must have my head in a basket these past few months. Who knew selling drugs in our small town would be a big deal."

"Well, it is. Kids everywhere and adults are looking for all kinds of drugs and these organizations are happy to provide them. Big bucks!"

"So, Ellis, you think Mickey's death is related to his drug activities?"

"You bet. Between the drugs, his abusive treatment of me, and the seedy characters who he called friends. Our divorce is not final-final, but now I guess it is." With a sad look, "What a waste. He really was a nice guy till the drugs took over."

CJ entered the conversation, "Not to make this conversation any more difficult for you, do you know anything about a woman named Suzanne Martinelli?"

A long pause as she slipped through names, "No. No I don't. But the Martinelli family is well known in Denver. Why?"

"She came to Oresville and got a job as receptionist for the County Offices last year. She and Mickey hooked up."

"We wondered what a Martinelli would be doing in Oresville."

"No good if she's related to the Denver Martinelli's. They're the drug gang Mickey worked for. I don't know the details of how they operate and I mentally left for good months ago."

Phoebe was watching Ellis avoid further conversation,

"Is there anyone we can call to help you with this news?"

"Nope. I'm sorry he ended up like this. I'll call my family. They'll help."

Ellis started filling a to-go bag for CJ with the remaining nuts, dried fruits, and cookies, "Let's get you two set for your drive. Somehow, my appetite is gone."

"Thanks for your time and the food. Sorry about this bad news. I'll be back in touch as we find out more about Mickey's death. Looks like you're next of kin, so I'll have the ME notify you when the body is released."

"Thanks, Phoebe. Bye for now. You too, CJ."

Climbing back into the behemoth, CJ circled back to the conversation, "I'm thinking if your last name is Martinelli and you live in Colorado, you are most likely related."

"Yea, I think you're right. And if this Suzanne is related to the Denver Martinelli's and she's really missing, there'll be hell to pay."

THE WHO'S WHO

Phoebe took a minute to absorb CJ's comment. The cell rang and it was the official Green County Coordinator, Roz. "Y'all aren't gonna believe what I found out about the Martinelli family. Oh yea. Conventional wisdom has it that Suzanne is the granddaughter of the head honcho in the Denver drug gang, mafia, whatever they call themselves these days. He sent her to Oresville to watch Mickey."

"How do you know that, Roz?"

"A lady never tells, unless she's pregnant." Roz let out a laugh and lowered her voice to a whisper, "My husband came from the Denver PD, remember? He's got some connections from his job there as a patrol sergeant. Now his connections are my connections too. Easy peasey."

"Got it."

Roz loved fresh gossip and continued the story, "She not only watched Mickey, but she also took it a step further and used all her girly charms to entice him. It worked. They hooked up and the rest is history."

"Well, not exactly history. I'm convinced Suzanne's missing, even though we don't have a missing person report. Her car's at the adventure park, her boyfriend's dead, and she's a no show at work. Any bets on where she is in this mess?"

"Let's see if she's hiding out with family. Here's the addresses for her parents and grandparents. Good luck. Hope ya find her. Say hi to CJ for me. Nice and quiet around here without her," she laughed at the bitchy comment.

"Thanks, Roz. You're a gem…except when it comes to picking rides. This truck's something else. It rattles, waddles, bounces—I've had more comfortable rides on mountain trails. Right, CJ?"

"For sure."

"Stop complaining, Pheb'. You could be stuck here wishing you were in Denver."

"You're right, but that doesn't make my butt feel any better on this poor excuse for a seat."

"Adios, Ladies. I have my own issues to deal with. These twins better get born soon. You think you have problems sitting."

Disconnecting, Phoebe plugged in the first address and followed the suggested route. "With a bit of luck, CJ, someone will be home at this first address—maybe Suzanne is there? Wouldn't that be a sweet resolution to my burning question."

"I hope so. This rattletrap's killing me too. Is there any padding in these seats at all?"

"Doubtful. What do ya expect for free?"

Fifteen minutes later, they arrived at Suzanne's family's home. The neighborhood was upscale with lawns like velvet covering half acre lots, multiple car garages, and a golf course visible through the structures. The Low Rider U-Haul-Em looked sketchy at best in this setting. Phoebe parked in front of the house. She knew if she parked on the driveway a puddle of oil would be a continual reminder of this visit. No need to piss off the Martinelli's.

Phoebe rang the bell twice to set the pace as an all business visit. The front door opened and there stood a forty-something woman whose face was a replica of Suzanne's. This woman was as wide as she was tall as a result of a steady Italian diet of pasta three times a day. Her hands had a sparkle that radiated light from the diamonds on several fingers. Phoebe was thinking, *It's only Wednesday morning and she's dressed big time as in "I'm a Nordstrom Private Shopper customer."*

"Mrs. Martinelli?"

The woman looked at Phoebe and CJ. She scanned their appearance, checked out the ride at the curb, and instantly plastered on a scowl. Mind made up, she started to close the door, "Yes and no thank you for whatever it is you're schlepping."

Phoebe was in no mood to play this game, "Hold on there, I'm Deputy Sheriff Phoebe Korneal from Oresville. And this is my colleague, Carrie Jean O'Brien-Friedrich. Do you have a moment to speak with us?"

"Oh, dear. Sorry. Sorry. Sorry. Oresville? Is this about Suzanne?"

"May we come in."

"Oh yes, excuse me. Please." She stepped back and swung the door wide. They entered into a large entryway, opening on the right to a well decorated sitting area.

She escorted them in. The room was washed in the southern light from a glass wall overlooking a patio and pristine lawn. The three of them stood awkwardly in the center of the room. CJ cleared her throat, "Is Suzanne here?"

The woman seemed to not hear the question, "Oh. Sorry.

Where are my manners? Please take a seat. May I get you some refreshments? If you're moving, I'm sure you could use some water."

Phoebe was confused by her statement, "No, We're not moving."

"But that's a moving truck, right?"

CJ explained, "Ah, that would be a solid no. We repurposed it for a ride to town, not for moving."

The woman looked at CJ waiting for a further explanation. Phoebe stepped into the direction of the drifting conversation, "We're here to ask you about Suzanne. Is she here with you?"

"Suzanne? No, it's Wednesday. She's at work in Oresville."

"Any chance she would be with another family member or on vacation."

"No. If that were the case, we'd know about it. She usually calls every Sunday and sometimes through the week. Why are you asking about her?"

"Mrs. Martinelli, her vehicle was found at the High Country Adventure Park in Oresville. It appears to be deserted. We checked her home and she wasn't there. And, she hasn't shown up for work for two days. We thought you or someone in your family might know where she is. Any friends or a boyfriend we could contact?"

"The usual working group of gals at her job would be my guess and no boyfriend I'm aware of. What are you saying? Is she a missing person? What should I do? I need to call my husband. He'll find her."

"Please, don't be hasty. We're working on locating her. She might have information for a case we are working on. My first act was to contact you. All I can say now is if you hear from her, please call me immediately. Here's my card. The offer of refreshments? Hard pass, we need to get going."

Mrs. Martinelli was suddenly in a hurry. She snatched

the offered card, tossed it on a side table, and hustled to the front door. CJ and Phoebe followed her, as it was clear Mrs. Martinelli wanted this visit over with, right now.

As they stepped to the front door, CJ whispered, "I guess we can take a hint."

CJ ventured, "Not assuming anything. Just wondering about a close friend, Mickey Walker."

"Mickey Walker? Never. That'd be a joke." Mrs. Martinelli was shaking her head enjoying an insider's joke.

CJ pressed on, "It's my understanding she was close to Mickey. Not casual friends."

"Not likely. Did she tell me he's a janitor or something? Now if you don't mind, I have pressing business." She swung the door wide indicating it was time for them to move on. The only thing missing was tapping her toe to speed up their departure.

Phoebe stood her ground, "Mickey Walker is dead as of yesterday."

Mrs. Martinelli stopped and looked at both of them. Doubt clouded her eyes, "Dead? How?"

"He was found hanging from a zipline, beaten, and nearly naked."

She skipped over the details regarding his death, pursed her lips, furrowed her botoxed brow, and chose to argue, "Nearly naked? How can someone be nearly naked. You are either naked or not. Simple." With that observation she again fanned the door as if to say, "Come on. Come on. Leave already."

They stepped out to the porch as the door slammed shut behind them. Phoebe let go, "If I hear anything, I'll contact you ASAP, *Mom*." She looked at CJ, "Well, that went well. Not."

"She couldn't wait to get us out of there. I'm betting she knows something, but we showed up with news she didn't have. No details about his death, just the lecture on the use of the term nearly naked or not. As a reporter I can tell you people like details on a death. The old who, what, why—but not this one. Maybe already expecting something happening to this Walker guy and already knew the who, what, why."

Phoebe was listening to CJ, looking to the street, and the wreck of the Low Rider U-Haul-Em sitting there. "Right. Let's trade this POS and get the new ride at the center. Then we can head to the meeting with this Wingate guy."

"Good plan, Phoebe, and on the way we can eat the snacks Ellis prepped for us." She tossed a high five to Phoebe.

EYEBROWS ARCHED

The Mile High City, Denver, is one of the sunniest metropolises in the United States, with 245 days of sunshine a year. The average in the rest of the US is 205 days. This particular day in Denver was becoming overcast with clouds moving in from the west and temperatures holding. Phoebe was thankful for the shadowed sunshine. The clunker of a truck would not be so obvious.

CJ made a call to the U-Haul-Em Center for a status on the exchange for a decent ride. The center would not have anything for them until mid-afternoon. Not a good sign and they would have to head to the SBI in the truck. It was now blowing a thick cloud of light blue out the dual tailpipes while accelerating.

They pulled into the parking ramp at the state headquarters. The attendant at the parking ramp entrance leaned out the window, surveyed the moving truck with barely a quick glance at Phoebe and announced, "Deliveries around back.

Follow the signs."

"We have an appointment with the SBI and a Detective Wingate."

"Your name?"

"Deputy Sheriff Phoebe Korneal and my colleague, Carrie Jean O'Brian-Friedrich."

"You're moving in? As I said, deliveries around back. Follow the signs." He went back to watching his laptop screen.

Phoebe was not happy and took a deep breath. CJ and Phoebe had been best friends growing up in the same Salt Lake City, Utah neighborhood. Over a period of thirty years, CJ recognized the early warning signs coming from Phoebe's deep breath, pursed lips, and a Frieda Kahlo continuous eyebrow. She was ready to rip the attendant up one side and down the other. It didn't happen often but when it did—not pretty.

CJ attempted to de-escalate, "Easy, Pheb'. He's just doin' his job."

Unfortunately, when they pulled in, the gate had been raised. Now the attendant had a 'holier than thou' smirk on his face, not looking at them, reached over to push a button and in slow motion the gate began its journey to its horizontal position.

Phoebe blew out the held breath with a huff, shouted a four letter expletive, and jammed on the gas pedal. The truck sprang forward, a cloud of whatever blasted out of the backend tailpipes, and they were launched into the parking ramp. The tip or more of the gate broke off and went flying. Somewhere overhead an alarm started blasting accompanied with lights strobing throughout the parking ramp. CJ let out a yip and grabbed the dash to steady herself. Phoebe was leaning forward into the steering wheel, urging the truck forward. Security guards were pouring through the side doors, hands on holsters, ready for action.

They squealed into a parking spot on the second floor, jerked to a full stop, sat back into the seat, and waited. The truck was quickly surrounded and a familiar face appeared on the driver's side window, Kate, from the State Forensics Team. Phoebe reached to the handle and slowly cranked down the window. The truck was manufactured when electric windows were an expensive option.

There was a tap on the door frame, "Hello there, Deputy Korneal. That was quite the entrance. When those sirens go off, everyone is on call, including the Forensics Team. The rest of the police force is on its way. I'm just the youngest and fastest of them. Are you alright?"

Phoebe was staring straight ahead, thinking about what had just happened. "We're fine, now that we're here."

Others arrived and Kate introduced them. CJ was called out as a colleague and no questions were asked for clarification. After their extreme entrance, people were careful to maintain the calm.

The last person Kate introduced was Chief Detective Wingate. Phoebe noted he was a Chief Detective, not just Detective Part Time like she was. She had visions of being a Chief Detective one day, if the election didn't turn out as CJ was predicting. *Gotta have a backup plan.*

DEVIL IN THE DETAILS

atie called off the assembled team of law enforcement. Guns were holstered. A few low level embarrassed chuckles were heard and the Oresville women were escorted into the building. They followed Wingate to his office. Kate explained they were to meet in ten minutes, two o'clock, in the conference room.

Cliff Wingate's office was painted a neutral, boring green. Similar to the green of the city office building back in Oresville. Phoebe looked at CJ, "I guess this green paint must be a standard for government buildings throughout the state of Colorado. Kate and CJ chuckled at this little insider joke.

Cliff carefully looked at Phoebe, sizing her up, "Hello, Deputy Korneal. Have you been in Oresville long or are you in the process of moving there?"

Phoebe responded without addressing the moving van they were driving, "First it's pronounced Cor-nell and I'm on temporary assignment as Detective Deputy. Our crime rate is low enough that we do not need full time detectives. I've been in law enforcement starting as a teenage police cadet in Salt Lake City then the SLC Police Department. Now Green County for several years. I assume you've been here a long time?" She was trying to make nice, but this guy was not making it easy.

The air left the room as Kate and CJ readied for the sparring contest.

Cliff looked at her without seeing her, "Yea, well, yes, my entire career has been in law enforcement and several years as Chief Detective for the entire State of Colorado."

CJ was thinking, *Chief Wingate, one. Deputy Phoebe, zero.*

He started shuffling papers on his desk, looked at his computer monitor, "I'll be in the conference room shortly." They were dismissed. The three ladies stood in unison and hustled out of his office.

Phoebe shifted her vest to get comfortable as they followed Kate to the room. Kate tried to smooth over the abrupt dismissal, "Don't take it personally. He's notorious for thinking only men can do law enforcement the right way. Women are limited to desk jobs."

Phoebe responded, "How did he make Chief Detective for all of Colorado with *the attitude*?"

"It's still a man's world. Despite the advances for women in the past decades, men are the alpha dogs. You know, the protectors of us fragile women. That's it in a nutshell. There are a few of us women here and there in law enforcement. but the rate is low and turnover's high. You get used to the constant judgment."

CJ responded, "What doesn't kill us makes us stronger, eh?"

Kate kept walking and responded over her shoulder,

"Something like that."

They sat together at the conference table. The room filled with the state team of male investigators. It was a comfortable group until "Chief Detective I Be The Boss" walked in, sat at the head of the table, checked his watch, and impatiently announced, "Alright. Let's roll."

The group at the table were gathered to hear Wingate's decision on the Oresville investigation. Would they take on Mickey Walker's passing or let the locals continue? Wingate gave no indication. His presence at the meeting indicated an interest in this becoming a case for the experts called into this meeting.

Kate was heading up the meeting with her findings, such as it was. The lab analysis would take several weeks. There was little new information for Phoebe and CJ. The cause of death was blunt force trauma to the head, compounded by a severe beating. Drugs were involved. No UNSUB on the horizon.

At this point, looking at Phoebe, Chief Detective Wingate clarified, "UNSUB means Unknown Subject."

Phoebe wondered, *Is he talking to me?* Kate continued her report describing the condition of the DB. Again, Chief raised an index finger and interrupted, "DB is short for Dead Body." The people at the table started looking around, wondering what this was all about.

Kate cleared her throat, "Yes, as I was saying, the Vic has a history with us."

Chief Wingate spoke up looking directly at Phoebe, ignoring Kate, "Vic is short for victim."

This time Phoebe could not pretend his comment wasn't meant for her and maybe CJ too. She quickly raised a hand, palm out to stop Kate's report, and eyes centered to the head of the table, "Chief Wingate, your clarification is unnecessary, unprofessional, and not welcomed. Kate, please continue without further interruption."

CJ adopted a smirk on her face, *Take that, buddy—Chief one. Deputy one.*

The men looked busy trying to avoid a reaction.

Kate gave a slight nod as an affirmative and smoothly continued the summary. The investigators were listening hard to her forensic summary. The team had been following Mickey Walker and were ready to take over the investigation into his death. He was associated with the Martinelli Family and had been run out of Denver for gambling debts. Greenstone was the next assignment and the drug trail followed. After two years he was moved to Oresville. The investigators gathered at the table were hitting various CIs to see if his death was a Martinelli punishment or competition.

To prove her familiarity with the lingo, Phoebe asked, "Have any of the confidential informants, the CIs, come back with anything yesterday or today?" She looked at the Chief to see if he got her meaning. He was looking at her with a haughty stare, but sat back into his chair, fingers tented in front of his chin.

Phoebe moved the conversation to Suzanne Martinelli, "Has anyone seen or heard anything?"

She went on to explain they believed Suzanne was involved with Mickey and had not been seen for two days. They had visited her mother and she had not heard anything either.

With the visit mentioned, Cliff Wingate sat up, "You what? Visited Mrs. Martinelli?"

"Sure we did. The daughter's missing and might be another Vic."

"Has someone made an MPR?"

Phoebe had to admit, no one had filed a missing person report to the Green County Sheriff's Department.

"What about the Oresville PD?"

"In Oresville there is no PD or Police Department."

Phoebe was being ornery and clarified the PD directed at the Chief. She added a crooked little smirk. *Two can play your game, Chief Detective Wingate.* "We do not have the problems you have along the Front Range." *Boom. Take that!* She continued, "A full time department is not needed. The town has an officer who's helping on this case." Her tone returned the Chief Detective's haughtiness. *Tit for tat, Chief.*

Keeping score, CJ tallied, *Chief one point, Pheb' two.*

Wingate was ready to conclude the meeting. His determination of the SBI involvement was clear, "We are not going after the Martinelli woman at this level. You can pursue it on your level. We'll be watching and listening for any additional drug organizations coming into Denver. The FBI works with us and Denver is where the action is. It fans out from here. And, the death of this Walker guy sounds like a drug hit, prank gone wrong, payback? Who knows. You have a problem in your small town. Our expertise is not warranted at this point. It's up to you, Deputy Korneal. Anything to add from anyone?"

His question was met with silence.

He looked around the table, stood up, "We're done here. Thank you for coming, Detective Korneal. Did I pronounce that correctly?" And he actually let out a silly cackle but added a real smile in his eyes.

The team of investigators rose and left the room without further conversation. It was clear they could not be bothered with investigating the death of Mickey Walker. Drugs, prank, or something, case closed at this level. Suzanne Martinelli was not of any interest and her connection to the family in Denver was a moot point.

Kate escorted them to the exit for the parking ramp. She looked at CJ and Phoebe. "Sorry you came all this way for no new information and no promise of help forthcoming."

"I'm sorry too, but at least we're cleared to check out Mickey's death without Chief Detective Cliff Wingate in the way or taking over." Phoebe stuck out her hand to Kate. CJ did the same and they left the building.

Kate was impressed with Deputy Korneal and how she handled herself at the all-male roundtable. Not often did someone stand up to the Chief and certainly not a female. She watched the two women climb aboard the moving van. *Gut instinct tells me this is not over til the fat guy sings.*

RIDE LIKE THE WIND

Phoebe and CJ hustled over to the rental center and asked for a decent vehicle to drive back to the citizens of Oresville. The dispatcher at the site chuckled and passed them a set of keys. The new ride was smaller, maybe cleaner, and again, no power windows. Phoebe decided this was not going to cut it. She marched back into the building, tossed the keys in front of the dispatcher.

In a low, even tone, "Try again, Pal."

The dispatcher took a long, serious look at her. When she did not blink first, he let out a sigh, plucked another set of keys from a board, "Tell Quarterback Joe Jackson hi for me."

"Not on your life," and with that she turned, repositioned her bullet-proof vest, and headed to the next vehicle in hopes it had the right windows.

This time CJ was driving and the route she took was the long way west on highway 285. They headed to Fairplay. CJ drove as if she were somehow channeling Mario Andretti in a previous life. They sailed through Conifer, Bailey, and passed everything in sight with the constant assistance of the truck's horn blasting for highway domination. In pedal to the metal form and the horn to intimidate others, the little truck's throttle was floored. It appeared there was no governor device on it and the speed limit was a suggestion. Kenosha Pass was a non-event and Red Hill even more so.

It was an hour of *thinking silence* inside the cab. Phoebe was trying to recoup what occurred through the day. With horn blasting outside and a white knuckle grip on the steering wheel, CJ started, "So, if I do say so, this day was less than productive."

"Now, now, CJ. Let's look at both sides. First, we got Old Lady Martinelli's attention and probably the whole damn family. They'll escalate the question of Suzanne. If the drug competition has moved in as TuTu and Jorge are thinking, then the family members are well aware of it and Suzanne is their problem. On the other side of the coin, if they're not involved, we'll see a MPR on her. Or as Chief Detective 'Jerk' Wingate would add, 'This means Missing Person Report.' That guy treated us like we are some kind of hicks out of the backwoods of the Rockies. I'm delighted this is a case not worth his time."

"Yup, he's a jerk and the Martinelli babe wasn't much better. I loved the lecture on the term *nearly naked* followed by the door slammed behind us. I should have gone into attack technique screaming, 'Help me! Help me! She's trying to kill me.' What a piece of work."

Phoebe was laughing for the first time today. In a tone laced with 'TV personality,' "Agreed. Now back to it. Number two. Since the big time state police don't see anything by way of 'value add' out of Oresville, this lowly little ole Deputy Phoebe Korneal, pronounced Core-nell, is now free to move ahead sans their nose up my business. In other words, 'free to move about the cabin,' as the airlines say. Gotta love it. If I can put all this together, I will hand it on a gold platter to his majesty, the Chief Detective Jerk-Wad Gate."

CJ was now in giggle-agreement, eyes intent on the road ahead, fingers ready to jam the horn, "In the end, the only decent interview was with Ellis Meredith. She sent us out the door with enough snacks to get us through the rest of the day. It looked like a military MRE, only better. I wondered if there was a P38 can opener buried in it."

"That's funny, but it got us out of there without wasting time and money on food. That POS vehicle wouldn't have fit into a drive-thru anyway. If I were writing tickets today, I would write us up a violation for *exceeding EPA standards*."

"There's a law for that?"

"No idea."

"In spite of the bad news for Ellis, did you wonder about her reaction? Good news? Bad news? Ellis did not shed a drop for the guy. Could she have off'd him?"

"I say, 'Doubtful,' but I'll check her whereabouts this week."

"Back to what you said on the good news. How so?"

"Well, CJ, since you are now married you probably know this is a joint property state. She is still legally married to the dearly departed Mr. Mickey Walker. Right? Therefore, everything he had is now hers—lock, stock, and barrel. House, fancy mountain bike, food truck, the works, including any liabilities. Something tells me his was a cash only business therefore no debt."

"Winner, Winner, Chicken Dinner."

"Exactly. Let's get on back to the ranch and see what develops."

BLACK OPS

R acing through the highway light at Fairplay, Phoebe's cell rang. "Hey y'all. I'm just doin' a little follow up on friends in high places. What's y'alls location, Ladies?"

"On the way home. We're in the clear here. Anything new on your end?"

"I just got a call from my newest BFF at the Alibi Car Rental counter in Albuquerque. The giant black, SUV got turned in this afternoon. One guy. Truck was dirty like it had been off-road and there was food all over the interior—floor, seats, door storage compartments, console. They think he lived in it."

"No kidding. Interesting. That was my one mission, 'Find that tank.' Now what do we have?"

"I called Billy Baldwin's Towing and asked them to pick up Suzanne's car in the lot over at the zipline. That'll happen tomorrow, maybe Friday. They're busy with all the tourists running around the mountain roads in low profile vehicles—flat tires, overheated engines, ruined vehicles from 'flat lands' naivety. We'll see if Suzie-Q shows up for work tomorrow. Sparkle and I are now on 'hot gossip' comparison terms. Today's another no-show. She'll call me if there's a sighting."

"Good help must be hard to find. Have you talked with Bart? Maybe he's seen her."

"No, but Augusta was in today. She's hot to trot over the survey lines of her property around the Last Hurrah mine. Her various properties predate statehood in 1876, back in the day when we were known as the Jefferson Territories."

"Very touchy subject for her. But why's she tracking this? Taxes or something?"

"Family Pride, I'd say. I'm guessing her great grandaddy Higgins was part of the unwashed hordes of adventurers. The East Coast Gentry declared these vagrant miners to not be on the same level as the representatives of Pennsylvania, New York, and the like. It took several tries for Colorado to become a state. No wonder we don't like President Andrew Johnson. He refused us statehood over a technicality. A picky, picky Southern gentleman. Ten years later, Grant got it together and the petition was signed, sealed, delivered. Hence the Centennial State."

"Great history talk, Roz, but what's got her riled up now?"

"Something about a falling down cabin on her property line. She thinks someone's living there, visiting, squatting, who knows. She wants to be sure the property lines are accurately recorded before she goes in with guns a-blazin'."

"Gads. She better not. Tell her to cool it. I'll help her after I get this Mickey-Suzanne thing figured out."

"Her sidekick, Queennie, is coming up Saturday to help campaign for y'all this weekend. The two of them will investigate in their spare time. I'd advise not to worry until after next Tuesday. The two of them will horse around, kick the tires, and go back to work in the end."

Augusta met Queennie Lewis at the memorial service for Old Al. Although Queennie was married to him, she had not lived with him for over thirty years. Augusta was a friend and business partner with Al for an equal amount of time.

The two women were now fast friends and closer companions. Independent businesswomen and like-minded thinkers, they were enjoying this new-found friendship with snowmobiling for Queennie and motorcycle riding for Augusta. It was observed that the rigid "business first" thinking of the Higgins family women seemed to be bending with the influence of Queennie. She was a business owner who put people first and made money at it.

The Rubik's Cube for Augusta was the gold she had recovered before she set fire to the family homestead last summer. No matter how many times it turned over in her mind, the solution would not align. The Higgins cabin had been the winter housing for Old Al and his pet mule, Rose, for thirty or so years. Augusta's Mom, Anne Louise, had a partner, Uncle Q—short for Quinton Garrett. Before they moved to France, unexpectedly, Uncle Q, a retired assayer, had taught Al how to turn the gold flakes and nuggets into coin. The machinery designed by old man Higgins back in the 1860s still worked and Al was welcome to make use of it. Every winter Al rolled his gold into coins, dated with the year of the yield.

She had not told Queennie about the many jars of gold tucked away now at an Oresville bank. The stash was a mental quandary and it intruded at the most unlikely moments—a bubble popped to the surface from her subconscious, *What about the gold?*

Augusta could think of several scenarios for the use of

Al's gold. But the foundation for any plan required a first step—telling Queennie about its existence. That had become a hurdle to be vaulted. So far the jump was more of a hop in thought only and at random, unexpected moments it crowded into the gray matter, demanding resolution.

Pregnant Roz let out a groan over the air waves. She had run out of steam this late afternoon, "One final question, Pheb', and I need to give it up for today. What's the latest on Mickey's death?"

"I'm not so sure about him. Way more than a prank with what he's been up to—no good. He was on the radar screen of the State Investigators. But they have bigger fish to fry than small-time operator Mickey Walker. Given his history, drug deal gone haywire. We got the 'don't let the door hit your backside on the way out' treatment."

"Alrighty then. This is it for me and these twins. I'm gonna put my feet up, my cell phone down, and hope a good fairy Godmother somewhere gets me through the next few days without losing much more sleep.

"Wait. Did I hear few days? I thought we were looking at twins in July. Right? Wrong? What's this a new earlier date?"

Roz gave out some aha, aha's, "Oops. I meant to say month. Please forget the slip. Just wishful thinking."

"Okay, I hope you're being honest here."

"Yup, no worries. By the way, the county auditors are coming in tomorrow. Don't expect much work to get done with this yearly event happenin.' They take all day. Demand tons of paper receipts, fiddle around over a nickel here, a dime there. And the highlight of the day is lunch being brought in courtesy of the auditors, so we can continue working while eating. Can hardly wait."

"Good luck with that, Roz. Looks like a busy tomorrow. Same for me. I have a list of things to do and hopefully will not need your help. Hang in there, Girlfriend."

Phoebe's plan was to get some background on the manager of the adventure park, the deHerrera guy. A quick call to the Albuquerque sheriff's office would be made to see what they could provide. *Then I'll talk with Oscar. He might have some insight on Mickey and what happened on his zipline. Maybe a clue about Suzanne. Or even about drugs in our small town.*

Much to do to get to the bottom of this crime. Or is it crimes?

CLEAN SLATE

Back in Oresville, Bart took advantage of the afternoon and knocked on the doors of businesses and homes surrounding the new park in hopes of finding a person who had seen or heard something the day Mickey was found. On Tuesday the deputies did some checking with the businesses in the area, but little information was gained. Bart felt a second review was in order.

This neighborhood was in the process of unwelcomed urban renewal. Rentals were in high demand from the workers needed to operate the park. There was competition between them and the Moly mine workers. If the new, young park workers could live in the immediate neighborhood they could skip vehicle ownership and walk, bike ride, hit the skateboard to work, shop, and party. And, at least in the past, the Moly mine workers could afford the rent.

Now though, the properties were being upgraded, resulting

in increased values. As always, the rent increases followed. Most folks living in the area were hard working citizens and fixed income retirees who went to bed early and rose before dawn. Bart knocked on doors in the area surrounding the park with no luck and no new information.

The sun was past the midafternoon mark in the true blue skies above. The neighborhood was settling in for the rituals of returning home from a long workday, refreshing for an evening meal, and catching up with overdue chores. He was about to quit for the day and knocked at one last house, Mrs. McGillicuddy's front door. She peered through the peephole to see the handsome constable standing on her porch. Cracking the door, with the chain still in place, she shouted, "I can't afford any donations today," and started to shut the door with a definitive force.

Removing his ball cap he yelled, "Officer Bart here. No donations, just need a minute of your time"

The door stopped, edged open again. A set of eyes peered out through thick lenses set in round red frame glasses. "Well, I suppose I can handle a minute of my time for you, Officer Bart."

He tipped the hat folded in his hand and smiled, "Just checking the neighborhood to see how everyone's doing."

"How nice. But, how about we make this an official call. I insist you come in and have tea with an old lady." A single syllable bark of a laugh and she led him to the small kitchenette.

This elderly little woman was looking sharp with a short, dyed red, head of spiked hair, a t-shirt from a long ago Rolling Stones concert—all tongue and lips. Her 501 Levi's were definitely originals and old as the babe wearing them. Topping off the ensemble, her feet were cuddled in pink, fuzzy slippers.

Bart followed her into the tight space of a kitchenette equipped with a little table covered in a pink antique crocheted tablecloth. As he squeezed onto one of the two chairs, the duty belt clanged the side arms and back. He balanced on the very front edge of the chair to make do. It was not sized for someone at six feet tall, two hundred pounds, weightlifter arms, and ham hocks for thighs. Bart's knees hit the center post of the table.

This visit was an event for Mrs. McGillicuddy. She stepped to the only countertop and whipped out a teapot, with matching demitasse cups. In under twenty seconds she had the table set, water boiling, and a big smile for the handsome officer. "Hello and welcome to Oresville and I'm doing mostly fine."

"Good. People treatin' you right? Neighborhood's quiet, comfortable?"

"Oh sure. The young whippersnappers here think old people are odd, so they stay out of my way. Every once in a while I act crazy to reinforce the theory."

"Sounds like a plan. Gotta have one, ya know."

"Can't complain, no one gives a damn anyway."

"True for most of us, right?"

"Yup." At that point, she had lifted a stick, pointed it to the window, and pulled back the curtain for a peek at the parking lot across the street. "I've got a direct view of the new adventure park."

"You sure do. I'm wondering if you saw or heard anything Monday night or Tuesday morning. You know we had an incident during that time period."

"Oh yea. I'm well aware of the event. As a matter of fact, I was awake most of the night. Sleep's hard to come by. This park comin' in keeps me awake with worry. Rents are going up here and new neighbors comin' in all the time. Most of them, I'll never meet. Thinkin' it's about time to leave, maybe rent out this old house, and head to my daughter in Arizona."

"I understand. Can we talk about the park yesterday?"

'Well, on Tuesday morning, before the sun even started

lighting up the sky—hmm, it must've been about five thirty in the morning—I was looking out the window cussing the park that's creatin' all this change. And there was some strange goin's on.

"You know, there's one thing you should know about. These young kids playing around on the zipline at night. If it keeps up, someone's gonna get hurt."

"Really? I'll check it out, for sure. But right now, I'd like to focus on Monday and Tuesday morning. What'd ya see?"

"Well, first, on Monday afternoon a tan colored sedan pulled into the parking lot. No big deal, but it's still there. See, look out this here window—perfect view. Two people got out, went into the food truck then put some bags into the trunk, pulled a bicycle from the backseat and rode away. Then on Tuesday morning before the butt crack of dawn, a huge black car, you know, those new gigantic, gas-guzzling box things?"

Sitting at the little table was a tight fit for Bart. A knee was pressed to the center support of the table. When she mentioned the same vehicle he and Phoebe were looking for, his foot jumped with excitement and threw a jolt to the center support and the table tipped. He reached out in a vain attempt to right the teacup and grab the table edge to stop a full out turnover but missed the edge. This slight movement eliminated the fraction of the inch his butt was balanced on the chair. He dropped to the floor. Without missing a beat and not distracted from her question he answered her on the way to the floor, "An SUV."

Eyes round with excitement she watched as Constable Bart landed on the threadbare linoleum. Years of working out in Zumba classes kept her reflexes sharp. She automatically grabbed each side of the table and the grip stopped it from tipping over but the teacup shot lightly over the edge and broke on impact.

She tilted to the side, looked at him as he was scrambling

to regain the chair, "Good heavens, are you okay?"

He stood up and carefully sat back on the edge of the chair, let out an embarrassed bark, "Couldn't be better. Looks like your teacup didn't make it though."

She tossed a hand, "It's not older than me, so no worries. Tell me, is the big vehicle important? Looks more like a hearse if you ask me. Do people live in those things?"

He laughed, "I suppose they could for what it cost."

"It's the only one like it in town that I've seen and I've noticed it parked over at the train depot, on and off, for the last week. Well, anyway, it pulled up and two men got out. They hauled out something from the back end and dragged it up to the zipline platform. I was a bit afraid and thought best to close the curtains and back away from the window. Sure, didn't want those guys to see me watching."

"Why didn't you call the Sheriff?"

"I'm an odd old lady, living alone. I didn't want to get involved."

Bart gently tipped his head to one side. "I understand. But, next time, if there ever is one, give us a call on nine one one. We'll take good care of you."

"If you say so."

He thought ahead. "How about I bring in Deputy Korneal for a visit with you. She's investigating the situation we're talkin' about. I'm sure she'd have some questions for you. How about it?"

"I'd be glad to talk with her. I was thinking about voting for her. Any ideas on that?"

"She's the right one for the job. Lots of experience. I think she's terrific, but then I'm prejudiced. She's the reason I moved to Oresville."

"Really? Got a thing goin' with her, eh? Well, good for you. Both of you. Everybody needs somebody."

"Nice of you to say that. Thanks, but you don't have to be spreading that news around. Not exactly a secret. But you know."

She let out a chuckle, "Aha. I get it. I can keep it to myself. I'm old and odd, remember?"

"I'll get your phone number and give you a call after I see what her schedule looks like."

"Glad to help. And I look forward to meeting her."

After tea in a new cup, three cookies, and some harmless neighborhood chit chat, Bart gave her a business card and quit for the day. He picked up his dirty clothes at the cabin and headed to Phoebe's place to do laundry. *With a bit of luck Phoebe'll get home and we can have dinner together.*

They dropped off the U-Haul-Em and headed to CJ's place. Phoebe's call to Bart went unanswered. Once she dropped CJ at home, she headed home with a slow, easy, comfortable drive, tunes blaring. When she arrived at the trailer, there was Bart, doing laundry. *What a great surprise. This long day is in the rear view mirror.*

"Hi, Honeybun. Glad to find you here." She walked up to him and put her arms around his neck. "Don't know if you know this, but you're the best part of this day." Leaning in for a breathtaking kiss, *Having him here when I come home is a game-changer. Terrific to have someone who cares.*

"I can ditto that, Sweet P. When I see your face, I'm a happy man. How about I mix us a cocktail while you go get comfortable. Then we can get caught up on the day."

"That'll help. Make mine a Mugshot—coffee with a light shot of amaretto. Lots of whipped cream. Be right back."

Soon as she was settled at the table in sweats and a tee shirt, "I tried to call you from the road, no answer."

"Sorry. I was canvassing the neighborhood around the park to see if anyone heard or saw anything and lucked out with one neighbor."

Bart gave her a short review of the interview minus his slide off the chair.

"You really got good info from her. Let's see if we can interview this person together?"

"You bet. Now, how about your day?"

Phoebe took a deep breath and related her day to Bart. He never took his eyes off her, did not interrupt, and took careful note of all she reported.

"Wow, what a day. Of all you shared I'm most shocked at the state's detective and his dismissal of this case. Disappointing. Nevertheless, we've got a murder here needing to be solved and a potential missing person. Seems to me, the onus of accountability is on us to get it figured out."

"Agreed." Phoebe took a sip of the Mugshot, "I wasted time thinking the state would take over the murder. We're back to square one. Let's plan tomorrow with both of us on it. What do you say?"

"You bet. Say the word."

"The county auditors are in the office tomorrow so Roz is out as a resource. Let's go see the park manager, deHerrera, tomorrow for a first interview. Before we go, I plan on getting some background on him and the deHerrera family down in New Mexico. Got a tip from TuTu."

"Sounds good. Tomorrow's the usual town council meeting in the morning. Short agenda so I'll meet you there. Let me know the time."

HELLO CAPTAIN

S uzanne had been raised in Denver by a loving family who had a long history of being dysfunctional. Most of the uncles and some of the aunts had been in and out of jail, making family gatherings lopsided in attendance. The question, "Where is such and such?" was answered with a single term, "Jail." And the meal and celebration would continue in spite of the short response.

The family delighted in her minor accomplishments through the school years. College was out as she was more interested in the opposite sex and achieving a MRS degree. Why waste time getting an education? No matter who she married she would always be financially sound. With giggles and bright personality, she was programmed into the business. This might increase the family's coffers and give her something to do away from the Denver limelight.

An opportunity came to move her to the Oresville

operation. The Family contact there was relocated south, closer to Super Max, the federal penitentiary in Florence, Colorado. This unaffiliated area East of Pueblo was a wide open opportunity for the Family. The goal was to grow the business. The dispersed town itself was so messed up in politics, poor bookkeeping, unauthorized loans to employees, and various "discounts," it would be years before anyone bothered to look into a drug organization blossoming within their boundaries.

With the relocation of the Family representative, Oresville needed a Family contact and Suzanne was designated. Her responsibilities included keeping track of Mickey. He had already been sent to Oresville from Greenstone to grow the drug business, but he was not Family and owed them money. Working for their business was the only way he was going to get out of debt.

Suzanne needed a place to land to re-learn the ropes—for the another chance. Decision made, the family bought her a little house and a practical unobtrusive vehicle. It was a neutral, boring, tan colored Ford Taurus begrudgingly named the Tan Travesty. She hated this vehicle. It was unlike any fashion statement she had ever driven. Where was her beloved Lexus? The Beemer? The wonderful little Mercedes? Living in the Denver suburbs and driving beautiful cars, valet attendants noticed her coming. They rushed to her aid for an opportunity to drive a real car—a Suzanne car. Being cast off to this small town in the middle of nowhere was her penance for past transgressions and a chance to redeem herself, but in a Taurus? Ultimate humiliation.

This favored daughter was put on an allowance to teach her, again, hopefully, some personal financial responsibility and of course, the necessary bookkeeping skills needed to track drug sales. In hopes of the former, they took away her Amazon card, the AmEx Black card, the multiple Visa cards, and stopped her line of credit at several banks. The Nordstrom's account remained open with direct billing to Momma Martinelli's account, *A girl had to have the basics*. As far as the latter, honing her bookkeeping skills, well, that was up for grabs.

Grandma Martinelli hoped her granddaughter would learn how to cook. Better yet, find a husband. She took on Suzanne's Pottery Barn and the Williams-Sonoma accounts in support of this granddaughter's future. The hope for a husband for Suzanne was like rolling a twelve in the game of craps. Seems like every potential husband disappeared after being introduced to the Family.

Suzanne had inherited the "entrepreneurial" gene from her grandfather, Papa Martinelli. He had come over from the old country in the early 1950s, when circumstances in the home country forced some hard decisions. The impetus to leave his native country was his ability to think outside the box. His girlfriend was unexpectedly expecting and he had to make a fast decision to relocate or be chased out by her God-fearing family. For Papa it was the former.

He hightailed it out of Northern Italy while his girlfriend's honor was somewhat intact and her father's shotgun was ready. The girlfriend was escorted to the cargo boat where Papa was ensconced in a third class cabin. The captain agreed to marry the young couple when the ship hit international waters. The newlyweds were headed for America to be embraced by the New York family.

The family business was opening new markets. Colorado and Vegas were promising. After all, the Martinelli Family had originally gone to Colorado as laborers for the mining industry in the 1880s. In the mining around Oresville, they had an established legitimate presence. The young couple went to Denver and introduced their brand of business along the Front Range—loansharking, gambling, and black-market resale were the money-makers of the day.

In 2012, Amendment 64 was passed in Colorado. Marijuana was now legal for recreational use. Other drugs were not legal, but certainly were in high demand. With their systems and distribution network in place, the Family easily stepped into the marketplace of the illicit drug trade.

While Suzanne's purpose was to keep an eye on the help and learn accounting for the Oresville business, she had additional plans of her own. As the newly hired innocuous reception desk employee at the county building, she had the perfect drug distribution setup—Monday through Friday, no evenings, weekends, or holidays. With a youthful, bubbly, and informative personality, the young lady not only endeared herself to the bosses but also the clients. She diffused even the most hostile, angry, citizens with friendliness and respect. And cheerfully, quietly, dispensed the citizen's illicit purchases.

It was like someone had flipped the switch on the drug flow into Green County, Colorado. At first she was losing money. After all, who would enter the county building for a drug purchase? With Papa's spirited genes, Suzanne took the initiative.

Under the law enforcement radar, news of her program spread like a nasty virus. She set up a line of credit for her frequent customers, discounted drugs with blue light specials for the occasional customer, frequent flier offers for her big time users, and decorated gift bags for holidays. In a few short months, loyalty became king—customers loved her and business was booming.

Cocaine was the drug of choice and an easy, quick exchange of a small item. It was marketable, sold itself really, and did not include the huge storage space required of marijuana. And despite being within twenty feet of the Sheriff's office entrance door, it was easily passed. Cash only, exact payment required, no change given.

Additionally, Suzanne was looking into going online as a 'members only' site, quarterly auto-renewal welcome for all. The Family business in Oresville was growing by leaps and bounds and she was saving up for a Tesla. The Denver dealer would take the Tan Travesty on an easy trade-in, off the record, of course. Papa Martinelli would be proud when she arrived in the Tesla for the family's Fourth of July celebration. America, land of the free and the brave and the out of the box thinkers.

ONLY THE LONELY

uzanne's situation at the cabin was dismal and she was at a loss as to what was going on. She laid on the rough floor, trussed, blindfolded, and chained to a large tree root growing through the broken floorboards of the shack. The captors took the tape off her mouth. The blindfold and chains stayed in place.

The minute the tape was removed, she begged, "Please let me go. I'll never say anything about what has happened to me."

"Shut up."

She could tell from the voice it was the big guy speaking, the one who had spent all night in her home office. *What was he looking for?*

In a louder, whining voice, "No one even knows I'm part of this. I promise to say nothin' to no one. No harm, no foul. Please, I need to go back to my job. They'll fire me if I don't show up and it'll be your fault."

The big guy became enraged and threw a roundhouse fist into her jaw. Blindfolded, she never saw it coming. She was left unconscious and bleeding.

Coming to, she cried with a screaming headache, loose teeth, and a nighttime stillness of the darkness shrouded in evil.

The kidnappers argued in their language. She could not understand what they were saying but picked up on the occasional word of senorita. She had the distinct feeling her abduction was unplanned. The target was Mickey, not her. She was the Gift With Purchase. But not so much of a gift, more like a pain in the butt for them.

The two men had stocked food, if you could call potato chips and cheese doodles edible. Suzanne was a picky eater and despite her stomach pains, the junk food was not in the least bit appealing. They also brought a dirty milk jug of water placed on the floor near Suzanne. Disgusting.

On day two of her captivity, their argument continued outside. She was chained to something on the floor and the mask was still tied in place. She worked it against a log on the side of the building, careful to inch it up to see around the little one room space, not so much for it to slip off her face. The walls were rotting logs, the floor broken wood and dirt, with one opening to the outside. The door itself was long gone. The chain at her waist and wrists was tied to the tree root. Rubbing the chain against the root in an effort to cut through it was a wasted effort.

Sitting in the big SUV, Mateo listened as Alejandro spoke into his cell phone. "We're stuck with this la perra Americano. Mickey is muerte. And Oscar nada help. What's next?" Alejandro was quiet as he listened to the instructions.

When she heard them coming toward the door, she slid away from the root, turned her head away as if asleep, ignoring their presence. Alejandro gave her a kick to wake her up.

She groaned from the sharp pain, pretended to wake up, and tried again. "Please, Senor, let me go. You can go. Leave me here. I'll figure out a way back to town. Just unchain me before you leave. That's all I ask. I promise to not say anything to anyone."

"No way, la perra. Just checking to make sure you're alive."

More arguing ensued as the men stood outside. Then a door slammed and she heard the roar of the SUV's engine as the tires spun in a fast departure. *Oh, Lordy, I'm thirsty. Where's the water? How can I escape? Why hasn't my family found me? Stop wondering and start working on this chain. Get it loose and head downhill to town.*

She had nothing but the clothes she was wearing on the night she and Mickey had been cornered. Remembering back to what happened, she tried to find some sense of it. They had been sitting at the kitchen table at her house discussing Family business while sharing a bottle of wine. It was Monday and the weekend had been busy.

Her drug supplies were low and customers be damned, she deserved the day off. Suzanne was an old hand at skipping out of work last minute in her previous jobs and did not think twice about calling at the last minute to report out. She had left a voicemail for her boss, confident it would suffice, but forgot he was out on vacation for the coming week. Plus, this boss knew the long history of the Martinelli family dating back to the miners in the 1800's. The name alone gave her leeway others would never enjoy.

The least busy day of the week for Mickey's Mountain Munchies was Monday and a trusted apprentice sent from Denver staffed it for business—legit and otherwise. Today Mickey was helping Suzanne with her accounting when his phone rang.

Listening for a minute he hung up and turned to Suzanne. "Hey, we need to drive over to the park. The pickup guy out of Denver hasn't shown up yet. I need to get the pile of weekend cash out of the food truck. Don't wanna be carrying all the money on my bicycle. Let's take your car and stash the cash in the trunk. We'll leave the car there so we'll have it after our fun ride tonight. That'll work for you?"

"I wonder what happened to the pickup. He's always here at daybreak, right?"

When they arrived at the park, Mickey slipped the car into the first available parking space at the base of the zipline ride. in front of the food truck. The food truck shared a parking lot with High Country Adventure Park. The zipline ride was the only ride open so far at the park and the patrons were limited on Mondays. The park plans were big, but the progress was miniscule. They would have to be careful that no one was nearby when they transferred the money. Mickey was thinking it was a good thing the Family was not here to see this unsecured transfer.

"Hey, we're here, but not for long. Where's the dough?"

The apprentice was waiting. "I stashed it into these frozen french fry bags. And I put the few drugs left from the weekend activity into this smaller hamburger box. A bit of disguise."

"Yea, I get it. Hand it over and you can close up anytime this afternoon. Thanks."

"You bet. Glad to have it out of my hands."

Mickey slipped the plastic bags under his arms and another to Suzanne for her to carry. "C'mon, let's go." Suzanne followed him to her car, the boring, tan Taurus. "Keep an eye out for anyone watching us. I'm gonna put these two bags in the trunk. You hold the bag you're carrying. That one we'll deposit at the bank in the food truck account. When we get back from the fun ride on the zipline we'll bury the rest in the usual place. I don't like to bury anything in daylight. Raises too many questions. Neighbors might want to know if we ran out of mattress space for it."

She laughed at the vision of stuffed money, "I love that thought, Mickey, but the pickup guy always comes on Monday morning. I wonder what happened today?"

"Who knows? I'm sure we'll get a call before the day is over. We can make it over to the bank, deposit the money in the bag you're holding. If we try to deposit these two other bags, we would raise more than an eyebrow at the bank."

"The cash in the trunk can go in my backyard garden plot with the rest of it. We're going to need more PVC pipe for the stash. People are going to start wondering why my garden doesn't grow anything. I'll just tell them I've had a crop failure." They chuckled at the thought.

The challenge with handling large amounts of cash from drug purchases is major, even with the legalization of recreational marijuana in Colorado. The sale of MJ is a federal crime. Therefore it is a cash only business like the other illicit businesses the Family runs. The banks are regulated federally, so in Colorado the legal amounts of cash gained from the business cannot be deposited into banks. At the national level, the money from MJ is considered illegal. Filling up a large safe or two happens quickly. The dilemma is where to put the stacks and stacks of cash. Money laundering becomes the necessity or buried in waterproof PVC pipe for a 'rainy day.'

Mickey's high end mountain bike was stashed in the backseat of her car. They hopped on and rode back to Suzanne's, both thinking about the plans for the late night ride. Mickey had invited Suzanne for a risqué zipline moonlight ride, nude, under the celestial lights of the midnight sky. He hoped the zipline would be free of the town's teenagers, who also enjoyed frolicking on the line after hours. With just the two of them, one thing could lead to another, the arguments of the day could be forgotten, and they could get back to Suzanne's house in a hurry in the Tan Travesty.

Once back in Suzanne's kitchen, they had a second go at 'Quackbooks 101' as he liked to call it. Her preferred term was, 'Not Accounting for Dummies.' She appreciated his modification and admired his way with words. As it turned out, taking the day off was the wrong thing to do. They had argued on and off all day as they struggled with her mountain of records incorrectly entered into the Quack System.

"Suzanne, your records are a disaster."

"Stop being so critical. I've done the best I can."

"I guess. But I've had enough of this mess. Let's quit for the day and pour some wine. I'm ready to get in the mood for tonight."

They moved into the kitchen where they were cautiously making up over the wine. He did not like her new marketing strategy for creating an online sales club. Too risky. Too out there. And he was frustrated with her so-called accounting. He had a record of experience, but she was Family and could do whatever she chose. One canceled out the other. Back to square one.

Coming in from New Mexico, Alejandro's mission was to get information on the Family's business and get out of town. Mateo held a photo of Suzanne and another of Mickey. They had been told it would be easy to locate these two in the small town of Oresville. Suzanne would have the records they wanted and Mickey would have the Family names. DeHerrera was supposed to be the Oresville contact. When the two men arrived in town nearly a week ago they found him at the adventure park office. Oscar knew nothing and wanted nothing to do with them. Alejandro was furious, made more calls, and in the end, no help was forthcoming. He decided then there would be some revenge.

Within several days of their arrival, they located Suzanne and followed her home from work. Mickey was easy to find, he worked six days a week near Oscar's park. The plan was to take each of them separately. On Monday they watched her house and saw the couple leave in her car and return on his bicycle. The plan changed.

MISSION IMPOSSIBLE

There was a noise at the back door and she thought it was her tough outdoor cat, Mister, who had decided the safety of the house would be necessary. Mister was a personality unto himself. He lived outside and came in every few days when the mouse hunting took a downturn. The local vet called him a Lean Mean Killing Machine.

At twenty plus pounds he was one tough kitty. Last winter he had stayed out too many days and Suzanne thought he was gone for sure. He showed up, ears frozen, and with full recovery the tips fell off—now his ears were square. The local vet had given up on this animal going tame with old age. He requested of her to "quit with the late night emergency calls" for Mister. The vet sent the heavy duty kitty home with a portable kit for sewing shut the open wounds from neighborhood escapades, along with a big supply of antibiotics.

Suzanne stood to open the door, but the door slammed

open and two men charged into the kitchen. Mickey jumped up. She was hit by the door and fell to the floor. The men were yelling at them in Spanish. It was a mess. Nothing made sense and Mister strutted through the open door, unfazed.

The large man was clearly in charge. With a huge fist, he punched Mickey in the heat of the moment. Mickey fell backward, banged his head on the frame of the door, and went limp. The two men started talking in rapid Spanish. The shorter of the two dropped to his knees slapping at Mickey's face. His slaps were not the vicious kind, just strong enough to awaken him, but stopped when Mickey did not respond. The big guy walked over and kicked Mickey's side, yelling in English, "Wake up. We need answers." Mickey did not respond.

Mickey and Suzanne were tied up, dragged into the front room and left on the floor. Several hours later the boss helped himself to the wine and was still rustling through the files in her office. Mickey was groaning at times, not speaking. Suzanne was in shock, confused, terrified, *What's going on?*

There was a pecking order between the two intruders. The second man did as told, sitting in a chair with a gun aimed at her. There was arguing in Spanish. The little man was irritated and did not like her looking at him. He tied a scarf around her head as a blindfold. He couldn't find a scarf to blindfold Mickey so instead fashioned a hood from a sofa pillow covering. Mickey could converse in the language, but he was unconscious. More heated discussion in Spanish between the two men. *Why, tell me, why, did I not learn to speak Spanish?*

Spanish is everywhere and Americans are so cavalier as to think the world revolves around them—as bad as the British, the sun never sets on them. Americans too? Suzanne had already traveled extensively in her twenty some years on this planet and liked to profess, "Ain't no place better than this US of A. Land of indoor toilets, ya just can't beat it." But learn another language? *Ha!*

The bigger of the two guys came in and said something to the guard. Frustrated, he went back into the office. Little did he know Suzanne was somewhere early on a steep learning curve with the art of accounting. She had no idea what she was doing or what she was supposed to track. Records were mostly the past history of what, not the who and where he was told to find. Expectations were high. Delivery was, well, not so much. Suzanne was not the bookkeeper the Family and the intruders had hoped for.

At the first signs of the promise of dawn, a decision was made. The big guy came out of her office and told the small guy the new plan. Because her records had not yielded the information he was after and Mickey was useless, he saw this as an opportunity to get even with deHerrera.

Mickey and Suzanne were dragged out of the house into a vehicle. The back seats were laid flat and the car stunk like week-old garbage. The men had been living in it. They drove to the adventure park. Suzanne could hear them talking in the front seat, but the only thing she could comprehend was zipline. *What are they doing? Why are we headed to the zipline?*

The sun was bringing first light to the sky, but it would be over an hour before it topped the mountain range to the east of Oresville. She was left in the SUV still blindfolded and hands tied. Mickey was dragged to the zipline platform. They wanted something from him but were yelling in Spanish. Mickey was still unresponsive. The frustration was palpable. Left in the back of the vehicle, with the big rear door open, Suzanne was desperate and attempted to call out to Mickey through her gag. "Mickey! Give them what they want. Tell them everything, whatever that is." Her voice came out as muffled, not to be heard beyond the vehicle.

Suzanne could only hear some kind of a thumping sound

in the distance. Then it was quiet. The noise she heard was the additional beating of Mickey. He had been stripped naked and strung up on the zipline, hood still in place. The plan was to do the same to Suzanne. They would kill two birds with one stone. Get rid of these two useless people and shut down deHerrera's operation. Revenge completed. The bosses back in Albuquerque would be very upset with deHerrara's performance or so Alejandro thought. His getting even was short term thinking, fueled by his anger and the mess this mission turned out to be.

The two men heard the distant hum of a vehicle. They quickly left the zipline platform, headed back to the SUV, and the rear door was slammed shut. The men got into the front seats—doors were quickly closed in panic. She could hear the voice of the little guy. He was rattled and very angry. Talking rapidly, using a low voice, and hitting the dashboard with something, a fist perhaps. The other man was breathing heavily and not talking.

A vehicle pulled into the area. She could hear the arrival, distant talking of one person, then many minutes later another vehicle arrived. The men sat still, listening. The air was thick, heavy with anger, tension, anxious sweat.

Suzanne was tempted to yell in spite of the scarf tied around her head, covering her eyes and mouth. *Would someone hear muffled cries? Were they close enough to even notice such a sound? Where was Mickey?* She heard another vehicle or truck arrive, something heavier by the sound of the engine.

The SUV was started and they were on the move. *It felt fast and swerving for what reason?* The men were no longer speaking to one another. She decided she had best make some kind of a move. She kicked herself up to her knees and pressed her covered face to the nearest window. Someone nearby might accidentally notice.

She heard the sharp sound of metal hitting her head a split second before the pain erupted. Her space went quiet, dark, and empty.

GETTING TO KNOW YOU

J une in the mountains held the smell of a pine forest. The scent floated on the wind with a strong, distant sound and the air felt spring fresh. They were holding Suzanne at a remote, isolated shack. When Suzanne came to, she could sense daylight, but a headache blew reality out of proportion. She laid still and listened to her surroundings. When she moved there was a noise, she was chained with hands to waist and from there to something nearby. Someone kicked her and added in halting English something about water.

The covering over her mouth had been lifted, "I have to go to the bathroom. Please, help me."

More Spanish and an argument erupted. At the end of the argument, the lesser of the two men tried to help her take care of personal business. One of the men undid her hands and released the chain which was attached to the tree root. He helped her outside to complete the request. In the great outdoors this was a challenge for a woman under the best of circumstances. She knew better than to complain but whined anyway about the difficulty of peeing in the woods, thinking they would eventually feel sorry for her.

"I can't pee with someone watching over me. Please go away."

No comment.

"How long am I stuck here with no proper toilet paper?"

No answer.

Whining at a nudge higher, "I'm going to start my period. Then what? Did you think about that? You guys are lame." She was saying anything she could think of to gross them out.

No reply. She gave up, shook off her tush as best she could and wiggled back into her pants. One last attempt, "Where's Mickey? I demand to know what's happened to him. He's the one with all the answers, go get him and I can coax answers out of him for you."

More angry words in Spanish and someone rushed over to where she sat and taped her mouth shut again. This time there was a mumble from the little guy guarding the door of the shack. She could make out something about *zipline*. She laid on the floor and cried herself to sleep.

On day two, she could hear them arguing outside the shack. They left only to return with a blanket, a bucket for a toilet, and some candy. When Alejandro was unable to complete his assignment, he had no choice but to inform the higher ups. They demanded he return to Albuquerque. The bosses were not happy with the big guy's failure to deliver. More arguing. The big SUV left and never came back.

On day three, she got answers from the soft spoken man and finally his name, Mateo.

He removed the tape from her mouth, unlinked her hands. He could speak English in careful words and she played to it now that the big guy was gone. Many of her customers were Spanish and spoke in halting English. Suzanne talked to him about his family, his work, his life wherever it was.

Mateo told her he lived in Mexico and his wife and children were there, waiting for his return. He worked for a powerful man, but he was a low level worker. He drove cars. He ran errands. He dropped envelopes into waiting hands. He was sent in to be Alejandro's chauffeur. The short drive from Albuquerque to the beautiful mountains of Colorado was a chance to see the other side of the border and offered his first flight in an airplane from Mexico to the US. This was a one-off trip and he would return home to tell his children about Colorado.

"Well, This blindfold hurts my eyes. I'm allergic to everything. Please take off the blindfold." She added some real tears to her plea for help. That should do it.

Without a word he lowered the scarf to her neck.

Suzanne looked around in the dim light, "Where are we, Mateo?"

"Sierras."

"Hum, of course, we're in the mountains. These are the Rockies not the Sierras. But where?"

A long, lingering look at her, "No comprende. Bad English."

He gestured to indicate driving a car. "Find casa." He added two hands under this tilted head, "Dormir," and highlighted with snoring noises and a light laugh.

"You found this place and slept here?"

A long pause, "Si."

As they tried to communicate in their languages, Suzanne was able to understand pieces of what was going on. Mateo tried to share his story with her, painfully using broken English. He used sign language where he could and made a valiant attempt to let her know how he and Alejandro found the remote cabin and used it as their base to implement Alejandro's assignment.

With hands up in a gesture of frustration, Mateo attempted to describe the lack of cooperation and knowledge from deHerrera.

"What's deHerrera got to do with anything?"

A big pause as Mateo was converting her words to his language, "Familia Albuquerque."

Suzanne was trying to put two and two together. *Is deHerrera part of this group trying to infiltrate our territory? What do they want with me? Where's Mickey?*

"Mateo, my friend Mickey, where is he?

Another pause. With a sad look upward, he made the sign of the cross and drew a quick line across his throat, "Merto."

"Dead? How? Why?" Suzanne was devastated. Although her job was to keep an eye on Mickey for her family, she had become attached to the guy.

Mateo stretched his hands in a wide circle and put both hands to his head on either side, "El error."

Her tears began to flow. All hope for a rescue was gone. *If they killed Mickey, am I next?*

With the information from Mateo, Suzanne believed time was short, she needed a plan, she needed to act. Late on the third night she tried to make a run for it, but Mateo was outside, guarding the door. He grabbed her, secured her feet to the chain around her waist, and said buenas noches.

On the next day, he told her about the return airline ticket. It was his way home, but he must get to Albuquerque to use it.

She decided the ticket was her way out. "Mateo, if you go to the parking lot, my car is there. The keys are hidden on the front tire. You can drive back to the airport and use the ticket to return to your family."

He tried to show walking with fingers on a palm, "Long

walk. Car ausente."

She put a hand to her mouth and showed it zipped shut with hand at her heart, "I promise no say." She pointed to the blindfold at her neck, "See nada." She never mentioned that she had a clear picture of both men when they broke into her kitchen and now she had their first names. Something to go on. *My family will want to hear every detail and I'll be the hero with the breaking news. Goodbye, Oresville.*

At sunset he left on the long walk to town. Her feet had been released from the waist chain, but both wrists were still linked to her waist and that in turn looped to the root. After a reasonable amount of time had passed, she was sure he was headed to the parking lot for her car.

Suzanne's face was scraped and bleeding. She had slid off the mask by rubbing it against the rough logs of the shack. The reality of where she was held hit her and now she was alone. Unable to move beyond a few feet around the root, she tried stretching to a gap in the logs, but could not raise up high enough to see out. The food left for her was enough for a short day and brought the rodents inside. She fell asleep and woke up with the beady eyes of a pack rat looking at her. The sound of her scream scared them both. The tears started and turned into sobs when she understood abandonment, just as the cabin had been over one hundred years ago.

Day four and no sounds beyond wind, pine branches sliding against one another, and the smell of dry mountain air. She was a happy, popular, entitled young woman. Certainly someone would be looking for her—the authorities, her family, co-workers? If she could hold out for another day, rescue would be reality and she prepared to sit tight, wait it out.

It never occurred to Suzanne that she might have to work at her own escape.

INCOMING

She checked the cell phone caller ID and announced, "Deputy Korneal."

"Hey, it's me, Kate, from state forensics. I just saw the results on the smear of blood we found at the house. Thought you'd want to know."

Phoebe was not clear on how she felt about Kate and the Denver team. "I hope this is good news, I'm not making much progress since the visit with you yesterday. We're back to the start of the investigation."

Kate was disappointed in the Chief Detective's ruling they would not help Green County. "Just so you know, some of us are not happy with the decision. That's why I'm calling instead of waiting until a full report can be issued with all the results. The blood smear on the door frame and on the floor in that front room both belong to Mickey Walker. I believed you'd want to know ASAP. That's short for as soon as possible."

They both let out a laugh harkening back to the fiasco of the meeting yesterday afternoon.

Phoebe picked up on the mocking train of thought, "Ah, yes, and so you know, there is no MPR, that's 'Missing Person's Report,' on Suzanne Martinelli. It tells me that her family is taking care of looking for her. She's a missing person only to some of us. The Oresville Constable and I are headed over to the adventure park to talk with the manager, Oscar deHerrera. This woman's car is parked there and maybe he knows something. Mickey's food truck is open and the assistant is running it, business as usual."

"Good luck with all of this. And I'm hoping Tuesday's election yields good news, whatever good news would be to you."

"Thanks for the call, Kate and your good wishes. I'll keep in touch with you as to events here. Hope we meet again, for sure."

The possible future Green County Sheriff ended the call as she went into Bill's office for advice.

"So far not much on who murdered Mickey. Anything you might have heard?"

"Nope, I'm busy with these auditors. Mickey's death is probably just a prank gone wrong."

Really, I came into THIS office for advice? "Hmm. I rather doubt that. The state people knew he was part of a drug network out of Denver and into Greenstone. Now up here. It's more than a prank, Bill, and not talking about it doesn't fix it."

"No one's asking, so why bother?"

"So, we only 'Do Crime' if someone asks? That dog don't hunt, as Grammie used to say."

"I'll help you after this audit's complete. Likely today, but I'm so stressed with these people, I plan to take tomorrow off to rest. I'll see ya on Monday."

She stood there looking at him, wondering when he mentally left law enforcement, "Okay, see you then."

At her desk in the deputy's bullpen, she looked at a note from Roz. It was the phone number for the Bernalillo County Sheriff in Albuquerque, New Mexico. He answered on the first ring and Phoebe introduced herself.

With the usual pleasantries she added the reason for the call. "I'm the Deputy Detective assigned to a murder case here in Oresville, Colorado. A vehicle rented in Albuquerque by Alejandro Martinez, no address, was spotted at a new tourist park here. The park is run by Oscar deHerrera from your area. Can you tell me anything you might have on him or the Martinez guy?"

"Everybody rents cars and travels these days, I'd say no connection. This Martinez guy is not on my radar screen, but I can stay tuned in."

She talked over him, "The vehicle is suspected to be connected to a missing person, but it's gone and deHerrera is still here."

The Sheriff took a long moment of silence and decision made, "Let me fill you in on the deHerrera Family."

He launched into the background—many generations dating back to before statehood in 1912. It was believed they had connections to a Mexican cartel and drugs were the constant underbelly of the county. Oscar had left the city when interest was high in recent drug lord quarreling. There was a death of a deHerrera family member and the case was still open. No leads were forthcoming.

Phoebe listened to the Sheriff's commentary and took notes. Nothing sounded promising, *But one never knows.* "If you happen to run across these guys, please keep me in mind." She thanked him and promised to keep him posted if anything came about from her investigation.

"One more thing. I got a call yesterday from the office of the Colorado State Detective, some Wingate guy. He wanted information on deHerrera too. Any connection? Seems like a coincidence."

"You know what they say, 'No such thing as coincidence' in crime." They shared a good laugh over this one and hung up. *Another contact—should I need one after Tuesday.*

She sat back and wondered what Chief Detective Jerk-Gate was up to. *Right now, who cares? Time to call Bart and get this visit to deHerrera on the road.*

"Hi Phoebe, ready to visit Mr. deHerrera?"

"You bet. That's why I'm calling. Meet you at the park in five?

"On my way."

HOWDY

Three minutes later they parked at the train depot and headed for the manager's office. The office for Oscar deHerrera was in the city owned Short Line Railroad Station—temporarily rented until the park's development was further along. The city was charging him an outrageous amount for this convenience and the citizens of Green County were happy.

The office was quiet, no one was waiting in the chairs lining the wall and the administrative assistant was reading a magazine, sipping a drink, a bag of chips on the side, and listening to something on wireless earbuds. When Phoebe and Bart came into the office, she tapped a bud, closed the magazine, and offered a disinterested, "Can I help you officers?"

They stood in front of the desk for this unannounced visit and asked to see Mr. deHerrera. She started flipping through a large paper appointment book, "As the High Mountain

Adventures Park Manager he's a busy man. How about an appointment in the next week or two?"

The appointment book looked bright white and vacant to Phoebe. They had seen his car parked outside the train station.

"I have fifteen minutes the week after next?"

Bart smiled and stepped towards the office door of deHerrera. He raised a hand to the doorknob and offered, "We have a murder investigation going on. We can talk with him here or down at the Sheriff's office. In fact, you might be able to add information also. We could all go to an interview room at the county building. You decide."

A shadow seemed to pass overhead with a tangle of thought processes. In under five seconds the decision was made. She quickly stood from the desk, plucked her handbag from the back of the office chair, and rushed from the room. Over her shoulder an announcement was added, "Excuse me, I need a short break. Must have been something I ate."

Her sudden change of mind with the thought of a visit to the Sheriff's department was not a surprise. They watched her exit. Phoebe leaned against Bart's arm and gave a slight nudge, "You are so nice and I might add you have a real way with words for the ladies, too."

He smiled at the compliment and extended his hand towards deHerrera's office door, "Shall we?"

They skipped a knock on the door and stepped into his office with a flourish of a fast door opening, announcing themselves. Phoebe started first, "Good afternoon, Mr. DeHerrera. We met on Tuesday, the day of the crime on your property."

His interested, fake smile left as he heard the mention of the crime. Seated at an oversized desk, his dark eyes stared at the officers. He wore a suit and tie, loosened at the neck, black hair slicked back into a low ponytail. There were random bills piled in front of him, one hand fully loaded with money and the other stacking it neatly into piles. He did not look at Phoebe and continued the sorting process, "You need an appointment. Please see the gal out front."

"No one's out front. We are investigating a murder and appointments or otherwise are not on our agenda." She stared at him and Bart followed up by dragging an additional chair to the front of the desk. They seated themselves without an invitation to do so.

She took out her cell and punched the Record App, "I'll just record our conversation if you don't mind."

He continued the sorting of the bills and glanced at Bart, "Whatever. You'll have to excuse me. I'm counting the money from last week's business and cannot be interrupted."

Looking around at the money she rested her eyes on him, added a slight tilt of her head, and lowered her voice to a steady level, "Again, Sir, we apologize for the interruption, but there has been a murder on your property and you as manager owe us a discussion. We can be here or over at the Sheriff's Department. What'll it be?"

No response. Phoebe let the silence drag. People cannot stand a prolonged silence. It's similar to playing chicken—who will "blink first" to fill the silence.

He glanced at Phoebe, rolled his eyes to the ceiling, took a deep sigh, "I'm trying to run a business here. Make it fast."

"Right. Let's start with a simple question. Where were you early Tuesday morning?"

DeHerrera started opening desk drawers and casually moved money into them from the desktop. He was unfazed and stared at Bart, ignoring Phoebe. With a deep breath and exhale as if buying time or dreading the explanation for the umpty-umpth time, Oscar pushed back from the desk, hefted himself up, and let out a harumph with the effort. He was a short man and heavy set. The effort was a display of irritation or boredom.

With a step to a three foot high architectural drawing on a tripod beside the desk, he waved a gold fountain pen at the dry mount board and smiled at Bart. It carried the title High Country Adventure Park in prominent curved gold lettering, large sized Algerian font. Below it in small print, nearly unreadable was Oresville, Colorado, no gold on the lettering. In fact, it looked like sticky lettering pasted over some other town's name.

Instead of answering Phoebe's question he launched into what could only be called *The Pitch*, "This is what I was doing on Tuesday morning and every morning, afternoon, and evening for the several months since I moved to this burg—building the future of Oresville."

His voice boomed with practiced excitement and confidence. He continued preaching to Bart, "The zipline is the only ride available this season. Even as we speak the bulldozers, the cement mixers, and forklifts are busy converting this architectural dream into reality. The added income to the fair hamlet of Oresville will provide benefits as never before seen with added tax revenues, population growth. The accompanying demands for housing, infrastructure, services, restaurants and all the associated benefits of economic development will be a milestone in this community's history. This adventure park will put Oresville on the map with a big gold star attracting tourists worldwide."

They listened politely to the sell job from Mr. DeHerrera and could not help but smile with his vision of what's to come. Phoebe put her elbows on the chair, fingers into a steeple, and leaned forward, "This is great and the town fathers are happy." Then the smile left as fast as it had arrived, "Let's try this again, just for the record you understand. Where were you early Tuesday morning?"

Following his Chamber of Commerce speech, Oscar was

obviously looking to unload his frustration. Standing at the Park's aerial view he waited a full fifteen seconds and finally looked squarely at Phoebe, "Look, I don't have anything to help you. I came to the office on Tuesday like any other day, eight in the morning. By that time, a crowd had gathered and the action in the parking lot was in full swing.

"Constable Masterson here told me the zipline ride is a crime scene. If you want to track my whereabouts, do your job. Check my cell phone pings, I was at my apartment. Check my credit card receipts, I was in your restaurants. Now, I'm shut down until you release the crime scene. The money you see here is the last of it until you small town hicks open me back up."

Phoebe was unfazed by his declarations and waited in the silence for the next round.

The silence continued. DeHerrera blinked first, "I might add that the next time you barge into my office unannounced to insinuate my involvement in a murder, my family's lawyer will be in touch. Case closed."

With a quick move, Phoebe was on her feet, business card in hand, "Mr. deHerrera, here's my card. If you think of anything to help solve the murder of Mickey Walker, call me. Since you just gave us permission to check your records, we will do so. By the way, the involvement of your family attorney, Mr. Sanchez, will not be necessary. I've already checked and he is not licensed to practice in the state of Colorado. Have a good day, deHerrera."

Bart returned the chair to the conference table and stepped back to the desk. He plucked a business card from the stack on the gold card holder and looked at it for a brief study. As he tipped the card to deHerrera he assured him, "We'll check this cell number on what you've mentioned and be in touch. Thanks for your time."

Phoebe held open the manager's office door for Bart. She stood holding the doorknob, back to the door stretched to nearly a proud six feet tall, chin out, and a challenging set to her eyes. One last look at deHerrera, *This ain't over.*

He stood at the tripod with a shocked look, mouth agape at her mention of the family attorney in New Mexico. As Phoebe closed the door, he stepped to the phone on the desk and dialed.

Phoebe and Bart were standing at her Sheriff's vehicle parked at Mickey's Mountain Munchies food truck for a midafternoon lunch. She watched him take a giant bite from a hotdog and appreciated how classy he could make the effort look. Three bites at the max and it would be gone. He had ordered three with a smear of jalapeno jelly.

As he moved in for bite number two, she took advantage of the moment of silence, "That went well. Was I even in the room?"

"Seems like our park manager is a bit of a misogynist."

"Ah-huh. Why am I not surprised?"

"He definitely is a front man for this park operation, but somehow I think his job description includes some additional activities."

"With all that cash on his desk, I think you're right."

"You know, I almost told him to answer your questions to you, not me."

She laughed and hesitated before taking a bite, "If you had spoken, he would have been encouraged to talk only to you."

"No worries, I figured it's your crime, your trip to Denver, your questions—your circus, your monkey. I'm playing catch up. How'd you come up with the name of the lawyer?"

"I talked with the Bernalillo County Sheriff in New Mexico. He was loaded with info on the deHerrera family. Just took a few notes and the lawyer's name popped. I checked it online to see if he practices in Colorado. Nope. When he threatened with the lawyer bit, it was the perfect opening to let him know."

Bart was onto the third dog, "DeHerrera's quite the talker."

"I'd say more like quite the salesman. Did you notice how he did the old distraction away from the money? My limited career with the Salt Lake City Police included an occasional loan into major crimes and lots of training. Good old Oscar used the Art of the Sale when we walked in and saw the money covering his desk. Before we knew it, he had us looking at the park's layout and thinking about economic development. Pretty slick."

"I guess. Can a zipline bring in that much money? He said it was last week's business."

"There's more to High Country Adventure Park than a single ride and a fancy presentation. I believe our Mr. deHerrera is dirty."

WEEKEND KICKOFF

O n Friday morning Roz reported the status of Suzanne's car. When Billy Baldwin went out to retrieve it and tow it to the impound lot, it was gone.

Phoebe was listening to Roz's update while multitasking. She was at the hallway coffee pot station, pouring coffee and listening, "Gone? How can it be gone? Do you think maybe Suzanne picked it up?"

"Hard to say. She's not been to work all week. It's registered to a Joseph Martinelli, maybe someone from that connection came and drove it back to Denver. Why don't we cut to the chase and put out a BOLO for Suzanne?"

"It can't be a formal lookout, she's not officially missing nor is she a person of interest. Yet. Let me take a minute to call her Mom and see if Suzanne's there. She might have picked up the car and headed to Denver."

Roz jabbed a finger in Phoebe's direction, "Excellent idea.

Let's see what they say, just for grins and giggles. You need to get ahead on this one."

A hesitant, "Hello?"

"Mrs. Martinelli, this is Deputy Phoebe Korneal calling from Oresville. I'm checking back to see if you've heard from Suzanne. Is she there with you?"

A deep humph with a conceited voice, "No, I haven't seen or heard from her. Our family is on the lookout and we have everything in control. With many resources around the state, we are on high alert. This is our family's business."

"I appreciate that, Mrs. Martinelli, but I'm concerned. It's been almost a week since we've heard from her. Upon checking, she's not been at work."

"Yes, but as I said, we're taking care of things from our end. You can stay out of it." With the curt comment, the mom hung up.

At the abrupt end to the call, Phoebe looked at Roz, "Sure seems odd the mom's not concerned about the daughter's whereabouts. Does she know something and not sharing it? Strange."

"Well, there you have it. A missing person who's not really missing."

"I'm going over to her house to check it out. Maybe Suzanne picked up the car, went home, and knows nothin' about nothin.' We call it the old CNK, Claim No Knowledge. If I don't see the vehicle, we'll put out an APB to see if it gets spotted somewhere in the state. Mom's nonexistent help isn't the end of the question. If the big SUV was rented and returned in Albuquerque, maybe the Taurus was driven down there too."

Suzanne's house was buttoned up with the feel and taste of empty and unused. The crime scene tape fluttered in the gentle breeze of the morning. A mighty cat meowed as Phoebe checked the lock on the back door. It was the same cat who nearly took her out the last time she came in the back door.

"Are you hungry, Buddy?" The cat rubbed its head on her leg and purred, *I guess the answer is yes.* In a moment of weakness, she hefted the twenty plus pound feline and took it with her.

The cat was escorted into the office. The few people around started hunting for scraps and water for the new guest. If the election swings her way on Tuesday, Phoebe envisioned the animal would become a fixture. It could make the atmosphere more friendly for the visitors doing business at the Green County Sheriff's office. But right now, the constant meowing, jumping on desks in the Deputy's bullpen, and creating distractions was not making it the welcome addition to the staff as Phoebe had hoped.

Roz finally offered a cookie to it and nearly lost a finger in the process. It was starved or seriously lacking in the household cat skills category. Roz observed, "Once Suzanne is found, she can donate the animal and visit him when she comes to work." In the meanwhile, Roz made a few calls to find a temporary home.

Bart arrived on the scene. "Hey, I need a mouser out on the ranch. I'll take him with me and make sure he's taken care of until you come up with another plan."

Roz was petting the cat, "Great idea, Bart. He's all yours for now. From the looks of him, you better stock up on cat food or your life could be at risk."

Chuckling Bart responded. "I'll keep one eye open when I sleep and a shotgun nearby. But, for sure, I have enough mice around my place to keep this big guy busy and full.

The APB went out for Suzanne's missing car. Now they would wait for a bit of luck.

By four o'clock, Phoebe was feeling worn out from the paperwork of the week with little or no progress on the death of Mickey Walker.

Before she could begin the weekend, Phoebe called Bill to give him an update on Mickey's death and Suzanne's absence. "Hey Bill, got a minute?"

"Sure. Just practicing a bit before the onslaught of two new infants. The new teaching is to 'sleep when you can' with two of them in the house. Just like the military teaches combat soldiers." He let out a worried giggle at the thought of practicing his new life with twins in it.

Phoebe wondered what combat had to do with babies, *Practice? Impossible.* "Hmm. Okay good advice, I suppose. I thought you should know what's going on here with the case. We have no solid clues as to who killed Mickey."

"What do you have as evidence at this point? Not a big time prank gone wrong?"

"Come on, Bill, even if this is a prank, those who did it are guilty of murder. We even got a hit from an elderly citizen who lives across from the adventure park, Mrs. McGillicuddy."

"Old Lady Mac? She's ancient, older than dirt. Why waste your time on her?"

"Bill, she's across from the park—location, location, location. Let's remember everyone and everything's in until it's ruled out. Also, Mickey's girlfriend, Suzanne. She's still missing, a no show all week here at work."

"Maybe she did it and took off? Did ya think of that?"

"I believe she could be in dire straits. I doubt she was strong enough to overpower Mickey. Remember too, Suzanne's prints were not found at the crime scene."

"Suzanne's just taking a vacation, a personal day, or something like that. It's a case that isn't a case. Even the State Detective Wingate has stepped back. The big boys in Denver have a tight grip on what goes on. Stop worrying about it."

"Bill, really? There's more to this situation. There's

been no communication from Suzanne for days. A dangerous assumption would be the family knows where she is. Her house is empty and the car hasn't been found. Just so you know, I took the liberty to put out an APB on her car this afternoon. No results yet, too early."

"Please don't be so dramatic, Pheb. I'm sure she'll show up. And Mickey's situation, well, who knows what happened there. I still think it was some shenanigans gone wrong."

"Murder is murder. I don't care if it's a 'good old boy', or some kids, or whoever, Mickey deserves justice. Someone killed him and they need to pay."

A long pause, "You're right. I'm over-listening to a certain someone at the Buns Up."

She exhaled a relieved whoosh, "Even our retired Sheriff Joe could not spin his way out of this one."

"You've got a point, Pheb. You run with it and let me know anything new. You know me. I've got a lot on my plate and am feeling overwhelmed. I can't think straight right now."

"Bill, I understand. If Tuesday finds me elected Sheriff, I believe you and I can build a team to manage this county. You as Undersheriff and me as Sheriff. What do ya think? Do you have it in you?"

He let loose with a smile over the air waves, "You bet, Phoebe. What a relief to know you would want to keep me on."

"We've known each other forever. Of course, I'd want to keep you on. Friends are friends. You have big time experience and training. You're the right guy for my Undersheriff position."

Bill took a deep breath, checked his profile in the nearby window, swept a hand over his hair, "I can't tell you how right you are. I can do this. With twins in another month, I'll have my hands full. But keeping my job is critical right now. Thanks, Pheb."

"No worries. I need to have you in place to make

this transition seamless and transparent. With this murder investigation and the possibility of drugs running rampant, the county needs a strong, united sheriff's department. Maybe it's time to do what we're paid for—stop shining a spin on crime and address the underbelly of Green County."

"... count on me. Promise."

"Great, I knew it. Make no mistake. Crime is here big time. We need to keep the bad guys away and the citizens safe."

"Got it, Pheb. You know I want Oresville and Green County to be a stellar example of small town livin'.

"Thanks, Bill. All for now. I'll let you know if I hear anything over the weekend. Continue to rest up, *Like you are always resting up.* I'll be in touch."

FEED THE FIRE

E very Friday brought a new round of tourists which usually lit up the phone lines in the sheriff's office. The short term visitors call for directions, lost animal alarms, mountain road mishaps, and assorted missing family members. Today the phones were unusually quiet. Noting this, she decided a relaxing evening starting with the Freakin' Friday Finally Happy Hour at the Club would be in order.

Phoebe headed home to change into weekend attire. She gave Bart a quick call as she rolled out of The Court. "I'm headed to the Club. Meet you there?"

"I'm a half hour ahead of you for the start of the weekend. We could both use some 'unwork' socializing. Tomorrow starts the final weekend of campaigning."

The rented trailer had been Phoebe's home since she came to town. She preferred to call her trailer a rental to disguise it from a more permanent placement. If another opportunity came along, she wanted to be ready for a move up the career ladder, regardless of location. Never having a rent increase, she was committed to staying there to make a workable budget.

Now with Bart in the picture and their relationship growing from the lust stage to the next step of romantic obsession, cohabitation was a new possibility. She could not see herself living in Bart's Bliss—a three room cabin on the side of a mountain near tree line. Now that she was running for the Sheriff position, a more permanent living abode might be needed. *I'll worry about living arrangements after Tuesday.*

The Club was a B.P.O.E. Elks Club, run by the past Exalted Ruler and Club Manager, Willie Friedrich. It was a staple for the community and Willie intended to keep it a recognized community resource—weddings, funerals, graduations, and card clubs both legal and otherwise. They did an outdoor barbeque every Monday evening, hamburgers fresh off the grill for five dollars, fries an extra buck. On Burger Madness Mondays, Happy Hour started at four for members only, all others paid full price, non-members welcome.

Willie's longtime partner and family mainstay, Rose Mary, ran the kitchen with a tight fist and free drinks for the help. The kitchen ladies were seriously loyal to her and turnover was nonexistent. Willie's daughters, Jennifer and Ann, were the waitstaff on this one evening each week. CJ's hubby, Brian, was the other sibling of the Friedrich family and the only bartender, seven days a week. The Club was a family run affair and the Elks membership never waned.

The only non-Friedrich family operations volunteer was Rosalind Marie Boudreaux-Diamond, Roz. The recently married Sheriff's dispatcher and receptionist was preceded by reputation—she put the P in Party. The gatherings coordinated by her shined like a beacon in the night, gathering all into the sanctity of a celebratory embrace. Even in the present state of extreme pregnancy with twins, Roz was weeks ahead in planning for Phoebe's win as Sheriff. The women of Oresville and the Greater Green County were in rare form.

Roz arrived at the Club's Freakin Friday Finally minutes before Phoebe and Bart. She started inspecting the bunting she ordered at the expense of the Club's Sunshine Committee, "Win, lose, or draw, we're gonna get out the vote and party hard on Tuesday. I'm predictin' the biggest voter turnout ever recorded for a Special Election."

An outsider would have thought her plans were for a massive church social event to welcome a new minister. Just short of bringing in a marching band, Roz had organized a playlist of music that would make John Philip Sousa proud—preceded by several tunes in the Zydeco flavor. Her native Louisiana background always found its way into the celebrations and the music was the accent.

Roz had directed a giant potluck beginning at six on election day. The red, white, and blue bunting would be draped around the Club on Sunday by a team of women. The food tables were to be set up on Tuesday morning. Through the election day anyone coming into the Club not displaying a Vote for Phoebe sticker would be interviewed as to their voting status.

Lined up at the corner of the bar top, The Regulars observed the preparations, murmured assent, and lifted a glass in agreement. Being members and daily visitors for years, even if just for a quick drink, The Regulars were seldom absent without extreme cause. This year they were all retired and there were long lingering looks and thorough discussions at the goings on around the Club. As viewed from their corner. The bar was an L shape and the Regulars sat at the far side bend.

They returned to the latest news circulating. No man at the bar or at home, for that matter, dared take issue with this Sheriff

Women's Movement. Vote for Phoebe. They got the message.

On Tuesday, election day, anyone not displaying the *I Voted* sticker would be escorted across the street to the Green County Clerk's office to vote. Once their civic duty was completed and the sticker was prominent, they would be escorted back to the Club and presented with a coupon for a free drink. The polling station was open until seven for the miners who worked the late shift at the Moly.

When Phoebe walked into the Club in time for Freakin Friday Finally, she had changed into jeans, t-shirt, and cowboy boots, putting her at an even six feet in height, inseam thirty six inches. Her chestnut hair gathered into a messy bun at the back of her head sans a ballcap. Seated next to Bart at the bar, she gave him a quick peck on the cheek and looked around. They always sat at the long arm of the L shaped bar. From there they could listen in to the latest from The Regulars, easily spot the front door and the community meeting room and establish enough seating should CJ, Augusta, and others show up.

Bartender Brian rushed over, put a napkin before her with a flourish, filled a glass with soda, snapped a lime on the top, and in a loud whisper, "Welcome to the weekend, Sheriff."

A reach for the glass, slow and deliberate, "Why thank you, Sir, don't forget to Vote for Phoebe." Both of them laughed at the little joke.

Minutes later, CJ and Augusta came through the doorway and headed for the bar. The Regulars at the end of the bar acknowledged their arrival. This Friday night ritual officially launched the weekend.

The entrance of CJ brought on a side bet discussion. Would she stand on the bar stool and lean over to give husband Brian a fast kiss? At just under five feet, she could barely see over the top of the bar. Or would Brian beat her to it and lean across the bar from his position as bartender? Brian was over six feet tall and could easily lean forward if she were seated on the bar stool. This evening she beat him to it and kneeled on the stool. A sigh went up from The Regulars who had guessed otherwise.

Brian was already setting up a pour for Augusta. She ordered nothing but Pappy Van Winkle Bourbon, neat. The Club stocked it for her, regardless of price. Club Manager, Willie, once tried to convince her to switch to something cheaper and easier to have shipped into Oresville.

"No, I like what the old guy, Pappy, said and I use it as my mantra in business, '... fine bourbon at a profit if I can, a loss if I must, but always fine bourbon.' It's how I run my businesses, quality and consistency first. You have stocked it for me for thirty years and we will not have this discussion again." Willie understood and never again questioned the wisdom of her bourbon selection.

At times, Augusta was generous to a fault. She paid for it, treated all at the "L" on special occasions, and enjoyed her special drink.

The Higgins family had a variety of businesses, property, sections of land holdings, and mining claims at a level unheard of for a single proprietor. Augusta's grandmother, Connie, took over the family's business in the late 1800s after the family was wiped out from an epidemic. As luck would have it, she was visiting family a hundred miles away for the summer when the virus took out her siblings and parents. Hardened from the deaths of parents and siblings, she became the wealthiest teenager west of the Missouri River.

The Higgins family fortune originated in Omaha based on cattle. When her parents and siblings died unexpectedly, Connie rose to the occasion. Grandma Higgins back in Omaha decided the family's demise was an excuse for a long vacation in Europe. This experience would be the foundation for Connie's sudden launch into adulthood.

By the time Connie returned from the trip with Grandma she was married, divorced, and set on making Colorado her home. The Omaha family and Grandma were relieved and since then the family attorneys visited once a year as far as Denver. They planned the family banking reviews around the schedule of the Denver Stock Show. Entertainment and business combined and they never figured out the location of the backwoods town of Oresville.

Connie bought sections of land and created mining claims to ensure the Higgins Family future. The talk and movement for prohibition went on twenty years before it became law. Connie anticipated the eventual success of the campaign and quietly went about turning her ranches into farms to produce the crops necessary for liquor production. Distribution problems for the Higgins liquor went away when she started buying up businesses on the main streets of nearby towns.

The depression brought opportunity for bargain prices on properties and businesses. She bought up businesses, houses, apartment buildings, and kept the families in them at a modest "work for rent" schedule. No one went without if the Higgins family bought your failing business or home. In the long haul, Connie intended to sell the property back to these people, but that day had not arrived.

Before she could begin the Friday night gathering of friends, Phoebe liked to clear the air of details at the end of the work week. There was one little nugget left unvisited. Augusta was shifting into her stool at the bar and declared, "Barkeep, you look like I need a drink." Brian stepped up to the request and poured her a heavy-handed shot of Pappy's, always neat. Phoebe watched the usual ritual for the kickoff of Finally

Friday and tilted her glass of soda to Augusta, "So what's up with the Higgins property lines I'm hearin' about?"

Augusta took a sip before replying, "Well, I'm thinkin' someone has helped themself to a falling' down shack on my property. Might be on or near my property line. Or it's the other property owner's land. I don't know at this point. I intend to have a talk with whomever—the squatters or the owner. We can't have people moving in regardless of my ownership or the next guy over."

"Did you check the assessor records for property lines?"

"Yes. I have a survey crew hired for next week to re-sight the lines. It's been over a hundred years since that was done."

"What makes you think someone is squatting? Could be some backpacker looking for shelter from the elements. Or needing a rest."

"Possibly. I'll stop the next time I see a car there and have a little talk."

"I'd appreciate it if you'd wait until I can be with you. How's about the surveyors first and then I can help with the follow up. We can set the record straight if someone has set up residency. After Tuesday would be a help to me."

CJ leaned into the conversation, "I'd be happy to join you ladies in this little outing. Can we agree on Thursday? I'm anticipating a late night of celebration on the voting day followed by a non-productive Wednesday."

Augusta smiled, took another sip, and exclaimed how good this tasted for the end of a trying week. They both knew she would do what she wanted, when she wanted. All three of them understood this but at least the play was on the pass line. Check that box.

CAMPAIGN TRAIL

Saturday morning at TuTu's Washeteria the crowd of supporters had gathered early. Jorge was operating at full steam in the little warming kitchen. CJ's husband, Brian, was mixing the Bloody's as a one person assembly line. CJ was playing barmaid for the deliveries and TuTu was the wait staff for breakfast plates.

Bart and Phoebe were running late to the rally due to an early morning distraction after the alarm went off. Today promised to be beautiful and bright at this altitude of 10-5— crisp, dry, warm. They were dressed in the standard of jeans, flannel shirts, and walking sneakers. She had added the Green County Sheriff's baseball cap. It was firmly leveled on her head, the buckram added an extra inch to her height, and scraped close to six feet to Bart's five eleven.

CJ's plan for this final weekend of campaigning was simple. Hit the doors, talk up Phoebe, and get out the vote. If this turned out as anticipated, CJ could have a new career in politics. She could see the headline, *I did it!*

By nine in the morning the crowd of volunteers had gathered and were ready to canvas the town. CJ distributed block by block assignment sheets and flyers to hang on doorknobs if no one answered. She asked the candidate to say a few words before they spread out to cover the county with Vote for Phoebe stickers and yard signs. Phoebe offered up a short paragraph thanking everyone. Last minute second-guessing crowded her thinking and she hoped their efforts were not in vain.

Queennie had come to town from Pikeview and was standing with Augusta at the back of the crowd, next to the dryers. They were not happy with the few words Phoebe shared. *This young woman does not know how to get people excited.*

Taking matters to the next level, Augusta pushed her way to the front and stood next to Phoebe, "Hold on. All of you. Now listen up. I want to add to what Phoebe just shared. Reminder! The women of this county have a long history of making it what it is today. Now we're at another turning point. We must elect a young, experienced woman as our next Sheriff. Vote for Phoebe." She fist-pumped into the air and let out a rebel yell, "Yahoo!"

The crowd got on the energy wave and rode with it, "Yes," and another, "Yes," and another louder, infectious, "YES!"

Augusta shouted over the yesses, "Now let's get the vote out and make this happen for the people in this county, for the daughters of Green County, and for us women."

Phoebe looked at Augusta with a mist in her eyes and shouted a laugh, "I couldn't have said it better myself."

The excited supporters laughed at this and exited the washeteria to spread the joy of what a new female Sheriff in town could mean for all of them.

It was mid-afternoon when Phoebe's cell rang. She checked the caller ID, "Phoebe Korneal speaking."

"Hello, Deputy Korneal, I'm calling from the Bernalillo County Sheriff's office. The Sheriff is out on an active crime scene and asked me to radio link you over to him. He's out of cell range."

After several minutes of clicks, pops, and hissing, "Hey, Phoebe. Thanks for taking my call. I'm with the Major Crime people at a scene. We've got a Vic here and it looks like it may have happened yesterday from what the forensics people are guessing."

"Is it a woman?"

"No, why?"

"The situation I called you about? Seems there's a young woman missing who might be tied into this investigation somehow."

"Well, this is a big guy, Alejandro Martinez, a known regular in the drug scene here. Shot execution style, a double tap. Looks like they tried to get him to talk before he was shot. But what might be interesting to you is the car rental agency document in his cell phone. It matches the vehicle you were looking for this week."

"That might be someone involved in this mess up here. Is there anything with him? Articles of clothing? A heavy board or a ball bat? Maybe lucky enough to have blood on them?"

"The lab has taken a small bag of clothing. Looks like dirty clothes maybe from a recent trip. We'll see what the agency can tell us about the rental. I'll get back to ya when we know more. I'm guessing he turned in the rented vehicle and met up with someone. It did not go well."

"I'd like to give you the name of a forensic contact at the Colorado state level who helped us this week. I'm especially interested in his fingerprints, blood type, and any latent blood samples."

"I'm in the field. Let me pass you back to my dispatcher. Give the info to him. We'll see about a rush on the testing. Maybe we get lucky, eh?"

FRESH TAKE

I n the late afternoon, campaigning was wrapped up. Phoebe headed home feeling good about the reception from the county voters. Bart was already waiting at the trailer. After a way too lengthy embrace, he leaned back from her, "You're always the highlight of my day, Sweet P."

Her brain did a snap on the register of beta waves when she heard this and a smile in reply got broader than humanly possible. "But first, let's get a bit of business out of the way." She went on to tell him about the report out of the Zia state, New Mexico.

He listened to the report and was excited. "Maybe this is the break we've been looking for?"

"We can only hope." She added a deep sigh to relax, thought it over and switched gears. But for now, I'm thinking we need a night of R and R. How's about some cocktails and hot sex? Ya with me on this?" She applied a wide open teasing grin, wiggled her eyebrows for fun, and held out welcoming arms.

"Wow. I'm down with that, for sure. In the meanwhile, I've planned ahead and was thinking along the lines of another conversation plus your well-deserved rest and relaxation. Interested?"

"Most assuredly." She gave his hand a squeeze.

"I packed a bottle of wine and two glasses in your cooler. How about we run over to my place, such as it is and have a talk over dinner."

Oh no. Not, 'the talk.' He just said it makes him happy to see my face. But maybe that's not enough. Oh crap, what did I do to turn him off? I thought we were doing so well. I'm not ready for this. I really thought he was going to be the forever one. Stop it, Phoebe. Listen first, worry later.

She kicked aside the doubts, "Excellent. I've had enough campaigning for one day. CJ and I ate nothing but crap, marching up and down streets, knocking on doors, and munching cookies between houses. Not the smartest of choices. I can use one of your healthy dinners."

It was a short hop down to Bart's place. Getting out of the truck, he grabbed the handle on the cooler with one hand and helped her out of the truck with the other. The borrowed kitty from Suzanne's house gave them a hostile look of a guard cat. It had taken up residence on the porch and was looking fatter in just one day. They slipped past him and entered the house.

Amazingly enough, despite the rough interior, Bart had set the mood with a tablecloth and small vase of flowers on the makeshift dining table. *Maybe this talk will be better than I thought.* "What a nice touch, Bart. It feels like home."

He took a bow, pulled out a chair, "I thought you'd like it, simple, comfortable, and away from the usual. I wanted to set a mood. Please be seated and I'll pour, Madam."

The dinner was a charcuterie board. He had taken extra care to artfully place the assortment of crackers, cheeses, meats, fruit, and nuts. She was reminded of his natural skill in preparing only the healthiest foods.

"You've really outdone yourself," smiled Phoebe as she started plucking what she would eat first. *Maybe I'll practice the Art of Distraction while attending to the charcuterie. Conversation avoided.*

He poured them a glass of chilled Pinot Grigio and sat across from her.

Watching him move easily around the rustic cabin, she realized how deeply she felt about him. Phoebe was wrapped up in every insecurity she ever had, especially about love interests gone haywire. *Please don't let this be the end of our relationship. When did it move from 'the' to 'our'? Later on that question, Girly-girl.*

It was quiet in the room. Each was in a relaxed state of mind, stress had drained. She turned her attention to the view from the kitchen table. Evening was a lovely time to be in the mountains after a long day. The sun was a few minutes from closing behind Mt. Massive sending up streaks of blue, pink, and purple. The aspen trees were quaking gently in the sinking heat. The air was crisp with pine aroma and the crème de la crème—glasses filled.

Sitting at the table, Bart reached over and held both of her hands, "I thought it was time to tell you how I feel, Phoebe. You're the best thing in my life since, well, forever. Each day I care about you more deeply. Moving here has been great. We've had time to get to know each other and more importantly, learn to trust. I've seen the kind of caring person you are. Sincerity and honesty are two of the things I love about you. We need time to get to know each other. I'm hoping you're willing to stick with me and see where we can take this. Phoebe, I love you."

She had been holding her breath and released it with a rush of relief. With a small tear balancing on the edge of an eyelid, finding a response was out of the question. She went with first thoughts, "Bart, you're the first man in several years I've even looked at. Once you moved here, I believed we had a chance. I trust you too. Every day I see what a quality person you are. Today when I got home and you were there, I realized how important you have become in my life. With all my heart I hope our relationship grows with no end in sight."

A smile ten feet wide grew on his face, "You've made my day, no, my year. We can take this one step at a time and have some fun along the way. Let's take advantage of being in the middle of the Rockies, explore the terrain, and each other. I've never had a relationship where I could share my life."

She squeezed his hands, matched his smile, "Wow, I couldn't have said it better myself."

Letting go of his hands she stood and looped her arms around his neck. "I have another thought right now. Guess we're going to leave another glass of wine in the kitchen."

A long, loving, luscious kiss to seal the deal turned into an impatient roar of hormones and they practically galloped into the bedroom.

At first daylight they were driving back to her place. Bart drove with one hand, while he held her hand with the other. The sun squeaked over the eastern peaks and this morning's sky looked brighter, bigger, and bluer with the promise of certainty between these two. She was confident, "What a night. I was nervous and distracted by your opening volley."

"Volley? Like a shot across the bow, volley?"

She squeezed his fingers and had to laugh in retrospect, "Sometimes I feel like I'm one step off the abyss. When you told me we'd have 'a talk' I was sure it was the end of us."

"I guess we can put away our fears and trust each other. What do ya say?"

"You bet. For now, let's hit the washateria and see if Jorge and TuTu can rustle up breakfast and hot coffee before our day takes off."

WHEN PIGS FLY

S/ unday was a redo of Saturday, albeit shorter due to sore feet, bad weather, and fewer homes to visit thanks to a productive day before. The Club was offering an extended Happy Hour. A pizza and beer party was paid for by Augusta. Anyone bearing a Vote for Phoebe sticker was invited and The Regulars were all wearing stickers. Club Manager Willie denied having a favorite among the candidates. Willie always had his eye on the profit and loss bottom line, so he did not want to offend anyone.

Sitting at the bar in the Club at noon, Queennie and Augusta were thinking about the squatters at the shack, possibly on the Last Hurrah's land. "I'm not clear if it is on my property or the neighboring owner's. I've been lucky to not have this question in the last hundred years or so. Grandma Connie never would have thought such a thing could happen."

Queennie counseled a more humanistic view, "Times are

different now and some people have it rough. A night or two of shelter in an out of the way spot does no harm."

As she lifted the Pappy's, Augusta nodded. "I suppose so, but I'm thinking a little talk is due. You up for a little ride and we check it out?"

"Didn't you mention Phoebe offered to go along and make it more of an official visit? And CJ would ride along for the record?"

"Yea, but CJ is busy as campaign manager, running the volunteers. And Phoebe has enough on her plate right now. So, I figure why wait for them, daylight's burning.' Let's do a little high mountain trail riding and we'll be back here before the pizza's cold."

"I'm with ya. Let's hit it."

Augusta ordered them a six pack of stout to go and signed the bar tab. They slid off the bar stools and left. The Rubicon was parked at the curb and it looked like rain in the forecast was more than a sure bet—cloudy, dark, light drizzle. Augusta had made the trip so many times in her life she could drive, chat, point out geological features, and balance a beer without spilling a drop or hitting the brakes. They strapped in for a fast roar up the mountain trails to a shack on somebody's property.

At the start of the rough forest service trail, a little bubble intruded into Augusta's thought waves, *What about the gold?* She jerked the wheel to the edge of the rocky trail, turned off the engine, looked at Queennie, and yelled, "To hell with it!"

"What?" Queennie grabbed the dashboard with both hands, looked around them with eyes exploding in fear, ducking for a low profile in the windows. "What is it? Where? Duck!" She yelled for an answer—knowing there was trouble brewing.

Augusta was at a maxed out anxiety peak with the sudden

decision to spill it regarding Al's gold stash, "Nothin,' nothin.'" She looked directly at Queennie who was ducking and bobbing her head, eyes scanning through all the windows. Augusta let out a slow, long breath and with a harrumph, "Wait, that's not right. I've something I must get off my chest before we can continue on up to the shack, the cabin, the hut. Whatever you'd call it."

"Key-rice, don't do that to me. I thought we killed someone, or someone shot at us, or engine trouble, I don't know what." Slumped into the passenger seat, she fanned herself with both hands. Queennie owned a radiator and auto repair shop, Queennie's Radiators Plus, down in Pikeview on the Colorado Front Range. There was not an engine she did not understand. Her motto was true to form, 'If it's got wheels, bring it on.'

She was a great employer, a kick-starter for careers for high school kids, an unflinching woman at five foot eight, with short gray stick straight hair and a strong build. Queennie's built-in DNA of contentment waifed from her with a sweet hint of pleasantness. Outfitted with unyielding confidence, she waded into situations to help others, looking for the facts followed by the fix. By itself this built many lasting friendships out of business relationships and her community reach was wide.

Augusta looked over the steering wheel, out the windshield as if confessing, "I've something to tell you and there's no way to do this gracefully, so I'll just get it over with."

"Fine, go. But can't it wait until we can be comfortable over a glass of your home brew at the house, decent music piped in overhead? My heart is banging here."

"Well, yes, I guess this is rather abrupt. Ah, just forget it, we can talk about this later, never, or somethin.' I need a cigarette."

"Okay, but news flash here, you don't smoke."

Looking and feeling around the driver's seat, opening the console for the illusive pack of butts, "Right you are, I do not. In this case, I should. There's an old pack of ciggies in here somewhere. I keep it for emergencies."

"Emergencies? This is an emergency? What're we talkin' here, Augusta?"

"We're talking about nothing here. That's what we're talkin' about."

Augusta had decided she would tell Queennie about the gold. Their relationship meant more to her than all the gold in Al's pickle jars. Sure, possession is half the battle. Plus, it was stored at her family cabin until Augusta burned it down. Her friend should know about it. *No, deserved to know.*

Albert Lewis was Queennie's husband and they had never bothered to get a divorce. He prospected for gold in the Arkansas Valley for thirty or so years and she lived a hundred miles away in Pikeview, ran a repair shop, rode a Harley, and generally lived her life with friends, employees, and neighbors.

Al died with few friends, but the town folks supported his awkward life, laughed over his choice of a pet mule, Rose, and bought him drinks at the Club where he rarely appeared. The need for a divorce was a moot point and Augusta never asked him about it. Nor did Queennie ever think they needed to divorce. It was a technicality.

Augusta powered down the windows to vent the smoke from the crooked cigarette, exhaled a long leisurely drag, "Nope, this cannot wait. Let me take back the statement that it's nothin.' I've been carryin' this since last year and need to unload."

"Go ahead. Speak your piece, See-sta. First let's open a

can of this stout beer. Give me one of those ciggies. I think I'm gonna need it."

In her jitters Augusta rambled, "First, let me just say, I have no intention of ill will for Al or his memory. But it turns out, Queenie, I'm too close with our friendship. Now it looks and feels different."

"Gads, spit it out. The prologue's killin' me." Queennie took a deep drag, coughed, sputtered, and released a line of smoke that drifted out the window, then was caught and tamped by the rain.

With a sip of the stout, Augusta continued, "Ah, okay. Okay, this is unrehearsed I hope you know." I burned down the family homestead cabin last fall."

A drag, "Yes, you told me about it. Old news."

"Well, that ship has sailed, but before I set it afire, I loosened the boards in the kitchen and found gold coins. Not just gold coins, but two jars of flakes, nuggets, dust."

"Well, hallelujah. I wondered if the old coot had something stashed for the day he could retire. That's it?"

"Ah, yes. I want you to know that I have it and it is safely tucked away at the bank."

"A few jars of the gold?"

A thoughtful drag and an exhale out the window, a sip of the beer, "Ah, ya. Actually, two pickle jars."

"What kind?"

"What kind of what?"

"Pickles."

"The Pickle jars? Oh, right. Bread and Butter."

Queennie let out a hoot and declared, "And it was his 'bread and butter' all along!" She started laughing. The pureness of it grew to a roar, accompanied with shouts, and into a physical grip of uncontrollable body-spasm laughter. Augusta stared at her with a growing, gentle smile but this type of laughter was contagious, uncontrollable. In under five seconds, Augusta followed—it's a laugh with its own short story, its own life. They were both gasping for breath, each holding a cigarette out the window, and balancing a can of stout with the other.

The feel-good endorphins peaked and tapered off, tears running down cheeks, they sat back into the seats. Augusta wiped her eyes with a sleeve, let loose with a deep exhale as the wave passed, "I guess I never thought of it that way." They sat in silence, absorbed in the high from the joint laugh.

"But wait, there's more."

Queennie took a deep breath, rubbed her face with a bent wrist, shook her head, and looked at Augusta, "Unbelievable, I feel like I'm the big winner on a game show. What's the *more*?"

"He also had several jars of coins. The coins were his, my family cabin, mind you, but his coins. More pickle jars." Augusta's mention of the ownership of the cabin slipped out before she could stop it and instantly regretted her Freudian slip, *What's mine is mine.*

"How do you know those are his coins?"

"Well, we were a partnership, strictly business. He could stay at the Higgins Cabin all winter, fix it up for me. Kind of like a rent payment. He used great-grandaddy's coining machinery to process the flakes and what have you into coins. The machinery burned with the cabin."

"Too bad, we could go back into the coin making business. Make Albert proud."

"Except for it's against the law to make your own money."

"Tell that to the people who are in the side-hustle bitcoin business."

"Not likely. Also, Al hated banks and coins were easier to carry around than raw gold. Safer too. Plus, he used a small amount of silver ore from my mine, the Last, to make the coins sturdy. Gold by itself is too soft as coinage. I got some of what he produced every winter. I never asked what percentage they were of the total. He insisted I take two or three coins every spring, like a rent payment for his winter lodging at the cabin, discounted for his work, of course. He was one of the few people on the planet that I trusted."

Queennie smiled at this memory of him, "Honest to a fault, that was Albert. He gave me a few coins every year too. I've got a friend who's a big time assayer in Pikeview, third generation. She converts the coin into real money and feeds the gold into the system from her shop. Last year Albert gave me enough to expand my radiator business. That's how I bought the auto mechanic business adjacent. Hence the name changed to Radiator's Plus."

"That was decent of him."

"Anyway, I wondered where he got the coins and that weird design on them. The year on one side I understand as the year of production. But the symbol of the sun rising and the words The Last Hurrah carefully etched on each coin—crude, like handwritten, I didn't understand. All this time I thought it was some kind of double entendre. Now that we're friends, I get the connection to your mine. Ya gotta love it, you can't make up this stuff. People are so interesting."

Augusta sat still and looked at Queennie, listening, then dropped the cigarette into the empty beer can, "You're not mad?"

"Why would I be mad?"

"It's probably yours now, you're the surviving spouse. What else did he have that you got from the years of him roaming the mountains prospecting? A pet mule?"

With a sober look at Augusta, "What did I get from him? You can't be serious." She held up a hand and ticked off the points, "I have a decent life. I have good friends. I met you because of Albert and my life has expanded. That's what I got. In the end, it is what it is and the same was true for Albert. Case closed."

Augusta stared at her listening, then turned to gaze out the windshield, "In the end I guess it's all about what we do in the here and now. Not what we leave behind."

"Now you get it." She dropped her cigarette into the can, "Ugh, these things are nasty. My mouth feels like a dirty sock."

"Roger that, but it does hit the spot if needed—timing is everything, my dear. Let's get on up to the shack and see what it holds for us."

Queennie powered up the passenger side window, "With this rain, it might have caved in."

"One can only hope. Ashes to ashes, back to Mother Earth, et cetera."

"One thing before we proceed. You are the host of this wrap up of the weekend campaigning for Phoebe, correct?"

"The least I can do to help move us off the Good Old Boy Easy Chair."

"I believe that you or we need to be there to welcome the volunteers, help serve the pizza, and keep the beer flowing. It's only right and it'll be fun. Personally, I have never held a party and did not show up for it."

In full whine mode, "I want to see about the abandoned cabin, shack, whatever."

"It's raining cats and dogs. Aren't you bringing a survey crew up there this week?"

A full minute of silence with thoughts banging against her head cavity, "Hmm, you're right. Entertaining is your forte. Let's get out of here. The rain alone makes for a miserable, short inspection. It can wait."

Queennie smiled at the decision, took out another can of beer for each of them, and declared, "Atta girl."

Augusta started the engine, cranked up the tunes, popped the clutch into gear, maneuvered a reverse in the track, and put the pedal to the floorboard. The big engine responded like a filly out of the gate. They bounced, slammed, and rocked over ruts, rocks, and ridges. The pizza would not be cold by the time they got back to the Club.

NOWHERE TO RUN

I t was a dark, windy, cold day in the shack for Suzanne. Mateo had brought her a blanket several days ago. With rain dripping through the mostly vacant roof, it was wet and no longer worked for what it was designed to do. The food she had was gone yesterday as was her snappy, entitled, spoiled attitude. *When I get out of here, I will track down those two guys and cause them great harm.* What the harm would be was unclear, but her family would see to it, *If I get out of here.*

The "If" in this thought was a sudden eye opener. Would she get out of here? She had heard nothing for a few days. On Friday she thought she heard a vehicle, heavy duty from the sound of it slamming through the woods. She yelled and screamed but it had not slowed and in a matter of seconds it was gone, quiet again. The weather had been warm during the day and cold at night, typical for the mountains. The June days grew longer on their way to the solstice.

She had worked the chain against the tree root with little progress. The latest nail job on her fingertips was a lost cause and she had given up on all manner of neat and tidy. *If Momma could see me now* and she cracked a wistful smile. Momma was someone who would never understand. She shifted her head side to side with a "nope" and tears inched down her cheeks.

She liked to call her Momma Bear to her face and Momma Bee-ach in her brain. Theirs was a conflict of age-related perspectives and neither were able to close a gap created by nature. Suzanne liked to live life without a direction yet full speed ahead. Any plan was short lived and vaporized within hours in favor of the American dream of life, liberty, and the pursuit of happiness—her rebuttal to Momma Bear's constant critique.

Visions of food danced across her brain. She watched the pack rats and chipmunks enjoy the leftover food scraps on Friday. What she wouldn't give to reclaim a flat-line, unexciting white bread sugar sandwich. When the hunger pains swelled and thudded against her rib cage, she was reminded of all the food in her life she had tossed, the half-finished drinks tipped into the kitchen drain, and the picky demands of someone who had never in her life felt hunger. She sobbed.

The vision of Mickey popped into her sight non-stop. He had made her understand the business of sales, the art of the deal, and the value of distraction. She had to laugh at his frustration with her. "Make the deal, take the cash, next." He did not cater to the value of customer service for increasing sales, "It sells itself. Just don't get caught." He used the food truck as his office offering take away food with a high. The special was a hamburger with a side. This was the signal for a single dose of cocaine. Two sides bought a double dose.

Her face squeezed in agony at the thought of Mickey. The dry sobs faded into a case of the hiccups.

The one comforting thought for her was the vision of her Grandma Martinelli. She had been the only babysitter Suzanne ever had. Grammie spoiled her and shaped her view of the world and what it owed her.

In the quiet of these hours, she wondered about Grandma Martinelli's life. She was older now and careful to always be cheerful, supporting, but watchful. Suzanne liked spending time with her shopping, watching her cook, and listening to stories about growing up in the valley of Northern Italy. Was she making the family look for her? Did she know Suzanne was missing or lost or even gone?

Thinking about others was all new. It startled her and yet was thought provoking, yielding to a breakthrough notion. If she got out of this place, she would turn over a new leaf, start over, and use her money to drop the pretense of being a legitimate entrepreneur—actually contribute to the world. An easy commitment when you are bound up and praying to be saved.

The Tan Travesty was probably parked in the Albuquerque airport lot never to be questioned nor found. If the Tesla was in at the Denver dealership, of course, she would do the right thing and keep it as a little "round about town" vehicle. The thought of a snappy little Tesla cheered her for the briefest of time but it would not bring Mickey back. She cried again.

What if no one was missing her? A missing person who no one missed. She was too sad and spent to release a single tear.

The weekend had come and gone before it had arrived, or so it seemed. The frenzy of last minute campaigning continued this beautiful Monday morning, but not for Phoebe. At the desk in the deputy bullpen at 6:00 a.m. she was reviewing "next steps" in the death of Mickey and the disappearance of Suzanne. The missing person was nagging at her. *Suzanne wouldn't just drop out of sight. It's been a week since she was last at work. Plus, it looks like she was Mickey's girlfriend. He's dead and is she connected to the murder? Or the second victim?*

The thought of the SUV at the zipline doing a fast exit had her wondering if there was a connection. *Didn't Augusta say there were some people camping out at a shack below the Last? Did she see any vehicles there?*

Just as the last thought flew through her mind, Phoebe picked up the desk phone and called Augusta.

It was answered on the first ring, "Good morning, Phoebe. What's up this bright early morn?"

"Hey, glad I didn't wake you. I was wondering if you and Queennie had planned to head up to your property line to check the abandoned cabin?"

"Yes, as a matter of fact, that's why we're up so early. Nothing like a quiet morning to head into the mountains."

"Exactly. How about I tag along like we talked about on Friday night. I've a gut feeling, Augusta. I don't want to wait until Thursday."

"We're heading through town in about twenty minutes. Meet you in the Sheriff's parking lot? You can follow us."

"Got it. I'm callin' CJ. She wanted to go along."

"Roger that, Phoebe. See you in a few."

After a quick call to CJ, Phoebe tightened her duty belt, adjusted the bullet proof vest, and called out, "Hey Roz, I'm headed up to some structure on Augusta's property. She's going to take the lead to get us up there. CJ's ridin' along."

"Is this a Girls Day Out and I'm gonna miss all the fun?"

"Ha. Just work. Responding to a citizen's complaint of an unknown truck on property."

"I thought she wasn't sure if that cabin was on her property or not. Survey crew hired for this week."

"Somethin' like that, but I'm thinking it needs to be checked out before we get preoccupied with tomorrow's election."

"There y'all go again. Preoccupied? This is more than preoccupied, Pheb'. This is a big deal. Y'all could be the next Sheriff of Green County."

"Or not. It's an election—one winner and the rest are losers."

"Don't go there. The women of this county are backing ya. The volunteers over the weekend were great. Don't second guess it."

"When it comes to an election ballot there are still women who are intimidated by the men around them and give up. They end up voting as their husbands and boyfriends do. It's the old, 'Vote my way because if you don't, my vote will just cancel out yours,' threat."

"I like to think we're smarter than that. Women's Lib and all. Hey, after all, I burned my bra a long time ago. Remember that movement back in the day?"

"Before our time, Roz. But it reads like it was fun. I'm trying to be realistic, not assume. You know what you and I say about assume—ass-u-me." The tension of the conversation was broken and the two women shared a relieved laugh.

"Okay, play nice with Citizen Augusta, take a morning ride following her dust, and don't worry. We're with y'all. Vote for Phoebe! No more old white guys!"

ANGLE OF REPOSE

R ight on time they met and headed up the mountain. The trail wound through the thick pine forest on either side. Augusta did her usual Pikes Peak Hill Climb Race imitation and disappeared up the trail slinging a wide ribbon of mud from yesterday's rain. Phoebe followed in the Sheriff's Wrangler in granny gear mode with CJ at shotgun.

Queennie and Augusta sat in her tricked out four-wheel drive vehicle surveying the dilapidated structure. They were sipping coffee from a thermos and munching on donuts from the Buns.

Augusta poured more coffee, "I can't believe the trash around here. Looks fresh."

"I said before, probably just backpackers needing a shelter."

"What backpacker has this much junk food packed in?

I'm thinkin' it's from that vehicle parked here from a week or so ago. I should've stopped when I saw it."

"Don't try to second guess your actions. Coulda, woulda, shoulda."

Phoebe and CJ pulled up. Phoebe told the women to stay in the vehicles until she could see if anyone was camped inside. She announced with a yell, "Hello! Anyone here? Deputy Korneal." She carefully stepped around the structure, pistol not drawn but ready, and headed for the uncovered door frame.

The yell was answered with silence. Not even the pines were moving in the morning stillness just below tree line. Phoebe stood outside the door opening and leaned in. The interior was dark and dank. There was an unpleasant odor. Eyes squinting to adjust from the bright sunshine, she reached for the mag light and scanned across the small space. She gasped at what she saw and waved at the women in their vehicles and screamed, "Need some help in here. There's a body."

They scrambled into the shack where Phoebe was leaning down on one knee, next to the body. "Augusta, can you get a signal out here?"

"Let me check. One bar. I can make a call."

"Call Roz. Tell her to get an ambulance up here ASAP. Give her directions. CJ, you hold this flashlight while I check for a pulse. Queennie, help me turn over the body."

Just then there was a slight groan and the person shifted into the light. Phoebe recognized the face, "Oh my God, it's Suzanne. Suzanne, it's me, Deputy Korneal. Can you hear me? What happened?"

"Water. Water." It came out as a rasping grunt.

"Queennie, get water in here. When Augusta finishes her call, have her hold the light for me. CJ, take my phone and get some pictures of this area."

In under a minute Queennie returned and handed over the open bottle, "Here, Pheb'."

Holding Suzanne's head up a bit, Phoebe gently coached, "It's gonna be okay now. We're here. I'm going to pour some water on your lips and into your mouth. Try not to choke, no gulping, it'll make you sick."

While she tried to get some water into her, Queennie inspected the chain around Suzanne's waist, "This chain's looped to a tree root and there's a lock on it."

With a fast, calm voice, Phoebe directed, "Find a way to release her."

Queennie told Augusta to direct the light over the chain and reported, "Without heavy duty tools it's impossible. Augusta, we need to get tools from your mine. We can be up to the Last and back with the right tools before the ambulance gets here."

"Do it."

Suzanne was beginning to come around. Her skin was a sallow color, cheeks sunken, lips cracked. Scratches, bruises, cuts, and dirt covered her face, neck, and hands. The water on her lips was heaven and she opened her eyes to look at Phoebe tending to her.

Barely able to speak, a garbled, "Thank God," came out.

Smoothing hair from her face and holding a hand, Phoebe assured, "Suzanne, hang in here with me. You're gonna be fine. The ambulance is on its way to take you to the hospital."

Queennie and Augusta roared back to the cabin with a hacksaw and giant wire cutter in hand. Queennie's strength and knowledge were a godsend and Suzanne was released in minutes.

The ambulance arrived and the EMTs hopped out. They entered, took in the situation, knelt at Suzanne's side, checked vitals while questioning her. An IV went into Suzanne's arm. Then they smoothly placed her on a gurney. Phoebe held her hand, "Can you say anything about how you got here?"

She mumbled, "Two guys. Mickey dead."

Phoebe stopped short of the ambulance, "Two guys?"

Suzanne was loaded into the rescue wagon, an EMT jumped in with her, doors were slammed, and they were headed down the mountain. *No more information from Suzanne for now.*

"CJ, grab the yellow crime scene tape out of the jeep, will ya? Help me get this whole area marked off."

CJ headed to the Sheriff's ride with a single thought on her mind, *The e-Blast! headline for today.* Body In Shack. ALIVE! She could feel the Pulitzer coming on.

Phoebe turned to Augusta, "Hey, when you saw the car or something here a few weeks ago, what kind was it? Do you remember?"

"I didn't get the make of it, but it was a giant box, black. Looks like someone was living here with all this trash. I should have checked it then."

"Not hardly. Next time you see somethin' out of the ordinary, let me know. This kind of thing could be dangerous. Look at poor Suzanne. It could have been you."

Augusta blew off the cautionary advice, "Whatever."

Phoebe was putting two and two together. The big SUV leaving the zipline crime scene a week ago today, Suzanne missing, and the vehicle Augusta saw up here. Now it appears the same vehicle was checked in at the rental place in Albuquerque and Suzanne was left here to die.

"Thanks ladies. It's a miracle we found Suzanne when we did. Now we need some deputies up here to tag and label this trash as evidence."

Queennie raised a finger and offered to help, "Thanks but

there are protocols for how and what to label, regardless of how simple it is on television crime shows."

Phoebe called Roz. "Hey, send two deputies up here to tag and label all the debris up here for the chain of evidence. We'll send it over to the state lab in Denver for analysis. Have the guys bring lots of evidence bags. It's a mess."

CONNECT THE DOTS

By noon Phoebe was headed back to Oresville to catch up with Bart at the Sheriff's office. Augusta, CJ, and Queennie had gone to the hospital to add comfort and support to Suzanne. CJ was searching for any sordid details Suzanne could share from her time in the shack. The noon e-Blast! headline was paramount.

As Phoebe drove into the edge of Oresville the cell rang. It was Kate from State Forensics, "You're gonna love this tidbit. The Albuquerque Sheriff ran the labs on their murder victim, Alejandro Martinez. The analysis of the blood on his clothes came back and it's a match to Mickey's. Looks like we found his murderer."

"Wow! It could be the same person or persons who also kidnapped Suzanne Martinelli. We found her this morning and I'm just coming back from where she was held."

"She's alive I assume?"

"Already at the hospital recovering."

"We also got some fingerprints from the New Mexico murder site. Unusual as the prints are defined as 'Unknown and Classified' in the FBI system. I turned that over to Chief Detective Wingate to work. There is also another set of prints from someone out of Denver. A lesser known figure connected to the Martinelli Family up there. This could be the person who killed Alejandro. Wingate will follow up on this too and his crew will investigate."

"Sounds like the families are not getting along."

"Cartels are always trying to expand, eliminate competition, and get rid of anyone in their way."

"We've got to do some fast learning in Green County. Looks like they are operating in our neck of the woods."

"Help is available to you from Denver, but your county is a couple of hours away for onsite work. Hey, do you need some help to process where ever you found the woman?"

"You bet. It was a shack off a rough mountain road. There is a ton of trash and sure could use an extra hand. It's tagged and bagged but needs analysis."

"You got it. Send it over. I'll run it as soon as it gets here."

"Many thanks, Kate. All for now?"

"One more item I've got for you. Guess who's headed your way?"

Phoebe let out a laugh, "More help I do not need?"

"Likely. It's Chief Wingate, with partners in tow."

"Really? Why?"

"Big news, stay tuned. I can't talk this minute. More later." Katie disconnected the call.

Phoebe was left looking at her phone wondering, *What the hell?*

She pulled into the parking lot behind the county office building. The Colorado State car was already there. Her first cup of morning coffee was now long overdue. She entered the back hallway and headed directly for the coffee station.

The coffee bar was located twenty steps into the building. It was the bright idea of a previous county administrator. He could not understand the need for a break room with chairs, tables, refrigerator, and a coffee pot. So, to improve productivity, the coffee pot was located in a hallway. The administrator had moved on and no one had bothered to spend the money needed to relocate it. Yet.

As she hustled past the conference room Bill called out, "Deputy Korneal, we have company. Grab a coffee and come on in."

Calling out over her shoulder, "On it." She took extra time with the coffee, adjusted the bulletproof vest, and spent a long minute deciding on her attitude for their visit. She stepped into the conference room and took a slow look at the occupants. Along with Bill, there was Bart, Chief Detective Wingate, a small Hispanic man, and a young man in a suit and tie. She ignored Wingate and looked at Bill, "What's up?"

"Have a seat. These three have quite a story to tell. First let me introduce you to Mateo Mendez."

With a shy smile, he stood and extended both hands toward Phoebe, "Buenos dias."

"And next, this is Special Agent Chris Carter from the FBI Regional office in Denver."

Special Agent Carter did not bother to stand. Looking over his papers in a folder he greeted her, "Pleased to meet you, Deputy." His eyes never leaving the papers.

Phoebe gave him a serious look, dipped her head in his direction, and pulled out a chair at the head of the table. *It's empty, why not?* A bit curious as to who was in the office and why, "Welcome and what brings you to Green County?"

Bill flashed a brilliant smile at Phoebe, "Great question."

An exaggerated silence waited. She put her elbows on the arms of the chair, folded her hands at the waist, and leaned back. She looked around the table and settled on Chief Detective Jerk-Wingate. "I understood you state folks had washed your hands of the murder and kidnapping here in Oresville. When did the FBI get involved?"

Special Agent Carter took over the explanation, "Phoebe. May I call you Phoebe?"

Phoebe tried to relax her serious Frieda Kahlo unibrow. *What's with this guy?* She looked directly at him, "No." Phoebe had worked hard to get to where she was and a little chat with her was not going to be informal or friendly. The Oresville crew at the table were law enforcement professionals and murder was serious business. Knowing Phoebe, Bart was unfazed by her response. Bill gave a quick tilt with his head as if to agree, *so there.* He had grown up with Phoebe and knew the sign of the straight-line brow.

Carter looked at Wingate who looked away and sat up straighter into his chair. He cleared his throat, "Ah, okay. Sorry. There's quite a story to tell here. Mateo here is our FBI informant embedded in a Mexican cartel. He has a photo of Mickey Walker and also one of Suzanne Martinelli. He has been very concerned about her in a cabin outside of Oresville.

"He had to leave her, get to town, and find a way to contact us. With limited resources and his English not being too good, it took him a while to get in touch. When he did, we headed over here to find her only to find out you were already on the job."

"Right. That ship has sailed. I found her this morning. One more day and I don't think she would have made it. Right now she's at our local hospital."

Mateo had been listening closely. When the words clicked in place for him, he made the sign of the cross, "Gracias."

Incredibly relieved with a deep sigh, "I worry."

Continuing, Agent Carter related how the FBI had been tracking the Albuquerque drug ring for a very long time. "Mateo is embedded in a cartel in Mexico as a reliable, trusted handyman who keeps his mouth shut. For several years he's been feeding us information about the cartel's activities. Then he was given a job. A big job. He was to be the driver for Alejandro. With a fake passport and a round trip ticket he came into the US via Albuquerque. Once there he met up with the man assigned to this little project, Alejandro Martinez. They were to go to Oresville and get information out of Mickey and Suzanne on the Martinelli Family. Safer for the cartel to have their own man partnered with someone out of the Albuquerque group."

Wingate interrupted, "No one trusts anyone in those circles."

Carter agreed, "Exactly. We know the plan is to infiltrate the Martinelli operation and take over the drug business from Oresville. Turns out Alejandro didn't get the info required and killed Mickey by mistake, accident, or otherwise. Then to avoid getting caught at the zipline, they hightailed it out of there, stuck with Suzanne who was tied up, stashed in the back of their vehicle. Mateo told me after some time and much arguing at the shack, Alejandro dumped him and headed back to Albuquerque."

Phoebe was frustrated and had listened enough. She drew a deep breath, fastened her eyebrows together again, and leveled a look at Special Agent Carter, "Then your man Mateo left her to die."

"Mateo did his best to take care of her and left her set up with food and water. He came today to show us where she was."

"She was chained to a tree root when I found her this

morning. Mostly unconscious—left to die."

The special agent leaned forward to emphasize, "He thought he could get help to her in time or maybe someone would have found her."

Mateo was following with the bits and pieces of his English, "Si. Get help. No listen. Alejandro gone."

"I talked with the Sheriff in Bernalillo County. Alejandro's dead."

Chief Wingate entered the discussion, "From your contact, we were able to find a match of the blood on his clothes to what we have on Mickey."

Bart put his hands on the table for emphasis, "It's because Deputy Korneal took the risk all along in this case. She believed Ms. Martinelli was in trouble and connected to the death on the zipline."

Bill harrumphed, "We might be a small town, nothin' fancy, but when someone's dead we don't wait for the state to figure it out. Same for someone missing—we look. Regardless of opinions of others and no MPR officially reported."

Phoebe backed off the attitude and looked at Wingate with a knowing little smile, "That's a Missing Person Report." She was surprised and pleased to hear Bill spout off, *Maybe he's back into law enforcement.* She sensed the state was in a tough position. They missed the significance of the death on a zipline and a mafia family member perhaps missing.

Wingate got the message, "You're right. We should have supported you on this from the very beginning. You called in forensics, then came all the way into Denver looking for help. I did not welcome you. In my defense, your U-Haul-Em van was quite an unusual vehicle. To say nothing of the aggressive entrance crashing through our gates, setting off lights and sirens. You engaged half of our police force in full tactical gear." His eyes relaxed into the memory. He then let out with a chuckle and the tension started to lift from the room.

Phoebe lifted one corner of her mouth in what could be considered the beginning of a smile. Before someone could overthink it, "Apology accepted."

Special Agent Carter looked confused, "U-Haul-Em truck? Are you moving to Denver?"

Deputy Korneal artfully dodged the question, "So why would New Mexico want to do business in little old Oresville?"

"Well, it's what we've been trying to find out. Our mission calls for 'gather facts to prevent crime.' We've uncovered a healthy, thriving drug business in the underbelly of this area. The Martinelli's have been the main suppliers. When the Mexican cartel realized there might be an opportunity for them to take over in the mountains, they sent up their go-to guy to get the lowdown on what was happening.

"Seems the assignment was messed up. Mateo told us they never intended to kill Mickey or kidnap Suzanne. But one thing led to the other and they were in deep trouble. Mateo couldn't blow his cover so he went along with Alejandro and kept Suzanne at the cabin. Watching the Albuquerque organization, we found out they want to expand into Colorado. The Martinelli Family has run their Denver mafia business the same for many years, 'If it ain't broke don't fix it,' mentality."

Bart added, "But it seems to be working for them. Drugs are the growing monster along the Front Range."

Carter added a hand gesture, "Eh, it could be way more if expanded. The Family's present operations in the mountains are old school and small scale—too distant from the Denver base to make a difference in their bottom line. So, they sent Suzanne. Little she could do to harm the operation. However, she and Mickey teamed up, landed a food truck, and a public drug business out of your county building, right outside the Sheriff's door. The Family business is growing enough to attract attention from the competition."

Phoebe was putting the pieces in order, "Enter the Albuquerque connection."

"Right. We hear the plan is for the Family to be overrun and eliminated by the cartel's new thinking and business model. The drugs would be shipped uninterrupted over the back roads out of Albuquerque, up to Oresville, and distributed into the skiing industry and points west of the Continental Divide including Utah, an untapped market for them. The money would be washed through cartel owned enterprises."

Bart raised a hand, "Excuse me. Like the High Country Adventure Park here in Oresville? The manager is a Mr. Oscar deHerrera. He's from Albuquerque, by the way."

Wingate and Carter traded a silent connection. Carter went ahead, "Ah, yea. That's their plan and deHerrera is the front man."

Bart looked at Carter, "I checked out his story in connection to the death on the zipline. It checks out. Not involved, directly anyway."

Bill gave out a quick smile, "Good catch, Constable Masterson."

Mateo heard the mention of the zipline and became agitated, "Oscar not help. Alejandro mad. Suzanne too. But jeep come."

Phoebe looked at Mateo, "When?"

Mateo turned around his thinking for her question, "Tuesday. With Senor Mickey. Zipline."

"So, Alejandro was going to hurt Suzanne too?"

Pause, "Si."

Phoebe lifted a wilted smile to Mateo, "Gracias. But why no come to police, us?" She added a pointer to herself and the others at the table.

A lengthy pause as Mateo converted her question.

Carter stepped in, "Not easy with his limited English. This

was his first trip into the states. Tough to navigate. He picked up Suzanne's car and drove to the Albuquerque airport with a return ticket to Mexico. We got wind of what was going on when he made contact with the airport police and TSA."

She listened carefully and gave Special Agent Carter a tough look, "Regarding the elephant in the room, let me ask, at what point were you going to tell us about all of this?"

Chief Wingate had been watching Phoebe, "That's why we're all here today."

DON'T STOP NOW

uzanne was in the hospital, being hydrated and fed as she could tolerate. Special Agent Carter and Detective Wingate, along with Deputy Korneal were anxious to talk with her. After concluding the meeting at the Sheriff's office, they drove over to the Oresville hospital. Bart remained in the conference room with Mateo.

The threesome stopped at the reception desk. "We're here to see Suzanne Martinelli."

The receptionist acknowledged Phoebe and looked over the records, "Room 208."

They quietly entered the room. She was lying in the bed, small and fragile. Her face was bruised, scratched, and hair was spread on a pillow like broken wheat stalks—eyes closed, breathing was shallow.

"Ms. Martinelli, are you awake?"

Slowly opening her eyes Suzanne tried to focus, "Hi,

Phoebe."

Carter stepped closer to the bed, "I'm Special Agent Carter and this is Detective Wingate. We have a few questions."

"Can't you see I'm practically dead? Leave me alone."

"We'll make this quick today, but we need some answers. What happened to you and Mickey?"

A long pause and then the decision to get this over with. She took a full ten seconds, deep sigh, and closed her eyes to replay the events, "We were at my house when two thugs burst into the kitchen. They knocked me to the floor and hit Mickey. He fell and his head cracked on the door frame. Tied up, they dragged us into the living room. The big guy went into my office and the other guy sat with us, gun in hand."

Suzanne looked at the little group of law enforcement officers and asked for water. She closed her eyes again. Apparently the story was over.

Carter was not interested in stopping the story, "Please, Ms. Martinelli, what happened next?"

Suddenly her energy returned with fresh anger, "Mickey couldn't talk, which pissed off the big guy. Before dawn, they loaded us into the back of a vehicle. A short ride and next thing I knew Mickey was pulled out. They left me tied up, gagged, and blindfolded and I heard thumps and then the two men slammed back into the SUV, arguing. It sounded like another car or something pulled in and when I tried to rise up to a window, they hit me with something. Lights out. When I came to, I was chained on a dirt floor, still blindfolded, and gagged. That's it. Leave me alone and get out of here."

Phoebe was thinking this young woman's age would help a fast recovery and stepped in with a firm tone, "Was anyone with you?"

"I told you, the two men. The big guy kicked me to see if I was awake. Then the other guy took off my gag. I begged them to let me go, but the big guy wasn't having any of that. They argued in Spanish and left."

"Do you have any idea who these men were and what they wanted?" Carter really wanted to make the connection to the cartel. "Did you hear any names?"

"No. Please, I'm tired. Are you done?"

"Almost. Here, have a sip of water. You need to stay with us so we can find these men. Let's hear it."

The whining started, "You wait till my Momma gets here. She'll get rid of you. I want my lawyer."

"Ms. Martinelli, you're not under arrest. What makes you think you need a lawyer?"

"Bull! On my TV crime shows, that's what you always have to ask for first."

"This isn't TV. Now let's hear it. Continue."

Another long pause, "Okay, I guess. I'm the victim here. After the big guy left, the other guy told me his name was Mateo. He was nice. We started up a conversation. Crappy English, but he told me he was from Mexico and had a return ticket. I told him to go get my car and drive to the airport so he could fly back home."

"Did the other man come back?"

"Nope. Mateo took off and left some food and water. There were yucky bugs and little rats everywhere. I thought I was gonna die. Then I heard a voice and there was Deputy Korneal. I was never so happy to see someone. Please, can we be done?" Suzanne's attitude was back in full force.

Special Agent Carter looked at Phoebe and gave a curt nod. Phoebe patted Suzanne's hand. She had one more question for the young woman, "Suzanne, there were drugs in small envelopes scattered all over the zipline platform where we found Mickey. Can you tell us where they came from?"

Long silence and decision made—throw Mickey under

the bus. "Probably from Mickey's Mountain Munchies. That's where everyone buys a special side with their burger."

"What's the special side?"

"Cocaine. I'm done with you. Get out and leave me alone."

Phoebe glanced at the other two, "Hmm. Get some rest and we'll be back this afternoon."

Suzanne turned her head, "Knock yourselves out. I won't be here."

As they were leaving the room, a woman was entering. "Well, hello Deputy Korneal. And who are you two?"

"I'm Detective Wingate from Denver and this is Special Agent Carter from the FBI. And who are you?"

The woman stood straighter, "I'm Suzanne's mother, here to take her back to Denver where she belongs."

"Mrs. Martinelli, I am not sure Suzanne needs to be moved right now. She's been through quite an ordeal."

"That's not up to you, Deputy. We Martinelli's take care of our own. I've told you several times to leave us alone. What part of this don't you get?"

Detective Wingate felt the tension. "We have a few more questions for her. If she's moved, we need to know where. She is the victim of a crime and a potential witness to a murder. I don't want to have to put her in protective custody. Here's my card. Let me know where she'll be."

Without a glance the card was shoved into a pocket, "If I remember."

The two officers look at each other. *What's her problem?* Phoebe just shook her head.

Sitting back in Wingate's car, they put together all they had learned.

"Deputy Korneal, you had a bead on this whole situation. I should have listened to you in Denver."

Carter was way ahead of the discussion, "Yes and we have

what's needed to get ahead of the Mexican cartel move into these mountains. The murderer and kidnapper connected to this crime, Alejandro Martinez, is dead. Now we need more info on the Martinelli operation in Oresville."

Phoebe had moved past the demise of Mickey. The murderer was identified and dead. But, still looming was Suzanne's involvement in the drug sales. "I can't believe she was selling drugs practically at the front door to our Sheriff's office. Amazing. Gutsy even. I think she'll be fired as a result of the no show at work for over a week."

"Extenuating circumstances like being kidnapped won't save the job?"

She flopped her hand back and forth, "Iffy and not likely. So that'll cut off the drug flow from the county office building, for now anyway."

"Regardless, her mom will probably put the kibosh on living in Oresville. Speaking of which, how did Suzanne's mother find out she was in the Oresville hospital and get here so fast?"

Phoebe was sitting in the back seat of the state vehicle. She leaned forward to be heard by the two, "I would bet Mickey had a network of helpers for his food truck business and the drugs. He had to trust someone to help him sell from the truck seven days a week. We know he took Mondays off. When the ambulance took off early this morning to get Suzanne from the shack, the news spread like wildfire. Small town network and all."

Wingate was following the conversation, "What say we pay a little visit to Mickey's Mountain Munchies and see what else is being sold along with a burger. We missed lunch so we can sample from the menu?"

When they arrived at the parking lot the yellow crime scene tape still surrounded the zipline and was fluttering in a gentle breeze. There were spray paint markings where pieces of evidence were found. The area around the food truck was quiet, no cars in sight or bicycles. The front cover was closed and food operations appeared to be shut down.

Carter and Phoebe climbed out of the vehicle and stood together looking over the vacant lot. He started snapping photos of the area, "I'm guessing the food truck attendant has 'left the auditorium'."

"Good help's hard to find."

"Probably pulled by the Family as a precaution. Everyone'll be on high alert back in Denver from what's gone on here. The granddaughter of the head honcho saved by the locals in Oresville? There'll be backpeddlin' like crazy to find the eddyline for a reason to avoid fault."

Phoebe's brain got stuck on his use of the word eddyline, "Eddyline as in?"

"I thought you were an outdoors lover. Livin' in Oresville. Isn't the headwaters of the Arkansas around here somewhere?"

"You're so right. It starts the long journey around here, but I don't get to use the great outdoors. Too much work to do. We're always short-handed thanks to the bad rep the big city cops make for those of us in safety management."

Carter skipped over her critique, "Eddyline's a term for kayaking through rough waters. What route to take into the main current flow. Forgive the assumption. If you win the election you will have even less time for enjoying Colorado's great outdoors. Just sayin'."

"Now you tell me."

They traded looks. Phoebe felt a faint passing of regret for stepping up to running for the opening.

Excitement yet the embers of doubt about her leadership if she were to win the election, *Better leave the whining to another time.*

Just then Wingate climbed out of the state's vehicle and tried the food truck's back door. It swung open and he yelled into the dark, empty space. No response. With cell phone in hand, he looked at Phoebe, "How about I call Kate. The forensics team can come in to process the truck and surroundings. We might be able to find the prints of someone already in the system who can tell us more about Mr. Mickey Walker's business plan."

Phoebe laughed at his terminology, "His business plan? Okay. I agree. Can Kate include the shack where we found Suzanne too? This'll save the sheriff's department here some headache. We don't have the expertise to do crime scene work ourselves." She decided to not mention that Kate had alredy offered to process whatever they had found and tagged at the shack.

"Sure, I say it's included. One other thing, from the state budget I can get some funding to amp up your training here in Green County. That is if you're interested."

"After tomorrow's election maybe we can talk. Or not. Hard to guess at this point. The Good Old White Guys are hard to beat in Green County. No offense intended, Chief Detective."

He had to smile at the comment around the old white guys in power, "Let's get back to the Sheriff's office, get a warrant, and tie up this mess."

They gathered again in the conference room where Bart and Mateo were eating. The table was loaded with sandwiches, coffee cups, chips, and Mateo was attempting to teach Bart Spanish from a menu.

Kate had been called out and the state forensics team would process the food truck and the shack. The State of Colorado and the FBI would take over the final pieces of the investigation and return to make the formal announcements.

LAY OF THE LAND

Tuesday dawned bright with the promise of temperatures into the sixties. The weather predicted a perfect day for high voter turnout. Roz had the day off and was already headed to the Club. It had been decorated with Phoebe signs, plenty of red, white, and blue bunting, and the playlist was ready to roll. Roz would supervise the potluck setup with the volunteers eager to help.

She had brought in a potato salad thanks to the help of her friend, Libby, who was in a learn-to-cook-potatoes mode. After a year she was still working to perfect Roz's potato salad recipe. The volunteers had been forewarned and the salad was safely tucked into the back of the kitchen refrigerator labeled "backup, last out."

Phoebe had decided it was her regular duty day and she would not take it off to worry, fret, and hide out so no one could witness her angst. She could blame Roz for feeling like a long-tailed cat in a room full of rocking chairs. "Just because running for sheriff is a half-baked idea doesn't mean it won't be a good time." *With the promise of a good time, I agreed. Stupid. Stupid. Stupid.*

TuTu's Washateria was Phoebe's first stop of the morning. TuTu and Jorge were counting the contributions from Monday. Jorge greeted Phoebe, "Here comes the next Green County Sheriff."

Phoebe smiled, accepted the steaming cup of coffee, "Thank you, but let's not talk about it. I already have butterflies. I'm not the usual political archetype."

He headed back to the kitchen, "What you need is a Jorge Breakfast Special. Be right back."

TuTu patted her on the shoulder, "There. There. Let's not go off the rails. You're the right person for the job even tho' you're not an old, white guy. They have a leg up but the women of the county have this one."

A smile of appreciation for the comment and the faith, "That's a big maybe. Let's get some work done today. You heard about Suzanne Martinelli?"

"Sure. It's all over town as of about two minutes after you found her. Small town gossip generally referred to as networking." They laughed at the euphemism.

A gentle blow over the hot coffee, "Contrary to popular opinion, she did not kill Mickey. It was an outsider from Albuquerque. Case closed."

"Appreciate the update. Jorge and I went to the hospital yesterday and her Momma had already checked her out, paid the tab, and generally ticked off the entire hospital staff. A big city entitled woman with an attitude."

"Oh yes, a real piece of work that one."

"Does the Sheriff of Green County have ideas on drug sources now that Martinelli and Mickey are gone? Likely for good."

"That's why I'm here this morning. When you get wind of drugs, TuTu, unusual people coming in, bad actors, can you give me a heads up?"

"I have the confidential thing goin' with my clients, as you know."

"Understand. This would be all on the lowdown, nothing official ever. I promise. I've got to get tuned in to what's happening and stop the spin doctrine implying all is copacetic in the small town of Oresville, USA."

"Let me think on it. My first thought is yes. Jorge and I have seen too much just this past year. Bad drugs, broken families, children overdosed, adults hooked, and desperate players. The underbelly is a not so Happy Town, USA."

"Yup and together we might be able to head off some hurt, humiliation, and humble pie. Your ears to the ground and my follow up."

"I'll talk with Jorge. It takes two and we love to tango." She let out a chuckle as Jorge popped the heated plate of buttery eggs, crispy bacon, and jellied toast in front of Phoebe, *A class act.*

He topped off the coffee, "Just what this doctor thinks is needed. We'll count the take from yesterday while you eat. You're gonna need sustenance. It promises to be a long day."

Phoebe looked from him to the meal in front of her and the butterflies fluttered.

Phoebe had posted a deputy at the parking lot to keep an eye on the closed truck and any activity in the area. This morning she went to talk with the deputy assigned to the park. He had been on duty overnight. Phoebe wanted an update and came bearing gifts of hot coffee and donuts.

"I did see someone pull up last night at the Train Depot. It was about eight in the evening and bright enough to see it was the guy who manages the park. We had to deal with him on Tuesday when this all started. He wasn't happy then and appears not too happy now."

Phoebe let out a decisive humph, "We had to close it down. It's a crime scene. He'll get over it—or he won't. His choice. Did he go up to his office?"

"Looked like it. Lights were seen from the second floor windows. He was in the building for a half hour and left. The vehicle was packed full in the back end. Maybe he's moving in or moving out."

"I'll check it," and she went over to the depot. There was a hand printed note taped on the locked door, "High Mountain Adventure Park is Closed for Repairs." No number to call for information. No date for reopening. No reason for closure. No name to contact. All was quiet and it felt deserted.

Phoebe made a call to Wingate and reported it seemed deHerrera had closed the park. Going forward the three agencies—State, FBI, and Green County—would share information to build a net around the drug business happening in her county. Wingate's office will be the distribution point to keep all three agencies current.

Her next stop was the food truck where Kate's team was already working. They had come in last night too late to get started. "Hey, Kate, thanks for coming out."

Kate was in a HazMat suit and lifted a face mask to talk, "No worries, we had a good night and your Coroner Watson had a bakery open up for a Chef's Choice Dinner in the kitchen. Fab-u-lo-so. One of my guys is offering to quit and come work for the owner, Rebecca Riney, if she'll marry him."

"I'm afraid he'll have to stand in line. Over the top culinary skills and her focaccia bread wins awards."

"She-ite! Makes the rest of us look bad next to a Sister who's talented like she is. I give up before I even start to think in that direction. I'm not sure how to turn on my stove. What about you?"

"I'm in your club. I can't cook but I am a cleaning machine somewhere light on the OCD spectrum. The Constable of Oresville is the squeeze of my life. You met him, Bart Masterson?"

Kate smiled at the name, "Oh yea. He's the cute, strong type. I did take a second look and a third and another. He's out of Greenstone. Just my luck he's already tabbed. Well, if you decide to dump him, be sure to call. I'll come runnin' with a net."

Phoebe saluted, "You got it, See-sta."

"I'm back to work. We won't have much, mostly samples for lab work and a few fingerprints out of the food truck and the shack. Stand by."

HARMONIC CONVERGENCE

Kate called Phoebe, "We're headed back to Denver. I wanted to tell you what we found in the food truck and the cabin. Early results for now, lab results later."

"Let me guess, frozen hamburger patties and french fries."

"Close but no cigar. The hamburger box was part of the search, but no burgers. Instead, the box held thirty-two small glassine envelopes. Cocaine is easily tested in the field. We got a positive."

Phoebe was quietly processing and quessed, "What else? Money? Guns?"

"Nada. We pulled some prints. Mickey's prints were matched in IAFIS. The other set was a guy named Mario Mattuci. Last known location is the Denver area. Must be the helper who worked for Mickey. I'd assume with all the excitement, that person has skedaddled. Interesting to note that his prints were also at the crime scene of the Martinez fellow down in Albuquerque. Chief Wingate is researching this guy."

"So, the food truck was a front for Mickey's drug business. If you ordered a double hamburger, no onions, you got cocaine on the side?"

Laughing, Kate responded. "Could be. Be careful what you order next time you sidle up to a food truck."

"For sure. Looks like we're getting this case together thanks to your help and believe it or not, Wingate's help, albeit late."

"Don't be so modest, Phoebe. You'll be given credit for this find. It's a murder with a big drug bust."

Phoebe took an extra few seconds, "Why? I didn't do much of anything."

"Don't cut yourself short on this. You're the one who called it, made the effort, created the link with New Mexico. You get the credit and the FBI will add it to their radar screen. Wingate and the state team, we'll stay in the background. Give yourself a pat on the back, smile, add it to the resumé, and move on. The tough part starts now. Law enforcement demands have just tripled for you with this big news of your perseverance—a drug bust and a murder, too."

"How does the news part work?"

"From what I've seen, the process is pretty straightforward along the Front Range anyway. Wingate comes up with the drug value numbers, FBI validates, they'll all parade to Oresville within a few days to make the statewide announcement of what's been going on here. Better let CJ know. She'll milk it for a week, I'd guess. The media being what they are."

She had worked all day haunted by election day jitters. Off on time, she went home only to stare at her closet assortment. Phoebe was unsure as to the right clothes for election results at the Club. Giving serious thought to attire was a tough call. The standard of jeans and t-shirt always made the cut. If, and granted, it's a long shot, but if she won an appropriate picture would be taken—confident, smiling, appreciative. Likewise, if she lost—brave and forward looking into an unknown future. Thanks be to the Rented Trailerhouse Gods, she was ready to get out of it, move on, leave the election behind, *Stop with the negative. Doesn't mean it won't be a good time. Thank you, Roz.*

The cut became jeans, black Tony Lama cowboy boots, a black pearl button shirt, and hair done up into a signature messy bun. One last look and she couldn't help asking, *Who are you and what's happening?*

Bart picked up on the first ring, "I'm at the county building helping people with the voting process. I'm an election volunteer. Kind of fun and working with the nicest bunch of ladies."

"Heads up, Bart. The ladies like you."

He had to laugh at the observation, "Not much happening now that dinner time's comin' up. The Moly workers are out at five, so that'll bring another wave. The final count starts at seven not a minute before."

Silence as she thought about the last statement, … *the count.*

"Are you there?"

"Yea. Just thinkin'."

"Hmm. Okay. Just hang in there. Don't overthink this. We're a couple of hours away from the results. Why don't you go to the Club and try to have some fun. Be with your friends."

Another long fifteen seconds of silence, a deep shaky

breath, "You're so right. Thanks. Later." She disconnected the call, stuck the phone in a back pocket, looked at herself again in the mirror, sat on the bed, and burst into tears—she had forgotten to vote! *Just great.*

Tears wiped away and makeup reapplied, she locked the Glock in the safe and grabbed a jacket. At nearly ten-five in altitude, late night was always cold. This early June evening could be in the high thirties by the time she left the Club. She jumped in the pickup, slammed the door, hit the starter, and the music blasted, "I Will Survive." Phoebe has that song set up on the truck's playlist to begin at the start of the day. *A girl has to have encouragement.* Today she needed the extra shot of bravery and sang full tilt to no one in the truck. She backed out, slammed the gear shift into first gear, "I'll lay down and die?" *Oh no I won't.*

The drive into town was invigorating. She had talked herself into some fun with friends. Vote first, fun will follow. She hustled into the county building. Thankfully the crowd was nowhere to be seen, "Hey, Bart. Thought I'd better get out to vote, right?" She added a gay little giggle, like this was the plan all along.

Bart offered her a quizzical look, "Ah, right you are." The process was in full swing when CJ showed up with her camera. *Is she psychic? Had someone called her? Oh wait, she's the ace reporter. Of course, she showed up at the right time.*

Her camera at the ready CJ got into position. "Let's get a shot of you with a voting card in hand. Sweetie, what's with your eyes? Red. Swollen. Are you doin' alright?"

She spit out an irritated rapid, "Fine. Fine. Fine. Allergies."

"I'm callin' it on this one. You're not happy. This is a big day for the women of Green County and you made it happen with a little help from Roz and me. Stand tall and remember even if all else fails, we'll still have a good time, right?"

Phoebe looked at CJ. She was her BFF for as many years as she had been able to speak. *Clueless or trying to cheer me up?*

"Now a big smile for the camera. Drop the ballot in the box. Smile, damn it. Stop with the frown ... please."

Phoebe mustered a corner lift to her lips. *Oh Lordy, why'd I let myself get into an election? I'm not a politician.*

CJ left the building headed out in search of the next terrific headline regarding this momentous day in the life of Green County.

Bart put an arm around Phoebe's shoulder, gave her a tight squeeze, and fastened a sticker to her shirt. "You voted and here's your free I Voted sticker, courtesy of the county clerk's office. You'll need this to get admittance to the Club. It's my job to be sure the stickers are handed out after the ballot goes into the box."

"You're a real sticker kind of guy. I never knew you for such talent."

"Ah, right you are. Another thing you have learned about me. Stick around and I'll demo some of my other talents later tonight." He wiggled his eyebrows in an effort to cheer her up.

The comment brought on a smile, "Promises, promises."

"Now go over to the Club with CJ. She's just out the door. Try to relax and get in the spirit of the night. No matter how this election turns out, it won't change how I feel about you. We have each other."

As Phoebe turned, Bart planted a quick kiss on her cheek. "I have a feeling things are going to work out well for you tonight, Sweet P. Keep the faith. And I'll be at the Club with the results after seven o'clock. I'm a judge on this last shift so I'll stay for the count. Watchful eyes to guarantee accuracy along with the cameras that are in the room, ya know."

Phoebe was grateful for his encouragement and support. He was such a breath of fresh air. She realized it didn't really matter if she won or not. He'd still be there for her.

IMPROMPTU DATES

This morning had brought worry and fast talk between Bill and Roz regarding an early birth of the twins. Bill thought she should stay home and rest, but Roz was adamant, "I set up tonight's party and I will not miss it, twins or no twins. I took the day off from work so I can rest and be ready. Besides y'all are over-worried about this. I do appreciate all your experience with the two kids down in Denver, but Sweetie, with that being said, times have changed. Babies are born regardless of the worries medical science in America charges us for. Let's have an enjoyable evening tonight, celebrate with Phoebe, and snack on some homemade goodies—sans alcohol. That part will be boring, but ... right?" She gave him a winning, convincing, assuring smile.

He had to agree, "We're overdue for a fun night. We already look and act like an old married couple. What happened to dancing, drinking, and talking through the night?"

"Gone, but not forgotten. We'll be back there before y'all know it. Besides my entire family is comin' in July to welcome the twins to the world. And that'll be a party, for sure." She broke away and rubbed her giant tummy, "Hear that you two? Y'all aren't comin' out for another month. So lay still, enjoy the free ride while yer able."

Bill had to laugh. Her positive attitude brought him to his senses and he already felt better for the day ahead. "Let's run over to the dollar store and see if we can buy some baby clothes, what'd ya say?"

"No way. What are y'all a-thinkin'? Sit back and relax. In fact, let's pick out some more names for these boys."

"What's the rush, we have a month to go. Maybe we start putting the names into a hat? Do a drawing on July Fourth? Have a big Reveal Party on the Fourth and tell everyone we have known all along its boys. Surprise! Surprise!"

"That'd be fun. A real shocker. Let me give some thought to a July party. How about we go with names that'd be somethin' catchy like … Firecracker and Cherrybomb?"

He handed her paper, pen, and a hat, "Fine, write it up and put 'em in the hat. I've got to head to work. We're short staffed with one of the deputies watching things over at the adventure park." He planted a quick kiss to her forehead, patted the baby tummy, and was out the door. Since Phoebe had assured him of the Undersheriff position, he was psyched anew with his law enforcement career and ready to be the daddy to these babies.

The excitement and stress of Joe retiring and Phoebe running for Sheriff put Bill over the top with worry. Adding the insecurity about his future with the Sheriff's office, along with being a new dad left him in a constant state of distress. Roz knew this, so she had kept the June due date to herself. Bill needed a July due date so he could focus on his job as acting sheriff. *A June birth? Well, he'd be stressed to the max and drive me over the edge.*

Roz leaned back into the comfy chair, put her feet up and released a sign of relief. She felt like Hubby Bill was sufficiently distracted by the promise of a reveal party. Now he could get through this day and the election. Earlier this morning she had called the doctor with the report of a regular, faint tightening in the lower abdomen.

The babies were full term and of a decent size to do well on their own. She could handle the unanticipated fanfare of the birth, likely today or tomorrow. "Just hold on little ones. Momma's got a party to attend," and rubbed her oversized baby bump.

ASTRAL EVENT

The Club was lit up like a disco dance hall with a multi-sided mirrored ball, bright lights, and crackling excitement this Tuesday evening. The Special Election had brought out all The Regulars and the not so regulars. Free food, a special Drink of the Day discounted for members only, and Roz's hoppin' good time Zydeco music made for a community event like no other. All were there anticipating the celebration of the first ever female sheriff of Green County, Phoebe Korneal.

As deputy sheriff and *as needed* detective for the past several years, Phoebe was well known and liked by the residents of the town and the county. She had a comfortable demeanor with the citizens and was tough on crime, such as it was. Law enforcement was her passion. She knew when to play nice and when to play not-so-nice. There seemed to be a desire in town to make a big change in the makeup of the county's leadership.

Electing Phoebe would fit the bill and be a first step.

The bar seats were filled with the usual crew Augusta, Queennie, and CJ. They had surrounded one empty chair, reserved for their candidate. This chair was draped in red, white, and blue bunting and the added flair of several Vote For Phoebe buttons. Convinced she would win the election they wanted her front and center in the room. Those gathered in the Club were all Phoebe supporters, volunteers, and workers. There was no doubt in the room as to the results. Like Roz reminded everyone, "Even if this run for sheriff turns out to be a bad idea, we'll still have a good time."

The party was in full swing before the polling was closed and votes counted. The supporters were checking out lapels, shirts, and t-shirts for "I Voted" stickers in case someone had slipped in without already voting. It was announced weeks before, anyone without the sticker would be escorted across the street and 'encouraged' to vote. Courtesy of Augusta, a free drink would be waiting upon their return from the Green County Clerk's Office. *Get out the vote.*

The newest commissioner, Joe Jackson, the other county commissioners, and their minions were seated at a large table, watching the crowd. Bill Diamond had joined them and was keeping a watchful eye on his wife. Roz was sitting down every chance she got and her volunteers were taking care of what was needed for the Election Celebration Party.

Retired Sheriff Joe was coaching the fellow commissioners on the etiquette of candidate treatment regardless of outcome. Phoebe had been invisible to the commissioners when Joe was Sheriff, now Joe coached them on pronunciation, "The last name is Korneal, pronounce it as in Core-Nell, no first name. You'll be head and shoulders above the game if you get her name right. Also never refer to how poorly her bullet proof vest fits her chest. That's a real no-no with women."

Joe's free advice was tolerated, barely. He was speculating on the election results—Phoebe would be the female top gun in the county. They had better get over it and learn to like it. There was a certain amount of pride in Joe's voice as he mentioned repeatedly to any audience, "She's my gal. I taught her everything I know about sheriffin' for Green County." This statement brought plenty of side glances along with the lip service expected, politics being what it is.

CJ, the Vote for Phoebe campaign manager, invited the other twelve candidates to the festivities. Her clever thought was if she had everyone together when Phoebe was announced as the new sheriff, they could each offer their congratulations and encouragement. And, more importantly, CJ would have the exclusive on all that was said and done by the candidates. Headline material galore.

The plan seemed to be working. As she looked around the room, every candidate was in attendance. They might be there to partake of the freebies and why not? Some still held out hope the election would go in their favor, but it wasn't looking good. Every person at the Club was wearing a Vote For Phoebe button, except for the other twelve candidates and a few of their spouses. Not to worry though, a Vote For Phoebe button would be passed to the losers when the results were announced.

Roz had asked Joe to make a short speech to congratulate Phoebe when she was announced as the winner. Joe had rehearsed favorite quotes such as, "Leap and the net will appear," and "A person hears only what they understand." Both of these were from some dead guy named von Goethe. Joe intended to use the quotes as advice for everybody in the room, not just the newly elected Sheriff. He was holding out hope that one of his childhood buddies might accidentally win so he was keeping the talk generic.

Bartender Brian was in top form with the high demand for beverages of all kinds and had the foresight to ready beer and soda in large tubs of ice. The champagne had been ordered in by Augusta. The bubbly was chilled beside the sparkling apple cider for those whose preference was restricted by the local court system.

The Drink of the Day was a cocktail named for the Oresville altitude, The Ten Five. Club manager, Willie Friedrich, had jacked up the price to nine dollars and discounted it to members as seven. *Someone has to pay the electricity bill.*

With less than five minutes to go the polls would close. The excitement of anticipation was rising to a fevered pitch. Of course, there was also the worry over the outcome. When the big hand on the clock over the bar hit the twelve and the small hand pointed to the seven, everyone took a deep breath and said a silent prayer. Voices had quieted and people were seated, many anxiously tapping their fingers. After all the hard work, planning, and hope for new leadership, these minutes of waiting were grueling. The constituents kept their eyes on the front door waiting impatiently for Bart to enter with the final count. The background music filled the void left by the lack of conversation. Roz's playlist had taken a slower, almost somber tone. Confidence had taken a step back from the line in the sand.

Phoebe exhaled a deep breath the minute she realized the polls were closed. She added a nail to bite, lips pressed into a tight line, and all sound faded to a low level tinnitus. The count would be started across the street. She had been careful to drink only her favorite, tonic and lime. Brian had been keeping an eye on her and knew tension and stress when he saw it. Talented bartenders know these kinds of things instinctively. He stepped in front of her, and using the Augusta favorite phrase, he announced, "You look like I need a drink."

The line brought relief to the tension in the room and a collective laugh. Queennie spoke up, "I second that." Augusta was caught up in the moment and her generosity was sparked, "Barkeep, a round of my favorite for the house." Those within hearing distance issued a relieved chortle.

Brian went to work. The shot glasses were lined up on the bar top. The Pappy's was poured. Augusta stood on the rungs of her bar stool with her shot extended into the air, "Salute! To Phoebe, the rest of you candidates, and all the hard workers who have made this night possible." A chorus rang out, "Hear. Hear." The shots were tossed to the back of throats and the glasses slammed on tabletops and bar tops alike—election done and dusted. Results, well not quite.

Across the street from the Club, the county clerk was in full-out modus operandi. The total population of Green County was slightly over two thousand and registered voters under seven hundred. The count would be fast.

All eyes were on the procedures for transparency, precision, and final certification. The paper ballots were opened and the machines were ready to be fed. The count was taken. Bart and the other poll watcher volunteers oversaw the procedure per the election laws. The County Clerk thanked the election team for their commitment, hard work, and volunteerism. Bart was handed a sealed envelope of the results for each candidate and total ballots. He headed across the street to the Club. With a deliberate walk and somber face, he jerked open the front door and stepped to the front of the room.

Bart had asked the Green County Clerk to not tell him the

results so he could be as surprised as everyone else awaiting the numbers, especially Phoebe. The future for him and Phoebe would be a path determined by this election. Their commitment to one another was solid, but the election results would determine the operational side of the relationship.

The room quieted, all faces turned to Bart. The oxygen was sucked out of the room as everyone took a deep breath as if to sanctify the results. If a pin dropped it would be heard. All were rapt, waiting for the report.

Except Phoebe. She could not move. She could not look at another living soul. She could not breathe. Instead, she zeroed in on the scuffed floor and blocked out all sound but for a slight tick with every half rotation of the disco light ball. Tick. Tick. Tick. *Can I shrink to a nugget and exit?* The music had stopped but the disco ball was slowly turning, casting crazy light patterns in sync with her heart rate—a flash, a skip, a vibration, *What if I don't win? What if I do? I'm a mess. Shoulda had the Pappy's. Maybe two.*

She lifted her eyes to Bart's face and couldn't read an expression, the news, or whatever. He had not told her the county clerk agreed to his idea of the sealed envelope. As Bart looked around at the full house, he tapped the envelope into his opened hand. He avoided looking at her. Instead, he purposely called out greetings to various people in the audience. *I've lost. Otherwise, he'd be smiling at me. Look pleasant Girly-girl.* Phoebe affixed a tight half smile to her face, unfastened the unibrow, and tried to look invisible.

Bart called for quiet in the room. "Thank you all for being here for this eventful night. The election committee, the county clerk, and the volunteer poll workers have gone through the procedures for a Special Election as mandated by the laws of this Great State of Colorado. It has been legally determined that this election has met the requirements. The results are valid and certified by the Clerk of Green County.

"Ladies and Gentlemen, drum roll please. Let me introduce you to the new sheriff in town." Just then he added, "Oops."

He had smoothly run a finger under the sealed flap. It caught at the far corner, a little nervous fumble, and he dropped it. A sigh from those gathered went up, willing him the grace and speed to "Get on with it." He emitted a short, embarrassed giggle as an apology. He quickly bent to retrieve the envelope and cast a watchful eye to the group in case mob rule would rush him for the envelope.

The tension was palpable with the redo on the opening of the envelope. He snatched the paper from the enclosure, unfolded it, and glanced at the written numbers. He did another take and the crowd started chanting, "What? What? What?"

Bart broke into a smile, a laugh, and added a battle cry, "Sheriff Phoebe Korneal, will you please step forward and receive a shiny new sheriff badge."

The crowd went wild. There was whoopin' and hollerin', huggin' and kissin.' Phoebe was in shock.

"Get up there, Pheb', it's your rightful place." CJ was over the moon with what they had accomplished in a short amount of time. She might consider a career change into politics should a story on this magic thirty day campaign result in a Pulitzer.

Roz had the best celebration song queued up and Katy Perry blasted into all corners with Roar. Phoebe slid off her stool and jogged to the front of the room. She stood next to Bart as he draped his arm over her shoulders. Slightly above a whisper for her ears only, "Congratulations, Sweet P. I couldn't be happier for us."

She stared at him and looked out to the crowd in disbelief, tears of relief slipping down her cheeks. "How can I thank all of you? This is incredible. Best I can do tonight is promise you I'll be the best sheriff I know how to be and take care of our town and county with every bone in my body."

Everyone cheered again. Retired Sheriff and now Green County Commissioner, Joe Jackson, took over the microphone and started his prepared remarks. Phoebe froze a smile at his comment about how she was his product with seven years training. Then one by one the other twelve candidates stepped to the microphone. In under ten seconds, each offered Phoebe best wishes, support, and conceded the election, noting there would be no contention about who won. CJ stepped to each defeated candidate, handed the old white guys a glass of bubbly one at a time and pinned a button on each lapel ... Vote for Phoebe. And the county did.

The party exploded into full gear.

FLIP SIDE OF DARKNESS

Roz was beyond happy. The thirty day campaign was a success and the election party signaled a great start for Green County. Once the twins were born and her twelve weeks of FMLA leave was completed, she'd be happy to return to work.

In the meanwhile, she knew the Sheriff's office would be in good hands. With her usual "a place for everything and everything in its place," Phoebe would quickly organize the office. A temporary replacement for Roz would be assigned to cover the front desk. The offices would be rearranged and some serious cleaning would take place. Once everything was in order, Phoebe would focus on her new job—law enforcement in the county.

Roz patted CJ on her back for pulling all of this together. "Can we live with our victory?"

CJ leaned over to her ear, "I'm thinkin' we can all breathe

easier for the time bein'. You know, the honeymoon of power—a newly promoted Sheriff from deputy. This fresh air will last a while."

"Ah, yes. We can start lookin' at campaignin' for the next woman wanting to be in an office. Got any candidates in mind?"

CJ raised her eyebrows in thought, "Nope, nothin' in the category of 'up and coming' possibilities. Keep your eyes open. We're quite the team."

Roz had joined Bill at the commissioner's table. The commissioners and their support staff were enjoying the last of the champagne. Bill was announcing a big reveal party for the twins which would be held on July 4th, "Mark your calendars, gentlemen."

After a few minutes Roz whispered out loud, "Drat. Gotta pee. Be right back." As she rose from her chair, she felt a stabbing pain in her belly, grabbed the table's edge, Bill's shoulder and yelled, "Guess what big guy? We're gonna have some babies tonight. My water just broke and another contraction. Oh-Lordy! With twins, I'm a-thinkin' this whole birthing event outta be quick. Call the Doc. Get the car. Get me to the hospital. Forget the appointment in Denver. Oh-Oh, NOW!"

The conversations in the room had slowed as the party wound down. The last minute goodbyes stopped at her alert. A baby's birth in a small town is big news. Even bigger news is the birth of twins—truly a community wide event. Everyone heard Roz and moved to hurry her to the door. Bill raced to the parking lot. Bart reached Roz and with a strong arm, guided her carefully. He knew little about babies, even less about the birthing process. "It'll be fine, Roz. Just breathe deep—slow and steady wins this race. Take care of these babies."

She rolled her eyes at his advice and snarled, "Easy-peasy,

right? Like y'all've been there."

Reaching the car, he opened the door and helped her into the back seat where she could be comfortable. No seat belt as she tried to assume the position of a flat board. No bending the beach ball at the waist.

Bart's smile of assurance to Roz disappeared as fast as it had started, "If you need anything call. This could be a long night."

Roz gave Bart a shake of her head, "I'm thinking it'll be a short deal. Honey, make this a fast ride. The boys are ready. Arrgg, there it goes again."

Bill hit the accelerator before the door was even closed. "We'll be there in five. Hang in there. Keep breathing, like we learned. I've got this. I've got this!"

With another contraction, she flared, "Y'all got this, Bill? You? How's about me?"

Bill punched the pedal to the metal and off they went leaving Bart standing at the curb. He had a perplexed pinch to his face and yelled at the departing car, "Boys? Boys?"

Back at the Club, most of the guests decided it was time to go home. After all, this was a weeknight and folks had early morning wakeups for the next workday. The county commissioners were holding a quick, off the record discussion. With Roz in labor, Bill would no longer be the Acting Sheriff. His FMLA leave of several weeks would put Phoebe in place immediately, but they would need to make it official.

Commissioner Joe surveyed the group, "How's about we declare her Sheriff right here, right now. Done deal?"

The staff minions offered to spin his suggestion into

something legal, "With the press watching, it'll never fly." They had learned from the failed attempt to appoint Bill as Sheriff. People are watching and the good old days of throwing around the power of a position were dead—for the time being. The quick discussion ended with a special meeting to be announced tomorrow. Phoebe would be Acting Sheriff until the proper swearing in. Discussion over.

At the bar with her buddies, "What a night," sighed Augusta. "First Phoebe wins the election and then Roz goes into labor. What next?"

"Nothing I hope." Queennie made the statement and everyone in the immediate proximity agreed.

"We've certainly had enough excitement for the evening. Perhaps the week." Phoebe was coming down from the personal high following the celebration. Her energy level was fading fast. Time to head home.

As the Club door opened and closed with departing celebrants, in walked two men. They were looking formal for a late Tuesday night in a small town. Each was dressed in a black suit and shirt sans a tie, wing tipped shoes, and they each sported unlit fat cigars. Bringing up the rear was one familiar woman— Suzanne.

Phoebe lifted a smile to Augusta, "I think your question 'what next' has just been answered."

Phoebe stood up and walked to Suzanne, "Hey, I'm surprised to see you. I thought you'd still be in a hospital somewhere."

Suzanne touched her face, still covered with scratches and light bruise marks, "Mom brought me to Denver and being around family helped speed my recovery. It looks worse than it is. A few glasses of water and I'm back to work."

"Good for you, Suzanne. Back to the county building?"

"I'm moving on from being a receptionist."

"Oh? What might that be?"

She side-stepped Phoebe's question and waved a hand at her guests, "Sorry. Let me introduce my cousin, Mario Martinelli, and uncle, Dino Martinelli."

As the introductions were in progress, Bart joined the group and shook hands, "Bart Masterson, Oresville Constable."

The trio claimed the first available table, inviting Phoebe and Bart to join them. Suzanne looked around the room, "Looks like you had a big celebration here tonight. Who won the election?"

"I did. I'm in shock. It was an amazing bit of work by the women in this town, led by CJ and Roz. In thirty days they created a successful campaign, rousted the vote, and here I am. I am woman, hear me roar." She raised a fist into the air and they all chuckled.

Dino called to Brian at the bar. "How about a round of drinks for the table here? Make mine a rum and coke. We need to congratulate your new sheriff."

Phoebe called to Brian, "Hey Brian, make that my usual, please."

With a quick smile, she looked directly at Dino. "Tonic and lime works wonders." She was hoping her refusal of a cocktail would let him know something about her. What that would be was 'to be determined.' She had not thought about the nuances of the position as Sheriff, but one thing for sure, *There will not be any quid pro quo while I'm Sheriff. No freebies, cocktails or otherwise.*

Brian delivered the drinks, Dino raised his glass and bellowed, "To Phoebe Korneal, the new sheriff in town."

"It's pronounced, Core-nell."

"Right." Everyone smiled at the correction and took a sip, a gulp, or a slug depending on the preference.

Phoebe decided to not let go of her question about

Suzanne's work. Trying to be casual, "You mentioned back to work. At the county building?"

"No way. Recreational marijuana is legal in Colorado. We're gonna open a shop for it here in Oresville. A community service, ya know." Suzanne beamed. "And I'll manage it."

"Just a reminder, marijuana for recreational use must be voted on by the town or in the county. It's up to each county or city, not an automatic green light. The next election's in November."

Suzanne's focus shifted to Bart and she lit up a big, flirtatious smile, "Yes, Uncle'll be workin' with the town to put it on the ballot. It has just worked out so well meeting Constable Masterson here tonight."

At the mention of his name, Bart turned to Dino. "If you are going to be in town for a while, come over to my office tomorrow. We can discuss the necessary procedures you need to follow."

"We'll be there. Thanks for taking the time for us."

Phoebe turned to Suzanne "So, what will you be doing in the meantime?"

"Choosing a place for the shop, cleaning it, and setting it up. You know, getting ready for business. That should take up quite a bit of my time."

Phoebe's senses were on high alert. *Something more is going on here. What's she up to? And why are these guys here tonight? Looks like I'll have some investigating for my first day on the job.*

Mario spoke up for the first time. "Looks like this county's in good hands with the two of you. Do you work together or do you take care of the town, Bart, while the lovely sheriff here takes care of the county?"

Phoebe registered a peg on the irritation scale with the 'lovely sheriff' reference. "It depends, Mr. Martinelli. Bart covers the basics in town. Something more serious than a traffic ticket or disorderly conduct, the sheriff's office is called in. Of course, we work with the state police and the FBI as necessary." *Get the message, Martinelli?*

"Good to know, Sheriff. Good to know. We'll keep that in mind. Constable, we'll stop by tomorrow." The family members finished their drinks and rose from the table. Dino smiled at Phoebe. Congratulations again, Sheriff. So nice to meet you tonight." Then the Martinelli's left the Club.

Bart and Phoebe looked around the quiet room—wilted banners, stickers, and little USA flags on sticks. The lighted disco ball was slowly, sadly turning, emitting a slight tick, tick, tick. The leftover fragments of a party.

The phone rang and Brian announced, "It's a celebration at 10-5 for Phoebe Korneal. Brian speaking." He always made a point of announcing the latest happenings at the Club plus the altitude of the town. In reality the altitude was overstated by a few hundred feet, but everyone liked to support the local Chamber of Commerce.

He listened, smiled, and handed the receiver to Bart, who listened, smiled, said goodbye. He turned to Phoebe. "Looks like it's twin boys. Mom and babies are doing well. Bill's a mess. He's in tears."

"How cool is that?" They sat back down at the bar. Brian poured a shot of leftover warm champagne for the three of them. Sheriff Korneal led a salute to the increase to Oresville's population and a fresh start for all. "Hear. Hear!"

INTO THE LIGHT

At the rented trailer, Bart and Phoebe shared a "contact high" over the day's events. It was nearly midnight and tomorrow was barreling down the road aimed at them. "How about a quick nightcap, Sweet P?"

"I'd enjoy some quiet time. Space to sink into the election and the past week."

"I'll mix us a cocktail. You, Madam Sheriff, take a well-deserved seat."

"Just a reminder, I'm still Deputy Korneal until the swearing in."

"I thought with Bill out on the sudden leave, you are automatically in. No?"

"Well, yes and no. It'll be sorted out in time. For now, I'll answer to Deputy, or Sheriff, or Hey You. It's all good."

At the kitchen table, she had a distant stare and was slumped into the chair. "I'm just now grasping what CJ called the fork in the road from the election. At work tomorrow, I'll be in charge. I'm excited and nervous. The good news is the state investigators and the FBI are following on the death of Mickey and the kidnapping of Suzanne, although we were the ones finding her. Anyway, glad I don't have to deal with that on my first day."

"Agreed. Just getting situated will keep you busy, especially not having Roz up front."

Phoebe had to smile with the thought, "Exciting to hear she delivered two boys and all's well. CJ'll have lots to write. Headlines for the coming week, maybe a month."

Bart put a cocktail in front of her, "There's something else. You know I'm expected to attend the town council meeting every Thursday. This last one, they're talking about building a police force. The town has the money and the Good Old Boys are thinking Mickey's death triggered a need for expanded law enforcement for Oresville. Talk is, they want to add two officers and have a Chief of Police. The coverage would not be round the clock but would take some of the burden from the Sheriff's office.

"Wow, that's news. Maybe it helps that Joe retired and moved over to the commissioner spot, ya think?"

"For sure. And I'm thinkin' with my degree in Law Enforcement, I could be a candidate for the Chief's spot. Plus, when I was in Greenstone I covered for the chief when she went on vacations, or any other absence. A good piece of experience."

Phoebe perked up with a wide smile and a spike of energy, "I'm stunned at the idea. If you made that and I'm Sheriff, we'd be working together keeping this town and county safe. This could be a giant career move for you and I love it. Exciting and scary at the same time."

Bart was tickled at her thinking out loud and laughed,

"Maybe, but this is all down the road. You know how elected officials work and now you're one of them. But a head's-up for you that the wheels of progress are turning, more like grinding. You need to be on top of it."

Phoebe thought about it and started to itemize, "So a jump into the political mixmaster, feet first on day one in the office? Just what I need on top of the fact we are short one deputy, one dispatcher and one undersheriff. Ho-ho! That's not all. I need to keep an eye on the Martinelli family members from tonight and their plans. The budget needs to be straightened out. The list grows from there."

"Don't get too ahead of yourself Phoebe. Take one thing at a time."

"This quiet time to absorb—now is shouting for attention. Life was much simpler when I was a beat cop in SL-Ick.

"We've never talked about your life before Oresville in Salt Lake City. Why do you call it SL-Ick?"

"That's a whole 'nother story for another time, another place. Ancient history but worth telling at some point down the road."

They listened to the silence of the summer night, sinking into the moment. She took a deep breath and reached out to hold Bart's hands. "What makes me happy about this whole election thing is I got to share it with you. Over the last thirty days, your support was my foundation when I could not breathe. Together we did this race. Since you moved to Oresville two months ago our relationship has taken on a life of its own. My fear of commitment has been replaced by trust for you. You're the person I want in my life. No doubt about it. I love you, Bart."

He stood up and pulled Phoebe to him. With one of his incredible hugs, he whispered in her ear, "I love you too, Sweet P."

And so, another late-night night-cap sat on the kitchen

table as they happily headed down the hallway. The promise of their future together like a shining beam in the midnight sky.

Just then her cell phone rang. It was the after-hours emergency center for the district. "Deputy Korneal? Dispatch here. Got a multiple accident on Fremont Pass."

Their immediate hot sex faded to a feeble spark and extinguished.

A long hesitation, "Korneal, are you with me?"

Phoebe pointed with her chin to Bart and let loose a sad smile, "Roger that. I'm on it. Call out the fire department response team. I'll need help."

THE END? THE END? THE END? THE END? THE END? THE END? THE END? THE END?

COZY CHARACTER COCKTAILS

ORESVILLE RESIDENTS

Augusta Higgins: *Third generation*
Pappy Van Winkle Bourbon
Pappy's neat
Add a water back, just in case…
Quality at a price!

Bart Masterson: *Beautiful but basic*
Margarita
1½ oz. Tequila
1 oz. Orange Liqueur
¾ oz. fresh lime juice
¼ oz. simple syrup
Rim glass: Lime juice and salt, fill with ice
Combine all in shaker of ice, shake, pour into glass
Garnish: Lime wheel on edge of glass
Cheers to a special occasion.

Bill Diamond: *Classic and self-absorbed*
Jack and Coke
2 oz. Jack Daniels
6 oz. Coke
Fill rocks glass with ice
Add the Jack, top with Coke
Garnish: Lime twist
Here's to me!

Carrie Jean AKA CJ: *Ace and only reporter*
The Journalist
2 oz. Dry Gin
½ oz. Dry Vermouth
½ oz. Sweet Vermouth
¼ tsp Grand Marnier
¼ tsp fresh lemon juice
1 dash Angostura bitters
All into mixing glass with ice, stir
Strain into chilled martini glass
Garnish: Lemon twist
There's a headline here.

Phoebe Korneal: *Caffeine and cops combo*
The Mugshot
Cup of strong coffee
Add 2 oz. shot of Amaretto
(Optional) Top with whipped cream
Garnish: Shave chocolate on the whipped!
Toast to straight arrow.

Queennie Lewis: *Loves her bike*
Sidecar
1½ oz. Cognac
¾ oz. Cointreau
¾ oz. fresh lemon juice
Rim a coupe glass with sugar
Combine all in shaker of ice, shake & feel the chill
Strain into coupe glass
Share and share alike.

Roz Boudreaux-Diamond: *Currently preggers*
Heartburn Be Gone
4 oz. Club or Lime Soda
2 oz. Ginger Beer
4 dashes of favorite bitters
Pour all over ice into highball glass
Garnish: Lime wedge
Vote for Phoebe!

BAD ACTORS

Alejandro Martinez: *Bad Guy*
Smash and Grab
2 oz. Bourbon
¼ oz. simple syrup
2 mint sprigs
2 orange wheels
In shaker, muddle syrup, mint, orange
Add Bourbon, fill with ice, shake
Strain over ice in Old Fashioned glass
Garnish: Lemon wheel
My way or the highway.

Mateo Mendez: *The better man*
Limoncello Lemon Drop Martini
2 oz. Limoncello
1 oz. Vodka
½ oz. fresh lemon juice
Combine in a shaker, add ice, shake 'til chilled
Rim martini glass with sugar
Strain shaker contents into glass
Garnish: Lemon slice
Ahhh, Buenas noches!

Mickey Walker: *RIP druggie*
VRB
2 oz. Vodka
1 (8 oz.) can of Red Bull
Pour vodka over ice to highball glass
Top with Red Bull
Garnish: Lime twist
One and done!

Suzanne Martinelli: *Spoiled rotten*
The Spoiled Brat
2 oz. Vodka
½ oz. Chocolate Liqueur
½ oz. Pear Liqueur
½ oz. fresh lime juice
2 dashes cherry bitters
Shake with ice and strain into cocktail glass
Feel free to whine a lot.

The Cozy Character Cocktails are drinks preferred by our main characters featured in The Last Line The Phoebe Korneal Mystery Trilogy. The cocktails are designed by Becky Riney Sloboda as a match to the unique personality of the character. We thank Becky for her creativity, careful consideration, and sharing! *Cheers!*

ACKNOWLEDGMENTS

First and foremost, we want to extend our appreciation to the law enforcement men and women of Chaffee and Lake Counties in Colorado and Pima County in Arizona, whose flexibility and diligence with the citizens in their respective areas make livin' large in these areas comfortable, interesting, and safe. We also want to acknowledge the dedicated volunteers of search and rescue organizations in Colorado. These brave people have the tough job of responding to the dire circumstances of residents and visitors who enjoy living and playing in the great outdoors.

We have come to the realization that every day is a new learning curve, just when we thought we were old enough to know it all. To this point, we wholeheartedly thank our friends and families who have supported us through the re-learning of the literary use of the English language and the use and application of family names and antidotes.

We thank our husbands for their loving support and perpetual patience. You helped to keep our heads on straight, pulled us back from the ledge as needed, and vetted Phoebe's adventures in life and law enforcement. We love you and thank you for maintaining a sense of humor through thick and thin as we created the third book in the trilogy. What a ride, eh?

Virtual hugs going to three especially talented ladies, Martha Kutas, Diane Newman, and Sue Grove. Their insights, grammatical expertise, and attention to detail combined with their encyclopedic knowledge made this a much better read. We want to publicly acknowledge Becky Sloboda for singlehandedly designing Character Cocktails appropriate to the narrative arc and character personalities. Nancy Taylor for lending us her creative thinking with designing the marketing, maps, and icons.

To each of our friends and allies who have graciously allowed us to use and grow from your experiences, our thanks. You have shown us that it's all about the amazing stories we accumulate through life. You have tolerated and critiqued our thinking out loud as we created this story and studiously ignored our whining through the laborious tasks of editing and rewriting—again, and again, and again.

We extend our thanks to our friend, Wendy Simms, Pima County, Arizona, Senior Forensic Technician. Our sincere appreciation to this sheriff's organization for allowing us to use Wendy's picture as the prototype of our gal Phoebe Korneal (pronounced Core-nell), and using their police vehicle as the backdrop for her photo.

The National Mining and Hall of Fame Museum in Leadville, Colorado, gave us the inspiration for this setting. Their collections highlight the brave women who helped make mining the anchor for the beginnings of Colorado in the 1800s. We live stronger in today's world with this firm understanding of our history as exemplified in museums. Thank you for capturing the essence of the Colorado mining life.

READING GROUPS

QUESTIONS AND TOPICS FOR DISCUSSION

1. Drugs are prevalent in many cities and towns. How prevalent is drug use in your town?

2. What do you think are the challenges for women in law enforcement today? In the story, Phoebe moves from a big city to a small mountain town in order to further her career. Can we speculate about the personal opportunities in a small town vs. a big city?

3. How do women relate to Augusta in her non-traditional role as owner of a working mine, her lifestyle, and her change of heart at the end of the story? What are the differences between women in nontraditional work in Corporate America vs. small town settings? Can we call out the examples as proof one way or the other—easier or not?

4. How do women relate to Queennie and her unique role in life? Queennie never divorced Old Al. She owns a radiator shop thanks to the funding from Al's gold prospecting. She rides a Harley for pleasure. Do these choices influence how others see her? What are your first thoughts regarding this character?

5. There are several unique women in this story. How do

they support each other? What are their differences? Can you give examples of how they support one another?

6. What do you think of the relationship between Queennie and Augusta? Will their relationship grow? What will make this relationship a challenge to develop? What examples could make it easier? Will distance help or hinder?

7. How is the Elks Club important to the culture of Oresville? What are examples from the story of how the Club "works" for Oresville?

8. Augusta finally tells Queennie about Old Al's gold stash of gold. Was this the right thing to do? Should she have kept part of it? What do you think Queennie should do with the money? In the story, what are the examples of her choices?

9. Green County is steeped in the mining tradition. What will be the challenges to Phoebe as the first female Sheriff? She is the first and recently the Good Old Boys have complicated their positions of power. Where will her challenges come from?

10. Who are your favorite characters in the story? Most interesting? There are several characters in this fiction work. Who would you like to see more of in the next book? Please let us know at phoebekorneal@gmail.com. We would love to hear from you! We appreciate your opinions and are happy to answer your questions and your pleas for more!

ABOUT THE AUTHORS

Judilee and GaGa at the Sloboda Summer Literary Salon

Judilee Butler

Telling a story is my passion albeit discovered late at twenty years into retirement. Co-authoring with GaGa is fantastic and we'll write until we can't. Using Colorado's mountains for our Phoebe Korneal Trilogy, we've built a relentless detective, quirky characters, and mystery to give you fun, cozy reads. Enjoy!

GaGa Gabardi

As a septuagenarian livin' large in the Rockies, I discovered writing with Judilee is a daily joy. Our gal, Deputy and Detective Phoebe (Cor-nell), works in law enforcement—a man's world. This makes a platform for our collection of stories and opinions on the way to solving crime. First step, complete this Phoebe Korneal cozy mystery trilogy, next … who knows!

CO-AUTHORS

As co-authors living high in the Colorado Rocky Mountains, GaGa Gabardi and Judilee Butler became fascinated with the state's mining history. For this they thank the National Mining Museum in Leadville, Colorado. On a Saturday morning in 2019, they collaborated on a short story cozy mystery and their first of a trilogy was born ... The Last Hurrah A Phoebe Korneal Mystery trilogy, followed by The Last Slide. The Last Line is up next.

This initial writing sparked a passion for developing quirky characters and strong women. They then added the value of life in small towns as a backdrop and an excuse for the fun use of Colorado history.

Modern technology has led these two septuagenarians down the yellow brick road of long distance collaborative storytelling—Judilee in Wyoming and Florida, GaGa in Colorado. Throw in a mystery, a relentless female deputy sheriff, the small town of Oresville at an altitude of ten-five, and you have a fun read. What a ride!

The Last Line is written as a cozy read—sit back, enjoy the story, and the characters, We invite you to share questions, comments, and extraneous outbursts at our website BnGbooks. com and by email at PhoebeKorneal@gmail.com.

How can you help us? We want to continue to expand on the world of women in law enforcement today and also the special culture in small communities throughout America.

Share your experiences with us! Even the tiniest of tales rolls into the next chuckle, the unexpected guffaw, or the next wonky tale. It's the stories you share that encourage us to pursue the platform of Phoebe and friends, the Sheriff Department of Green County, and communities in every state in this great country of America.

Please tell your friends, family and the world about this book. Write a review about *The Last Line, A Phoebe Korneal Mystery* on Amazon.com. Don't forget our first book, *The Last Hurrah, A Phoebe Korneal Mystery*, that set up the story for this second book, *The Last Slide.* We also thank the judges of the Colorado Authors League for the Finalist Award for Book 1 and also the Bronze Award from the Colorado Independent Publishers Association.

Visit us on our website at BnGbooks.com and share your feedback at PhoebeKoeneal@gmail.com. We are always looking for the next storyline, the next character cocktail, and the next laugh.

GaGa and Judilee are available for discussions, lectures, and select readings: In person, via radio, Zoom, or television. We travel readily over the internet! To inquire about a possible visit, interview, or literary salon, please contact: phoebekorneal@gmail.com

They favor locations such as Colorado, Florida, Wyoming, Minnesota, North Carolina, and Arizona. Inquire soon; scheduling time is of the essence.

phoebekorneal@gmail.com

ABOUT THE AUTHORS

BnGBooks.com

LOOKING FOR MORE PHOEBE?

CHECK OUT THE PHOEBE

KORNEAL MYSTERIES!

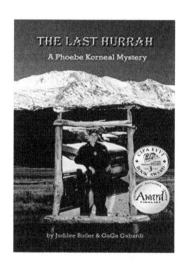

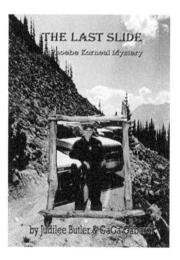

THE LAST HURRAH

BOOK 1

THE LAST SLIDE

BOOK 2

Made in the USA
Monee, IL
16 May 2023

33392670R00188